PENGUIN BOOKS

FIGHT FOR HER

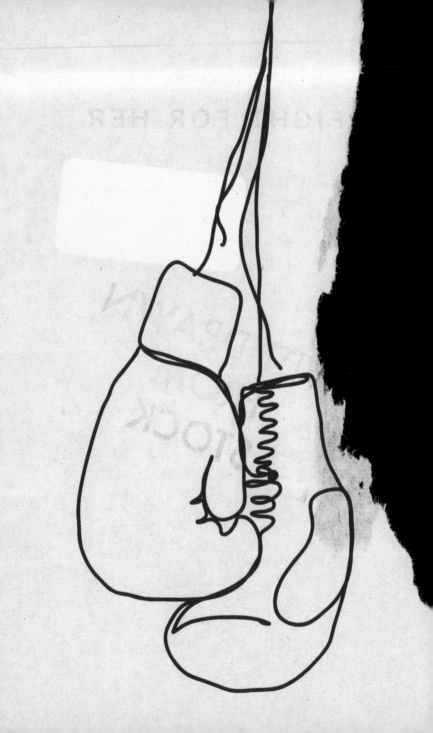

FIGHT FOR HER

LIZ PLUM

PENGUIN BOOKS

PENGUIN BOOKS

UK | USA | Canada | Ireland | Australia
India | New Zealand | South Africa

Penguin Books is part of the Penguin Random House group of companies
whose addresses can be found at global.penguinrandomhouse.com.

www.penguin.co.uk   www.puffin.co.uk   www.ladybird.co.uk

Published in Great Britain by Penguin Books in association
with Wattpad Books, a division of Wattpad Corp., 2021

001

Text copyright © Liz Plum, 2021

Cover design by Laura Mensinga
Cover images © Nejron Photo via Adobe Stock
Interior images © art is me on iStock
Typesetting by Sarah Salomon

Wattpad, Wattpad Books, and associated logos are trademarks
and/or registered trademarks of Wattpad Corp.
All rights reserved

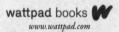

wattpad books
www.wattpad.com

Printed and bound in Great Britain by Clays Ltd, Elcograf S.p.A.

The authorized representative in the EEA is Penguin Random House Ireland,
Morrison Chambers, 32 Nassau Street, Dublin D02 YH68

A CIP catalogue record for this book is available from the British Library

ISBN: 978–0–241–46075–7

All correspondence to:
Penguin Books, Penguin Random House Children's
One Embassy Gardens, 8 Viaduct Gardens
London SW11 7BW

MIX
Paper from
responsible sources
FSC
www.fsc.org   FSC® C018179

Penguin Random House is committed to a
sustainable future for our business, our readers
and our planet. This book is made from Forest
Stewardship Council® certified paper.

To my parents, teachers, and readers. This one's for you.

Content Warning: mention of bullying, fighting, and accidental death

PROLOGUE

The knock at the door pulls me away from the television. It's late; too late for us to have any guests. I turn down the volume, being the only one downstairs, and debate whether to open the door or wait for whomever it is to knock often enough to wake my parents. The latter option presents itself first when heavy footsteps run down the stairs, and then my dad appears downstairs, his figure a silhouette against the late-hour darkness.

"Who's knocking?"

"Maybe Max forgot his key," I say.

But the moment my dad opens the door, time stops for all of us. A man dressed in blue walks into our house, his face sorrowful. They are speaking so quietly I can't make out a single word but I'd have to be pretty dense not to realize something seriously bad has happened.

The way my father's expression falls and his face turns white makes goose bumps rise on my skin, and the strain in his voice as he calls for my mom makes my hands shake.

Why is Max not home? Why is there a cop here with his hat respectfully held in his hands and not in place on his head? Why does my dad appear like he's about to cry?

My mom comes down the stairs with the same worried look on her face that I have on mine. My dad talks to her, holding her calmly while he speaks.

For a second after he finishes, it looks as though his arms around her is the only thing holding her up. But then he starts talking to her again, his expression sterner as he speaks. Then their eyes suddenly land on me, and the second I meet their gaze, I know what happened.

Max is gone. My brother is gone.

Suddenly, my rapidly beating heart stops, and I don't think I've ever truly felt it beat the same way since. My breathing grows heavy and fast and my vision blurs with tears. My parents run into the room to hold me, but my body has gone numb and I can barely feel their touch.

We're so sorry, Scarlet.

It will be okay, I'm so sorry.

Small nothings to reassure me that it's going to be all right. Empty words to create the facade of strength and stability even though they were just told that their only son is dead. All too soon the officer comes in, using a hushed voice again as he pulls my father into another room.

I don't know how long he talks to my father while my mom and I cry in one another's arms, but soon the two of them come back. Though my mind is clouded with heartbreak and my eyes are glossy with tears, I notice how their expressions have changed.

"It was a motorcycle accident," the officer begins, and my dad nods along, chin quivering as he bites back his tears.

"The driver of an eighteen-wheeler was drunk. He rounded the corner over on Boundary Lane, you know how bad the blind spot there is . . . I'm so sorry. Max died on impact; I was told he was never in pain."

He speaks as though what he's saying is supposed to make me feel better. As though hearing that my brother was plowed down by an eighteen-wheeler will make this easier somehow. As though there could be worse news, and this should come as a blessing.

All I know is that my brother is gone.

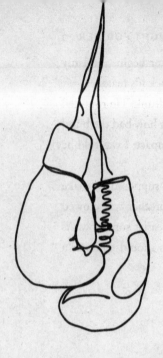

CHAPTER
ONE

Looking in from the outside, it would appear that high school has really been the *best* four years of my life. Every day people in our small town see the muscled arm of our school's star quarterback wrapped around me and friends surrounding me on all sides. The view from the outside, however, only scrapes the surface of who I, Scarlet, really am. The inside paints a much different picture; a picture that only my eyes see.

My boyfriend, Jack Dallas, captain and quarterback of our football team, is on his way to becoming an NFL superstar. He's got three state titles and has offers from colleges up and down the East and West Coasts. All the girls at school, including me, drool over his looks, southern charm, and the gentle accent that makes his voice sound sweet as honey. By chance, he and I hit it off from the beginning—I was just a girl in the crowd at his football game and he was just a player looking for a cute girl to give the winning ball to. After that, he and I clicked, and I waited for the day he would finally ask me to be his girlfriend, which took weeks of agonizing flirtatious "just friend" hangouts. When he finally did ask me out, everyone at school called us the *Cinderella Story* couple of Royal Eastwood High School, just like the movie with Hilary Duff and Chad Michael Murray.

It happened moments after he and the rest of the Royal Eastwood Warriors won the play-off game last season against our rivals, the West Side Knights. I was in the stands with the rest of the student body, soaked to the core from the torrential downpour that started during the second half of the game. No one wanted to leave because we were down by only one touchdown. With seconds left, Jack ran the ball into the end for the win. The crowd went ballistic because we were going to the state championships; we were yelling and screaming his name, and amid all the chaos, he ran into the bleachers to find me, wrapped his arms around me, and kissed me. After that, we became the it couple.

Even now, sitting in the middle of the crowded cafeteria during lunch, all eyes are on us. Jack moves his arm from my shoulders down to my waist as he laughs with his best friend and go-to wide receiver, Bryce. I look at Jack and get caught up in his perfect smile. His teeth shine, his jawline is sharp, and his bright-blue eyes are slightly narrowed, yet they still find a way to sparkle.

"Nah, bro, I totally shotgunned mine faster than you!" Bryce says, slapping Jack on the back while talking about the party a few nights ago.

"Are you kidding, Bryce? I had mine crushed before you were even halfway through!" Jack says.

"I had three before that. Hell, dude, I went to my car to do another instead of taking my test first period."

"Bryce, how do you expect to take over your parents' law firm if the only thing you do is try to beat people in drinking competitions?" I ask.

"I'm not worried about it, Scar. It's not like my parents have anyone else to give it to. Being the only child has its benefits. I'm only seventeen—right now it's all about partying hard."

"Same. I bombed my econ test last week, but my dad didn't care. I'm getting the company no matter what," one of the girls in our group, Katie, says.

I tune out the rest of their ridiculous conversation; it's all posturing and bragging. Royal Eastwood is known for educating the richest teenagers in the area. We come from a wealthy section of Texas—Conroe County, about forty miles outside of Houston. We are known for Lake Conroe, where the wealthiest students live the waterfront lifestyle.

Living in a richer county leads to an expensive lifestyle, and going to a high school with wealthy kids feeds into that way of life. Everyone in Jack's clique has parents who own a major business—his dad owns the Houston Texans football team. And because they are all so rich, not a single one of them tries in school, as Katie summarized with her entitled econ comment. They have some sort of weird mind-set that they don't have to try to succeed in life.

They don't know it, but I'm top twenty in our class. Yes, my parents have a family-owned business, too, Tucker Auto—a chain of auto shops spanning the Midwest—and my dad intends to give it to me when he retires, but my parents would kill me if I let my GPA drop too low. Not to mention I like the satisfaction of getting an A on a test or seeing the pleased look in my teachers' eyes when I answer a question correctly.

The business has to continue to do well when I take it over, and to do that requires a good education. There's no better place to do that than here at Royal Eastwood High—with nationally acclaimed teachers and an almost perfect graduation rate, it's the best public school to get an education at. My plan is to attend Virginia Tech after I graduate; a school states away but with a stellar business program.

Jack will go straight into football after high school, to whatever college gives him the best offer and provides the quickest path to the NFL. He was raised on football, on *Friday Night Lights*. The NFL is the only path in his life.

As for the others, I'm not sure what their immediate future holds. I know they will never make it in a world where their income is any less than six figures, but as to how they'll get there, I'm at a loss.

Katie's high-pitched laughter bubbles from the back of her throat and I fake laugh to cover the fact that I wasn't paying attention to the joke. Bryce and Jack don't notice my laughter is artificial, and Katie is stuck in her own bubble. The loud noises of the students mingling around us take away from the forced aspects of my laugh. Part of me wishes that I wasn't part of a popular group at Royal Eastwood—I don't relate to half of their conversations, I actually try in school, and I don't necessarily like partying *all* the time. They're nice, for the most part, but it's hard to call people your friends if you have absolutely nothing in common. Well, we have Jack in common, and being with him makes it worth it.

There's really only one girl in the group that I truly like, Jessica. She's got short brown curls, and I can tell she's just as disinterested as I am in whatever Katie said and is *still* laughing about. Even though Jessica's family is rich, she averages As and Bs in all of her classes, and doesn't care to know if Bryce got a haircut or switched colognes.

As lunch comes to the end, we venture past the garbage bins at the corner of the cafe to toss our leftovers and move to the halls to walk to our respective classes. Royal Eastwood never fails to impress me with its beauty. The roof is composed of skylights that brighten up the black lockers, which contrast with the orange and white floor tiles.

Jack and his football friends have most of their classes together, and though I don't have a class close to Jack's, we tend not to turn down walking with one another. On the way down the hall after lunch, Jack's telling the group about Texans training camp again, but while they're hanging on his every word, I notice something else. Elijah Black's at his locker.

Every school has a bad boy. Whether he comes from a group of bad boys or is the lone leather-jacket wearing idol, no school that I've come across seems vacant of one. Royal Eastwood fits the same stereotype, only we don't have the classic sex god that every other school seems to have.

No, being the bad boy at our school has the negative connotation the name is meant to have. He doesn't rule the school with a leather jacket and motorcycle, he doesn't sleep with an endless supply of girls, and he most certainly doesn't get into fights. No, he's labeled as a drug-addled freak no one has bothered to get to know.

Elijah Black.

When other students see him, they associate him with his deadbeat older brother—their words not mine—who died a few years ago due to a heroin overdose. No one in Jack's clique of friends has bothered to get to know Elijah. They're too judg-mental to care.

There are times when I catch sight of Elijah and I feel myself wanting to talk to him, ask why he doesn't refute anything said about him, find out what the truth is, and try to set the record straight so people can stop being down on him both through their ruthless gossip and the words sneered at him every day. It's unfair that people treat him this way based on rumors. It's unfair the rumors twist such a tragic event in his life into something that reflects poorly on *his* character.

His good looks don't seem to matter to any girls here. His seemingly vile lifestyle is enough to keep them away. It doesn't matter that his sharp jawline contrasts with his prominent cheek-bones, or that his green eyes, no matter how dark, always shim-mer. All they can focus on is the stigma of who he is. Normally, girls are attracted to mystery, but with Elijah they try their hard-est to stay away.

Jack's voice rips down the hallway toward Elijah. "Hey, look, guys, it's Eli the freak! He left his drugs long enough to actually come to school."

The group snickers but I don't react to my boyfriend. I never do when he starts this stuff. There are few things that I don't love about Jack, but his bullying is the most prominent. He says things like this to Elijah nearly every time we see him, and I don't understand it. Jack always has some new reason to attack Elijah, and the hate in his voice sometimes makes me wonder who Jack truly is.

If someone can harbor that much hate for someone they don't really know, how can they have love in their hearts? How can he hate Elijah this much yet still find it in him to share any love with me? But then I remind myself this is Jack I'm talking about, and I should never doubt his love for me. He says it every day.

Per usual, Elijah doesn't say anything or offer any reaction. He slams his locker shut, his lips pulled into their usual tight line. Jack laughs and we continue walking down the hall as the topic moves on to something other than bashing Elijah, but my eyes remain on him. All he ever does is grimace.

Elijah senses my eyes on him because he glances back, and despite how crowded the hallway is, his eyes meet mine and slowly narrow. I quickly look away and keep walking, but Elijah's eyes burn into me. My heart races for almost no reason, and I risk a glance back, once again meeting shockingly dark, shimmering green eyes.

The closer we get to my class the more the group fans out so that it's just me and Jack. He stops just before we reach my classroom and leans his back against the wall, pulling me against him. When apart from his friends, Jack shifts from cocky shenanigans to a loving desire to be with me. I melt into his arms, reveling in the hardness of his muscles as he gives me a soft squeeze, making it easy to forget the fact he spoke to Elijah with such disdain.

With Bryce, Katie, and the others, Jack puts up a facade of who he thinks he has to be. With me, he can be himself, and I forget about the hateful things he can say to and about others; because he's so sweet it's hard to believe those words really came from him.

"Katie and Bryce can talk your ear off, can't they?" He chuckles and tucks some hair behind my ear.

"They've got a lot to say, but not much worth saying," I joke.

"I think you should skip history class. I have the house all to myself, just you and me."

He places his hand back down on my hip and slowly massages circles into my skin. "We could get in the hot tub, I could give you a massage, slowly take your bikini off . . ."

"You know I can't skip, Jack," I say.

"Come on, babe, just this once?"

Laughing, I lean forward to kiss him and he melts into it, smiling against my lips. "No."

"That's okay, I'll just watch porn or—" Jack says. "Ow! Don't hit me, I'm only kidding!"

"*Sure* you are . . . I've seen your browser history. I had no clue you were so into blonds."

"Maybe you could experiment with some dye. I wouldn't be able to keep my hands off of a blond version of you."

"Maybe you could experiment with being accepting of your girlfriend."

"I am. She's the only one I want or need."

Such simple words, yet they're enough to have any girl falling in love at dangerous speeds. This is the Jack his friends don't see. A sweet, gentle man who holds his true personality only for those he trusts most.

"Keep the sweet talk up." I kiss him. "It may work in your favor. I have to go to history, though. I'll see you later."

Jack playfully smacks my butt as I head into my classroom. Of course, just as he does, one of the guys on the team catcalls and yells for us to keep it PG. I love Jack, but I definitely do not adore his friends.

Once the final bell rings, people usually hightail it out of school rather than stop at their lockers. The traffic to get off school grounds for student drivers is bonkers. If you don't beat the buses, you'll sit at a standstill for fifteen minutes, and even after that it takes forever to get home. In order to avoid the traffic, kids sprint to their vehicles and race onto the main roads to get home.

It's really a safety hazard if you think about it; a bunch of teenagers who just got their licenses speeding around trying to either look cool or beat the traffic. That's why I avoid it by staying a bit later to get my things in the peace and quiet of an area that's normally loud and rowdy. I lazily try the combination to my locker, getting it wrong a total of three times before I'm actually able to open it. Almost everyone has cleared out of the hallway now, and I'm away from Jack's friends mocking me for caring about doing my homework and assignments.

Bryce and a few other football buddies saunter past some kid. They stop in their tracks when they notice the boy stuffing his homework into his backpack, trying to escape their eyes as quickly as possible. Bryce reaches forward to snag the boy's backpack, and the boy quickly pulls it out of reach and shuffles away with his head tucked down low. My heartstrings tug painfully when he runs past me but what can I do? They're my boyfriend's best friends, and to them I'm just the girl attached to Jack's arm.

"What a loser," Bryce says as he walks by. "He doesn't even have the money to 'donate' to the school and get out of homework."

"His dad's probably the janitor, I heard he lives over off of Tenth Street."

Though we live in a wealthy suburb, our town has its rougher areas. The poorer district is at our south end, full of crumbling houses, a crumbling economy, and crumbling socioeconomic status. It's just beyond our version of a downtown, though we don't live in a big city. Students like Bryce would never cross the invisible border into that side of town.

Bryce laughs, and from the grunts of the other players I assume he punched him in approval, the way jocks do.

"That was funny, bro. Wait till we tell Jack about this, he'll freak!"

If you do your homework, it somehow correlates with being poor. Because if you do the work, then you must not have the money to "donate" to your teachers. And if you're poor? Then you don't belong and can be ridiculed. My parents would never let me write a check to pass high school. I do my work diligently, and in doing so I've gained respect from my teachers.

I choose the single textbook I will need tonight and shut my black locker. It closes with a satisfying slam that echoes down the empty hallway.

As I head outside to where I know Jack is waiting for me, I run smack into someone, dropping my textbook and folders as a gust of wind carries my papers halfway down the hall. The guy I ran into bends down to pick them up, and his voice startles me.

"Are you going to help?" His voice is deep and surprisingly rugged.

Elijah Black.

It takes me a few seconds to register that he's kneeling down on the floor picking up my papers without my help, and I quickly bend down too.

"I'm so sorry! I don't mean to make you pick them up," I say. "I was startled by our collision."

"You must be pretty clumsy to run into me when we're the only two people in the hallway," he teases as he stands up.

I stand there like a fish out of water, unsure of what to say. Elijah takes my silence as his cue to turn and walk away.

"I've always sort of been a klutz!" I blabber, and he stops walking, glancing back at me with one brow raised. "It may stem from when I was a baby. My very first steps were me falling down the front porch steps, and ever since then my balance has been way off. I blame my dad for not putting up a guardrail and baby proofing the front porch. Now that I think about it, he didn't really baby proof any of the house, and—"

"I'll see you around, Scarlet."

He disappears around a corner, and my face reddens from his amusement. What just happened? Elijah's certainly not a freak—there wasn't a hint of the smell of drugs or alcohol on him. Maybe the only rumor that's true is about his brother, and that one is hard for me to hear. I wanted to go to Elijah and comfort him after hearing what happened, because I knew how hard it was to lose a brother. I knew what he was going through. But I've always thought Elijah was an uninviting personality. So I never took the risk, and he had to deal with it all alone.

Adjusting my things in my arms, I head out to the parking lot, curiosity sparking through my mind.

Jack's waiting for me by his giant, jacked-up black truck. As soon as his parents got it for him, he went and lifted it by at least another two feet and installed a loud-as-hell exhaust system complete with pipes coming out of the bed, and installed a stereo that part of me thinks should be illegal because of how low the bass drops. But are you really in Texas if you don't own a lifted, pimped-out truck?

A few junior girls are huddled around him, probably gushing over his muscles, his eyes, or his truck. News flash, ladies, he's taken. But I can't blame them for gawking. He *is* a sight to look at. But as he sees me, he steps away from them as though they've turned invisible.

"Hey, babe, what took you so long? I've been out here for fifteen minutes," he says, effortlessly taking my textbook and folders from my arms so that I don't have to carry as much weight.

"I ran into Elijah by accident and my papers flew everywhere so I had to pick them up."

Jack stops in his tracks and I realize my slipup. He's the one guy who for some reason finds the most joy in making fun of Elijah.

"Delilah, I mean." I lie lamely, and Jack sees right through it.

"What are you doing talking to that freak?"

"I literally smacked into him and then he helped pick up my papers," I say quickly.

"That *freak* ran into you?" Jack repeats, as though Elijah personally insulted him. "He's going to get it. When I see him, I'm going to shove my fist up his—"

"Jack, don't worry about it. He didn't even talk to me."

Anger dances across Jack's face despite my words, so I lean forward and softly kiss him to try and calm him down. It works, and he lengthens the kiss.

"I don't want a freak talking to you, he has no business. You're my girl, Scar."

I decide not to reply, and he takes the rest of my stuff and places it in the back seat of the truck. If I could, I would drive myself to and from school, but sadly, I don't have a car. I'm waiting to buy one myself, and with how much I have in my savings I'm really close, but I'm not quite there. My parents offered to buy me a car but I really want to purchase one on my own—

there's something about buying something big like a car without my parents' help that makes me feel independent, I guess.

My dad has our garage stocked with vintage cars, like the 1960 Corvette, 1940 Ford Coupe, and 1970 Camaro he's collected over the years and fixed up as a hobby. For a man who runs a national chain of auto-body shops, an obsession with cars is a prerequisite to success. There are six cars, all of which are most likely better than anything I could buy on my own, but pride keeps me from grabbing a set of keys and making one of his cars mine.

Jack leans over the middle console and kisses me sweetly after helping me into the truck, and then starts it up while the diesel engine makes an excess of noise pollution.

"Ice cream before I take you home?" he asks. He sets his hand on my thigh, revs the engine for the entire *country* to hear, and then drives off to take me home, cranking the bass up with the windows down.

I'm suddenly deep in my thoughts, and my eyes go to the passing fields as Jack drives. Elijah was nothing like people described; he seemed friendly enough to try and make a conversation, which I instantly ruined by rambling. As Jack drives along the road with one hand on the wheel and the other on my thigh, I wonder why he is so critical toward Elijah. I saw no reason to be mean.

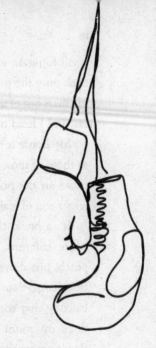

CHAPTER
TWO

Stepping down from what feels like a thousand feet above the ground after getting ice cream, I get out of Jack's truck and land with a thud that sends a jolt up my legs. Jack gets out of his own side and walks around to me, settling his arms naturally around my waist as he pouts.

"Are you sure you can't come over, babe?"

"You know my dad wants me home, *and* you have practice with the guys."

"I'd skip it for you."

"We both know you wouldn't."

He chuckles and swoops his head down to kiss me. "It's the thought that counts, though, right?" he asks, tapping my nose with his. "I'll see you tomorrow morning with my famous blueberry pancakes. I know they're your favorite. Love you."

Jack hops back into the truck, and then loops around the

small fountain in my driveway before driving straight out and back onto the road, his diesel engine making the ground shake. He roars out of sight, blasting some sort of music from his speakers, and I head to my front door.

My house is not new and, compared to Jack's house, as well as those of most of his friends, it could be considered small. To those on the poor end of town, however, it would be on the larger end of real estate.

It's a brick, three-story home with stark black shutters and white columns that decorate the large, stone-finished front porch. Just above the porch lives a beautiful yet tiny balcony that the second-floor master leads out to, and there is one smaller balcony that comes off of the back of the house on the third floor, my room. Our driveway extends for nearly half a mile, flowing from the road through our bright green yard, accentuating how large our property is, and ends at a beautiful black fountain placed in the middle of an array of yellow and red flowers that make up a *T* for Tucker, our last name.

I have loved growing up here. My neighborhood is friendly and I could ride my bike to and from old friends' houses when I was a kid, seeing other modest houses and realizing how fortunate my family is. But does it really matter where you live as long as you are able to call it home?

Wow, my philosophy class this morning must have really gotten to me.

As I walk inside, I call out that I'm home and I'm greeted by my mother, who is sitting on the couch in the den watching some competitive cooking show. Our den is filled with a wrap-around tan-colored leather sectional, a large flat-screen TV settled comfortably above our mantle, and beautiful paintings that intermingle with the pictures of our family that line the walls. The room is completed with my dad's dark-blue and red plaid recliner, which he refuses to get rid of.

"Hey, Scarlet, you're getting home late," my mom observes. "Long day?"

"Jack and I got ice cream after school. How was your day?"

"Same old, learned a few new recipes." She nods at the cooking channel playing on the TV. "I figured you'd like to try one out with me."

"Oh! What type of recipe?"

Taking a spot next to her as we talk, I throw my feet up on the ottoman and kick my shoes onto the floor next to it. My mom is nothing short of gorgeous, and if you didn't see the love between her and my father and didn't know how unbelievably smart she is, you might consider her a trophy wife. She has shoulder-length brown hair with naturally lighter streaks running through it. Her eyes are perfectly proportional to the rest of her face and are a light shade of brown. And her smile is the softest smile you will ever see on anyone. After everything my family has been through, my mom has proven how strong she is. She's had the hardest time of us all, but she has never let life's tragedies impact her love for me and my father. With some parents it's hard to tell what they looked like back in their glory days, but I think my mom is still living hers.

Just as we finish discussing our new recipe, the front door opens and my dad walks in, his suit jacket draped over his arm and his dress shirt wrinkled from the day's work. He looks tired from his no doubt long and tiring day at the office, but once he sees me and my mom, his tired eyes light up and he instantly smiles.

My dad is the perfect match for my mom. Her beauty could have gotten the attention of any guy she wanted, but she settled for my father. He has a contagious laugh, caring actions, and a determination to live life to the fullest. That would be hard for any girl to turn away. He's not the most attractive of men, with his receding hairline, black hair already thinning, and a slight beer belly growing on him, but he has beautiful blue eyes that draw her in and an amazing, caring personality to seal the deal.

"There they are, my two favorite girls in the whole world."

He walks over to my mom and sets a sweet kiss on her lips and then ruffles my hair like I'm still his little five-year-old.

"What was on your agenda today?" my mom asks.

"I just came from the store on Avenue F." He sighs as he sits down on his decades-old recliner, kicks off his work shoes, and throws them in a pile with my own that I'm sure has my mom preparing a scolding for us. "Archie asked if you wanted any more hours, sweetheart," he says to me.

My attention perks up at his words and I find myself instantly agreeing to the opportunity to work some more hours.

My parents own an expanding chain of auto shops, and I work part time in the closest one to us, on Avenue F. It was the first-ever location for the business. Thanks to my dad's countless hours of hard work and my mother's unwavering support, Tucker Auto now spans the entire Midwest, and we're trying to expand to locations on the East Coast to become nationwide.

Archie is my boss, as well as the head mechanic. He doesn't have much of a brain for business but he can fix nearly any car brought his way. He and my dad have a great bond, because although my dad is the CEO of the entire company, he loves to stay in touch with every store, Archie's especially, since that location was the first one for the business.

"You think you can help Archie later?" Dad asks, putting the chair back and lifting the footrest with a relaxed sigh.

"I would love to—you know I'd never turn down an extra hour or two at the shop."

My dad grins. "How was your day, sweetheart?"

"Same old, good and full of time spent with Jack."

"Why don't you invite him over for dinner? I can talk to him about what his game plan is, see if that coach of yours is doing his job right."

This is Texas. High school coaches take their jobs as seriously as NFL coaches vying for a Super Bowl win.

"He would but he's going to be at the field getting in extra practice with the guys."

"Another time then."

My parents fell in love with Jack the moment they met him. He charmed them with his passionate talk of pursuing football, his southern manners, and words of affection for me. They could easily see how happy he made me. With everything that had happened just before he and I met they were appreciative of someone who could get me smiling again.

That's one of the reasons I fell for Jack so hard. He was the only light I saw when I was stuck in a tunnel of darkness.

Standing up and stretching, I grab my backpack and head upstairs to do the little bit of homework I have. Passing the vacant room sends a shiver down my spine and reminds me of the sadness that ate at my heart before Jack came along. This used to be Max's room.

The phone rings somewhere in the distance, and my dad

comes up the stairs behind me a moment later. "You okay, sweet-heart?" my dad says.

It's been three years since my brother passed, and I've learned to mask the pain. It's what one has to do in order to move on. I'm only seventeen; I can't live the rest of my life hanging on to the sadness Max's death instilled in my life.

"Yeah, I'm all right."

Dad stares at me for a moment or two longer, judging whether or not to believe me. I learned how to fake happiness, and then Jack came to remind me I didn't have to by keeping my mind off of the troubles in my life. There were still ways to grasp happiness, and he was one of them when we first met.

"Archie just called about a car he's too busy to fix. Do you want to come with me, and we can have a look?" He's already changed into jeans and a T-shirt.

It's great not having to worry about money because your fam-ily owns a successful business, but the kind of dedication it takes to run a big company leads to one's parents rarely being around. I was in middle school when the business took off and my dad was constantly out at meetings and flying states away for work pur-poses, and I rarely saw him. When I did, I only ever saw the busi-ness side of him. I didn't get to see the fun, ripped T-shirt wearing, dad-jean sporting, goofy parent that I had grown up with.

He wore a suit every day and never wore it with a smile. But after my brother passed away during my freshman year of high school, my dad realized how little he was actually around and started staying home more and more, and morphed back into the dad I remembered as a little kid.

"Scarlet?" my dad asks.

"I'd love to come," I say. I've been going to the shop with my dad since I could stand on my own two feet. It's like a second home to me, and Archie like an uncle.

Despite all of the choices of cars to drive to the shop, my dad chooses his old pickup, which I suppose keeps him tied to his country roots. It looks odd in our magnificent driveway, the rusting red paint job chipping away, but neither of us care as we drive down the road to the shop. Dad keeps the windows down, letting the warm fall air whip my hair around, so that he can rest his arm out the window.

"Look there, Scar," Dad says, pointing to a house I have seen thousands of times. "That's the house—"

"That you grew up in. You've only told me that every single time we drive to the shop."

"It's important. I grew up there and opened a shop close enough to walk to, stayed home to save up while I worked on my business, got enough money to eventually move out, met your mom, and was able to slowly start expanding while raising two kids."

My parents have always taught me the importance of a good work ethic.

My dad taught me how to change a tire when I was ten. After getting home from the shop, I boasted to Max that I knew how to do something he didn't, only to learn my dad had taught him when he was eight and he knew ten times the number of auto repairs I did.

After that, I would spend every moment I could at the shop watching the three of them work—Archie, my dad, and Max. Once the shop expanded, I rarely worked with the three of them, so I cherished that time while I had it. Eventually, I forced my way in and then they had to teach me what they were doing. I wouldn't let them get anything done if they didn't.

Since then, my dad has only challenged me further. He let me work at the shop when I was thirteen years old, first with Max and Archie as their helper until I was promoted to a trustworthy mechanic who didn't need help from her big brother.

Archie grins when he sees my dad, a handshake ensues, and then he pulls me in for a side-hug.

"There's my favorite little worker," he says with a thick, Texan accent, ruffling my hair just like my dad had earlier. "This car is causing me a headache. It's constantly slipping as the owner switches gears."

"You check the transmission fluid? Sounds like it may be low," I say.

"That was my first thought too. I checked, it's fine. I can't seem to figure out what it may be, and I haven't got time to do the deep dive, got three other cars racked up and owners that'll be here any minute."

My dad glances at me and wraps his arm around my shoulders. "All right, Scar, what's the solution?"

Together, he and I lift the hood and start digging around to see if maybe there's something Archie missed. It creaks as I open it, a comforting squeak that bellows throughout the shop as I prop it up. Dad goes to grab us some gloves, and the dusty scent of them fills my senses as he tosses me my own beaten-up pair.

I know my dad likes coming to the shop to work on cars like he used to; the business side of owning auto shops means he deals with numbers and corporate officials. He doesn't get a whiff of the rubber scent of the garage, to worry about Mom yelling at him for getting grease and oil on his clothes, or hear the satisfying roar of an engine he fixed. No, he just sees our customers as dollar signs on a spreadsheet and sinks back into the stiff, business style.

He's already got an oil stain on his ratty T-shirt, and his forehead is crinkled as he tugs at a wrench to get into the problem. My own gray jumpsuit gains a matching stain the more we work on the transmission, and eventually my forehead is dusted with sweat and I have hair falling out of my loose ponytail.

"You figure it out?" Dad asks.

I know why he asked. He's diagnosed the problem, and he's challenging me to find it as quickly as he has.

"Not quite yet."

"Look here," he says, stepping closer to me as he points down at the spark plug. "Notice anything odd?"

"It looks normal to me? The terminal nut is perfectly intact."

"Look again."

He's right. Though the terminal is in fine condition, the area around it, known as the corrugations, is corroded.

"How did I not notice before . . ." I sigh.

"Don't worry, Scarlet, you would have gotten there. It's important to check even what you least expect, remember that."

"So simple I didn't even think to look either," Archie says. "Thanks, boss, easy fix."

Dad removes his gloves and tosses them on the table in the corner of the shop, dusting his hands off on his jeans.

"Keep up the good work here, Archie. Let me know if you have any other problems."

We head back home just as the sun begins to set and Dad keeps the windows down in the truck. The sun sets beyond the fields, setting a golden shadow over the town. We pass Dad's childhood home just as the last of the sunlight disappears, but I don't need the sun to know what every blade of grass looks like or to see the bump in the road as we turn into our neighborhood. I know this town too well; it's small enough for me to memorize everything about it. Small enough for memories to be tied to every street, every building, every person.

Dad pulls into our driveway, winding around the fountain in the middle, and we head back inside where Mom has made dinner. The savory scent of oven-roasted chicken drifts through the hall as we enter the house. After dinner, I make my way to my room to finish my homework and get ready for bed, noting a text from Jack reminding me to prepare for tomorrow's pep rally. A perfectly normal day.

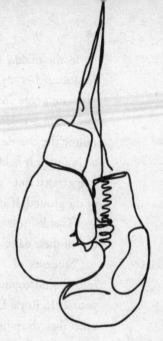

CHAPTER
THREE

I prepare all morning for the pep rally today at school. Fridays in the fall are every student's favorite day—we look forward to them all week long. The student body crowds into the steamy gym, where the are lights bright against the orange gym floor. You can actually feel the entire gym vibrating from the way we come together with dances and chants, an electric vibe in the air. This year the team, led by none other than Jack, has another chance to go to state and win.

At Royal Eastwood, it's a thing for the girlfriend of a player to wear her boyfriend's jersey at every home game, and of course I'm going to wear Jack's loud and proud. Not every girl has the honor of wearing the number one quarterback in the state of Texas's jersey. Our school colors are orange and black; Jack's jersey has a white *#1* outlined in orange against a black background that my hair practically blends in with.

In the middle of the cheerleader's famous Aggressive cheer, Jessica catches my arm and saves me from plummeting to my ultimate doom from the gym bleachers when some rowdy fellow senior accidentally shoves me from behind while trying to mimic the cheerleaders' moves. We're standing on the first row, an honor only held by seniors, so "ultimate doom" may be a little exaggerated since the first row of bleachers is less than a foot off of the ground. If anything, I would have only stumbled forward.

"Thanks, Jess. I swear these pep rallies are going to kill me one of these days."

"Students of Royal Eastwood!" Principal Meyers exclaims into the microphone, and the entire gym goes nuts. "Here is your 2018 Royal Eastwood Warriors football team! Led by none other than three-time state champion quarterback and team captain Jack Dallas!"

The screams grow somehow louder than they were five seconds ago.

Jack runs out, and my throat is already hoarse from shouting. He leads the whole football team into the center of the gym. He's a natural-born leader, and the team has no issue letting him carry the banner and be in the limelight. They look up to him in the same way most of this town does: as a leader, a hero, and the way to get our town known across the country for being home to the next greatest quarterback of all time.

The bleachers shake from the excitement that radiates off of the students; my community *lives* for football. Friday nights are the highlight of almost everyone's week. I mean, stores literally close for these games. Jack winks in my direction, mouthing an I love you to me before he addresses the rest of the school.

"Are y'all ready for tonight?" he shouts into the mic, spinning around to look at every single section in the gym. And then louder again, "I can't hear you! I said, *are y'all ready for tonight?!*"

The band echoes the excitement in the room, and I cover my ears as every instrument blares out random notes to add to the cacophony.

"That's what I like to hear!"

He's wearing his other jersey with jeans and boots, looking undeniably sexy in such a simple outfit. The jeans hug him comfortably in all spots, and his jersey reveals the muscles in his arms. The orange and black contrast his blue eyes, and I nearly melt in my shoes every time he catches my gaze.

"We play our rivals tonight," he says. "They've been saying how they're going to break our undefeated streak, two seasons worth of games. Now, how does that make y'all feel?" The crowd erupts into a chorus of boos.

"I don't like it either! Which is why we aren't going to let them put a single point up on that board!" Once again the crowd in the gym goes ballistic.

It's a big promise to say they aren't going to score at all on us, but everyone has so much faith in Jack's abilities, as well as those of the rest of the team, that he has us all believing him.

"But you know what the best part about tonight will be? Not only are we going to wipe the floor with them, but afterward I get to go home and celebrate with my gorgeous girl, Ms. Scarlet Tucker."

I hear a coo of awws from all around, and I'm mortified knowing almost every single person in the school is probably staring at me. And if I'm being honest, I'm not sure how I feel about the double meaning behind his words, which I'm sure people caught onto.

Though Jack makes me happy and likes to show me off, there are times he goes too far. He's a showboat—that's just the type of person he is, and I know that. But it isn't just football he brags about. While I don't kiss and tell, the same most definitely cannot be said for Jack. His friends have asked me intimate questions suggesting they know way too many details, and I've asked Jack to stop, which he did for about a week, but then he was back to his old self. People are who they are, and you either love all of them or none of them.

With Jack, I have to love all of him, even if there are parts I don't want to. Not every relationship is perfect; the important thing is that he kept me happy when all I wanted to do was cry after Max died. If Jack and I were to break up, although it's different, I'm not sure I could handle losing someone else that close to me.

The band kicks in with our fight song, and not a second later every single person in the stands joins in. We wrap our arms around one another and scream every word at the top of our lungs, radiating school pride. Texas schools may just be the most prideful bunch in the entire country.

As usual, while everyone in the bleachers filters back to their classes, I wait outside the gym for Jack to come out. Jessica waits with me for a little but eventually even she has to scurry off to class. I lean with my back against the orange and black painted concrete, eyeing the doors to the gym as I wait for Jack to emerge.

He finally does, laughing with Bryce before they bro hug and

Bryce walks away while Jack walks over to me. He lifts me into his arms, twirls me around, and laughter spills from my lips.

"You were great," I say.

"I have to be. The school expects me to lead us to another state championship."

"You sure did make a big promise."

"What, to not let them score? Babe, we've got the best defense around, there is no way in hell they're going to get down to the end zone. I've got confidence in my boys."

"That so?"

"You know I'm not one to disappoint," he whispers, pressing his lips to mine. "You look absolutely beautiful representing me." He lets his hand dip dangerously low on my back. "It's kind of a major turn-on."

Elijah's at the other end of the hallway, wearing a dark-gray hoodie zipped all the way up, his hands deep in his pockets. When we ran into one another a few days ago, he seemed so different up close. He was more welcoming. There was a softer atmosphere surrounding him than I was expecting. Jack catches sight of him right before Elijah turns the corner. He doesn't pull away from me completely, instead settling for resting his arm around my waist.

"Hey, freak!" Jack calls. "How come you weren't cheering? Too high to realize what was going on?"

Elijah stops walking, his body stiff and unwavering, but then he continues on his way. The pause lasts for mere seconds, and then he's out of sight. My heart drops for him.

"Thanks for cheering so loud during the rally, babe," Jack says, kissing my cheek. "But I'm going to go find the guys. See you later."

I watch him go, a part of me glad he's gone so I don't have to fake a response to his teasing. My eyes travel back to where

Elijah walked off and I recall how stiff his body became when Jack addressed him like that.

Maybe I should go find Elijah and apologize for Jack. I mean, he and I did have a conversation the other day, even if it only really consisted of me rambling on about *baby proofing* my house. But if we held (sort of) that conversation, doesn't he deserve for me to go and apologize to him now? I begin walking toward the hallway he went down, but then Jessica runs up with a few of the other girls and they engulf me in their conversation about what to pregame with for tonight.

After grabbing all of my books for the weekend from my locker, I head out to call my mom to see if she can pick me up. Jack usually drops me off after school but he's busy with the team. There's a heavy trail of smoke rising into the air in the distance, and I can't help but think that a Friday pep-rally afternoon is an odd time for a bonfire.

The line of smoke leads to an old, beat-up Ford truck, and it sort of excites me to realize I could potentially make someone's day (and mine) by helping them fix their car. Wandering over, I find Elijah messing around under the hood. My stomach flips at the sight of him, since he's the last person I was expecting. His hoodie is off, revealing a stained white T-shirt, but my eyes zero in on some white tape on his knuckles.

"Car troubles?" I ask once I'm close enough to him, knowing full well Jack would not want me talking to him.

Elijah lifts his head from the hood and looks over at me with surprise. "What was your first clue?"

"May I?" I ask.

"Be my guest."

Waving the smoke out of my face, I touch a few wires here and there as the smoke starts to dissipate, flinching from the heat. I can see the problem right away.

"Hey, so . . . I'm sorry about Jack," I say. "You're in luck, it just overheated. Get some coolant and you'll be good to go. There's a shop about a mile down the road."

"Thanks, Scarlet."

My breath catches in my throat when he says my name. It sounds so foreign coming from him, and it's odd to hear your name from someone as reclusive as Elijah. He pushes off of his truck and walks off in the direction I pointed.

I jog the few feet needed to catch up. "I work at the shop and my shift is starting soon anyway. Plus, I can get you a discount."

"Right, Tucker Auto. Your family owns it," Elijah says. "Scarlet . . . Tucker," he repeats to himself a little ominously, as though he put something together.

"It's my dad's business," I say, kicking a rock. "But I work at the one down the road, which is why I get the discount."

"Why work there at that level when you own the whole thing?"

"I have to make money somehow."

Elijah stares at me for a few seconds and then he averts his gaze to the walk in front of us.

"Do you really like walking or is your car not working?"

"Right, I come from money so I must own a Mercedes or a BMW," I mutter. "That's why I work at the auto shop. I'm saving up to buy my own car. I didn't want my parents to buy me one. Call it pride or whatever, but I don't have a car."

I sense his surprise. "You stereotype me pretty hard."

"Don't you do the same to me?"

When I don't reply, he moves past that topic and looks at the road next to us. "Considering who you hang out with, I assumed."

I kick the rock one more time and it passes into Elijah's path and then onto the road. "I'm not really like them. I'm only friends with them because of Jack. I know he can be a jerk to you, and I don't like that he does that. Sure, he can be too cocky at times, he can flirt with other girls too often, and he can be pretty rude—"

"Are you going to get to the but soon?"

"But," I emphasize, sensing his teasing, "he's a good boyfriend."

"I never said he wasn't."

"Still, I'm sorry for the way he treats you—" I start.

"You shouldn't have to be."

The neon Tucker Auto sign is up ahead, just beyond this small hill, and I say nothing in response. We stay silent as we walk up the hill, avoiding deep cracks in the sidewalk that could "break your momma's back." I can already smell the gas from the garage, but we avoid that part of the store and instead go to the shopping portion attached, hearing the familiar ring of the doorbell as we enter.

"Let me guess, that truck of yours is a 1980?" I ask, and he confirms it. "I figured. It really is a beautiful truck, just looks like it has a few engine problems."

"You really know everything about cars, don't you?"

"My dad's been teaching me the ins and outs since I was a kid." I pass him my favorite brand of coolant. "He brought me to the shop when I was only ten to fix a tire, and, for some reason, I absolutely loved cars. I'd whine until he'd let me look under the hood with him and then I'd pretend to diagnose the problem, even if I had no clue what I was doing. He says I was quite the whiny child, but I feel like he only says that to get under my skin at times. I—"

"Is rambling a thing you do often or . . . ?" Elijah pokes fun.

"Long story short, my dad actually started the business in this very shop."

I tell Archie to take Elijah's coolant from my paycheck. Elijah was quick to object but I shoved the bottle in his hands before he could say any more and gave him instructions on where to put it and how long to wait until driving off.

"Thanks for this."

I wave it off. "Take it as my apology for running into you the other day and making you pick up practically all of my papers."

A car roars by on the street in front of the shop, drowning out Elijah's chuckle.

"Have fun at the game."

The coolant in his hand sloshes against the sides of the dark container as he turns to head back the way we came, leaving me to my thoughts about how long after my shift I'll have to get ready for the football game tonight.

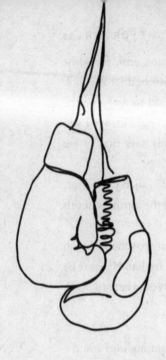

CHAPTER
FOUR

Jack, of course, led the football team to victory on Friday and kept his promise to the school. Our rivals didn't put a single point up on the scoreboard, and Jack was all over the news for promising such a hefty outcome and keeping it true. After a 35–0 total domination, he's in every newspaper and on every news channel within a fifty-mile radius. He celebrated his win during the weekend with his team, and I took on extra hours at work. I didn't mind at all; his happiness is on the field, and mine is in the shop. We didn't hang out all weekend, and that was fine.

He came to pick me up this morning for school, and it was the first I'd seen him since his big win. I appreciated the ride, considering the heavy rain that was pattering down loudly on the pavement. It had been pouring since last night, when the storm was the worst. Before fourth period, I'm back at my locker exchanging books and paying little attention to the hustle and bustle in the hallway surrounding me.

"Hey, beautiful," Jack breathes, coming up behind me and wrapping his arms around my torso. "You ran off this morning once we got to school, I didn't even get my good morning kiss."

"Someone got to my house ten minutes late—it didn't leave much time to do anything except rush to class."

"Couldn't have been me. I'm a great boyfriend so I'm always on time."

Lies.

I turn all the way around in his arms and stand on my tiptoes to kiss him.

"There you go, that's your good morning kiss."

"Now it's the afternoon, Scar. I need my *afternoon* kiss."

I oblige and lean forward to kiss him, but when I pull away after a short peck of our lips he practically growls and tries to steal another. Yes, teenage guys are complete horndogs, and Jack is the horniest of them all. He walks us a few feet back so that he's leaning against the wall of black lockers, painted with orange numbers to provide more school spirit, as he holds me in his arms.

"We go any further and you won't be able to stop," I joke, though a part of me is being serious.

"Less talking, more kissing."

I keep my lips away from his, though. "Speaking of words, I had this thing in English—"

"Aye, Jack!" a guy calls from down the hallway. "That was a great win Friday night."

"Thanks, man, I do what I have to," Jack says.

"Keep doing it—we are going to go all the way this year!"

"As long as I'm the QB, I promise it'll happen." He winks, and the guy stomps off shouting the Warriors chant.

Suddenly, a crowd of football players walk by and call for Jack. His attention goes to them as they all shout his name and make remarks about the two of us.

"I'll see you later, babe," he says dismissively as he goes after them.

"What about my story?"

He walks back to me, takes my hands, and rests them on his shoulders after kissing my palm. "I'm sorry, Scar. Tell me tonight and I'll be all ears, promise. Don't pout like that, you know I love you."

"Yeah, yeah, yeah, just go."

It's not like this is the first time this has happened, anyway.

"I can't wait to hear it, honest," he says, catching up to the large crowd of giant, mangy football players.

My eyes catch sight of a hoodie down the hall and the bounce in my step comes back. "Elijah!" I call without a second thought.

His shoulders stiffen, but he doesn't stop walking, so I shout his name again and jog to catch up with him.

"What are you doing?" he asks.

"Walking with you."

"Why?"

"We're friends, aren't we?"

"Friends?"

"I thought since I helped you out on Friday and we walked practically a mile together that we could be considered friends."

When he doesn't reply, I feel the need to fill the silence. "I mean, of course if things are moving too fast for you, I understand. That sounded like we were in a relationship, which we clearly aren't. Not that I think you're gross! Quite the opposite! Okay, I'm making this worse. It's just that we've only just met, and you know I have a boyfriend and—"

"Wall." Elijah's voice is calm, yet amused.

My face collides with the concrete and I slightly ricochet. I lift my hand to my poor nose and scrunch my face up from the sharp pain.

Oh. *Wall.*

"Okay, *ouch*."

I swear, if I just broke my nose all of the girls in Jack's group are going to go berserk telling me where I can get it done for the best results, and that's the last thing I want. And the fact I hit it on the trophy pillar in the main hall of all things; this thing is very hard to miss.

Elijah leans against the same pillar that just attacked my face. "You all right?"

I rub my throbbing forehead. "Just peachy."

"You want to be friends?"

"Why wouldn't I?"

"I could name a few reasons."

"What? What people say about you? Just rumors. And I try not to listen to them. You're mysterious."

"Mysterious?"

"That's practically the only thing I know for sure about you other than the fact you wear this hoodie quite often. The days you don't wear this one, you wear another oversized black one, and those are the days you hide your face. Oh, I also know that some-times your knuckles are taped up. Everything else: mysterious."

Elijah throws up an extra wall even stronger than the col-umn that destroyed my nose, and his lips morph back into that straight line. Before I can apologize for possibly offending him, the warning bell sounds for us to get to fourth period and he pushes off of the pillar, walking away.

"I'll see you around, Scarlet."

Elijah is just getting absorbed into the dissipating crowd of students when someone hisses my name and Jessica runs over to me. She grabs my arm, not so gently might I add, and drags me down the hall for who knows what reason.

"What are you *doing*?" she hisses.

"I should ask you the same thing!"

She notices her hand on my arm and quickly takes it away with an apology. "What are you doing with Eli? Does Jack know you two are friends?"

"I don't know if we're friends," I mutter as I realize that he never gave me a specific answer on that topic. "Why does it matter if Jack knows?"

"It doesn't matter, I just don't want to see you get hurt."

"You don't actually believe those rumors about Elijah, do you?"

"I didn't mean by Eli—though still be careful, he's a little creepy—I meant Jack. We all know he hates Eli, I can't imagine what he would say if he saw you with him."

Avoiding a freshman rushing to avoid being tardy, we make it to English class right as the bell rings. The thought of Jack and Elijah weighs heavily on me, taking away from my participation in the daily edits. Instead of focusing on my teacher preaching the correct use of who versus whom, my thoughts are consumed with Jessica's warning.

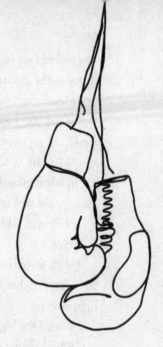

CHAPTER
FIVE

After Jessica's caution, I kept to myself for the remainder of the day. She made me think—am I doing something wrong? What she said is still on my mind even now, at the auto shop, echoing louder than the sound of the rain hitting the fallen leaves outside the garage doors. It hasn't stopped raining all day.

"Archie, could you pass me a rag?" I ask as I roll out from under an old, rusted truck someone brought into the shop a few days ago. Suddenly, a rag lands on my face instead of my outstretched hand. "Gee, thanks."

"You're welcome, darlin'," he says. "It looks like that Jack fellow of yours is about to drive on up here."

I slowly sit up from my creeper, the skateboard-like contraption mechanics use to go underneath cars when they are on a lift, and wipe my hands free of grease. I hear the roar of Jack's truck way before I see it, and after he stops in the parking lot, he jumps down to the ground and darts inside to escape the rain.

"Hey, babe, what are you—" I start to say.

"What the hell were you doing walking around with that freak?" he says accusingly.

"What are you talking about?" I ask, wringing the towel in my hands nervously.

Who the heck snitched on me?

"Eli! Bryce told me he saw you walking with him to class."

Bryce.

I walk across the garage to throw the rag down on a cluttered table, and Archie hightails it into the shop as soon as he sees a fight rising.

"What's the big deal?" I ask, avoiding eye contact.

"*What's the big deal?*" Jack repeats incredulously, throwing his hands into the air. "All that shit about him being such a druggy, Scar! His brother overdosed on God knows what; Eli's a freak!"

"Those are just rumors, Jack."

"Rumors ruin reputations. The things this could do to mine are detrimental."

"Did you come here just to yell at me? Because if so, you are welcome to leave until you've cooled down," I suggest.

"No."

"Then stop."

He takes a deep breath and closes his eyes for a few moments to calm himself down. "My dad needed me to pick something up for his car, that's why I came."

"What does he need?"

"Not sure," he mutters as he walks toward the shop, me following him. "It's some sort of water thing, I think. It was supposed to, like, clean the hood or the windshield or something. I don't know."

"Washer fluid?"

"That's it!" He snaps his fingers and I give him a kiss. "Thanks, babe, this is what my dad needed. I'm sorry about my temper. Can you take this out of your paycheck? I left my wallet in my game bag."

I don't want to fight anymore but I also hate it when he takes advantage of my hard work.

"Look, Scar, I don't like arguing with you. Why don't you come over tonight and I can make it up to you? I'll have Linda make us a nice steak dinner, we can watch your favorite movie, and then we can go upstairs and make up some more," he suggests, pulling me closer to him.

I debate what I should say. Linda, his family's personal chef, is a phenomenal cook, and her steak dinner is quite possibly my favorite meal ever.

"I see the answer already in your eyes, Scar." He smirks. "I'll come get you at eight; love you."

Jack leaves the shop, shielding himself from the rain by holding his jacket over his head the best he can, and hops into his truck. It roars to life and he drives off.

Archie reappears. "Don't worry, I'll pretend I didn't see him take that fluid."

~

"Scarlet, do you mind going into the shop? We've got a customer and I'm still working on Ms. Betty's car," Archie asks as he messes around the hood of her old Chevy.

I'm cleaning a few of our tools over on the worktable, but I set my things down and walk toward the shop.

"Yes, sir," I say, and he huffs. He hates it when I call him sir, but manners are number one.

The scent of tires fades only slightly and mixes with the air freshener I made Archie buy so that customers wouldn't get a headache from rubber fumes in the entrance where they wait. The garage reeks of oil and tires, and I know the smell sticks to me for hours even after I've gone home and showered, so I don't want that in the store.

A jolt of surprise shoots up my body when I see a familiar gray hoodie searching our array of windshield wipers along the back wall.

"You know, Elijah, now that we're friends you don't have to watch me at work. You can actually come and talk to me," I tease.

When he hears my voice Elijah doesn't jump, he just coolly turns around and his piercing green eyes land on me. I note that his short brown hair is matted down in random places from the rain, which drips down his slight sideburns and trickles off his jaw.

"My windshield wipers flew off after the storm last night," he explains, holding a new pair in his hands.

"These are for a 2014 and up sedan, plus they're winter wipers. That 1980 Ford of yours is going to need . . ."—I trail off as I grab the proper wipers—"these. I'm surprised we even have the proper blades on the shelf. Do you know how to install these?"

He scratches the back of his neck. "No, I don't."

"I'll help."

He opens the door for me and I quickly shuffle outside,

noting that the downpour has turned into a gentle drizzle and the dark clouds have lightened. We walk across the parking lot, dodging a puddle, and I get to work on installing the new wipers.

"Your truck is every mechanic's dream," I joke. "I mean, it's already had two problems in the span of one week." *Even though he technically didn't pay for the coolant, and we kind of walked out without paying for the wipers . . . oops, sorry, Dad.*

"That reminds me." Elijah reaches into his wallet to pay for the coolant from last week, but I stop him.

"It's really okay."

"Take it, please." He pushes the money into my hands.

"Thanks." His hands are rough and covered in cuts and scars but before I can ask about them, he shoves his hands back into his pockets.

"You're all set," I say as I finish with the wipers.

My eyes wander to the passenger side of his truck and I notice a giant, worn-out blue duffel bag laying on the torn leather seats. "Running away from home or something?"

"It's for the gym."

"I don't work out much. I went with Jack once, but he was with Bryce and all of his friends, so I felt like a fish out of water with no guidance," I say.

Elijah doesn't reply to my little story, so I clear my throat. "Anyway, what gym?"

"Thanks again for the help, Scarlet," he says before he opens the door, earning a loud creak in response, and drives off without another word.

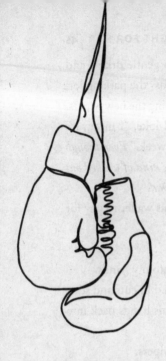

CHAPTER
SIX

As I round the corner on my way to lunch at school the next day, getting lost in the art students' mural of Lake Conroe on the wall that different classes have been expanding on throughout the years, a pair of arms suddenly wrap behind me and pull me strongly, yet gently, into a solid chest, and I let out a small noise of surprise. A deep laugh sounds in my ear and warm breath fans down my neck.

"Didn't mean to startle you, beautiful," Jack says.

"You'd think I'd get used to it, considering you do it almost every day."

"It's my thing."

The rowdy football players who double as Jack's best friends saunter over and my sweet Jack turns into a macho, football playing jock.

"Dude, have you gotten everything for the party Friday?"

Bryce asks, slapping Jack's shoulder, taking him away from my side. Well, it was nice while it lasted.

"Is that even a question? I've got enough kegs for everyone to have their own."

"Party?" I say.

"Shit, I forgot to tell you, I'm hosting a party Friday night after the game."

Before I respond, we reach the cafe and shuffle to our spot. The way it's set up is basically made to create the popular people—one giant table in the center of the room, big enough for our group, and then a bunch of smaller circular tables on the sides of the cafe for others.

As soon as we sit down, Katie pulls out her Kate Spade lunch box, a gourmet meal of sushi inside waiting for her, while Bryce pulls out a bag filled with three sandwiches packed full of meat. It's nearly identical to the lunch scene in *The Breakfast Club*, and if I was to pull out my dad's homemade sloppy joe, I would be the equivalent of the oddball in the back pouring Pixy Stix over her cereal sandwich. So instead, I pull out my salad. I mean, they're *fine*. I wouldn't eat anything I didn't like to impress them, but I'd prefer a juicy chicken or even a taco or *something* with a little more protein, which is why I toss enough grilled chicken in my salad to cover up all of the greens.

"Ugh, what should we do if Carson tries to show up," Katie complains.

I try to listen to their conversation about who would ruin the party's reputation if they were to show up, but I lose all interest and my mind goes to current news.

"Did you guys hear about the recent fall in the stock market? My dad said it may harm a lot of small businesses and—" They all cut me off with more stories about the party and I deflate. I could try again, but there would be no point.

"What about businesses, babe?" Jack asks, sending me his attention.

"The Dow fell this morning. My dad said it may not be a huge deal but to keep an eye on it. The Fed might be raising interest rates."

"Oh, the Fed?" he jokes.

"It could impact a lot of our parent's businesses, shouldn't we keep up with that stuff? It's basic econ, aren't you all taking that this semester—"

He smiles but his voice doesn't register any excitement. "Sure, babe. I'll make sure to let my dad know to be careful when he's negotiating salaries for the upcoming draft."

I don't even know why I try.

Elijah's sitting across the cafeteria with a wrinkled and ripped brown paper bag as his only companion, but he doesn't seem bothered by it at all. I wonder if *he* has a sloppy joe that his dad made for him as his lunch. Even though being alone doesn't seem to bother him, it bothers me. No one should sit by themselves. What would Jack say if I got up and walked over and sat down next to Elijah? What would everyone else at my table say? Why does it matter?

"Why are you staring at Elijah?" Jack growls in my ear.

I jump from the shock and look up at him with wide eyes. "What?"

"You're staring."

"He looks lonely."

"He's not a charity case, Scar. Quit staring."

I deflate and take one last look at Elijah before directing my attention back to the party conversations, which has moved on now to speculate on who can get drunk the quickest. That's their topic of conversation for the remainder of the day. On every transition between classes, the party is all I hear about. In fact, it's all anyone talks about until the end of the day when it's finally time to leave.

Holding my books against my chest, I head to the parking lot. Jack was unable to drive me home today, but my dad said to give him a call when I got out of school. He finished up at the office early today.

I am about to pull out my phone when a hand taps my shoulder from behind, and I turn around.

"Hey, Elijah."

He thrusts out his other hand, awkwardly holding a notebook that looks strangely familiar.

"You dropped this back there."

That's why I recognize it.

"Thanks!" I delicately take it from him and clumsily toss it on the top of the stack I'm carrying.

He nods and throws his hands comfortably into his pockets, completely fine with the constant silence that seems to fall between us. A BMW in the parking lot nearly crashes into a custom-painted pink Audi, which would have ruined the paint job, and the noise of expensive horns fills the air.

"Are you headed to the parking lot?" I ask, and he raises a brow at me and nods. "Let's walk together, then."

His lips move up from their usual straight line as he responds, "I planned on it."

I feel embarrassment sneak up my spine. He doesn't need my permission. I have the right to think I need to ask him, though;

he's never been the type of guy who seems as if he would want to walk with someone. He does almost everything alone, and I don't understand it. Sure, I'm independent, but that doesn't mean I don't like the attention of others. I like being with my friends and laughing with someone else, or just having someone to talk to. I don't understand why he doesn't.

"Do you like sitting alone at lunch?" I ask.

"It doesn't bother me."

"I wouldn't be able to do it."

"No?"

"I don't think so. I don't need a bunch of people surrounding me to be happy, but it's always nice to have someone to talk to. Like before Jack, when I was all alone, it was difficult to stay happy, I think. Then Jack came along and I realized how much easier things are when you're not by yourself. When you are . . . it's hard to stay away from the thoughts that have potential to eat away at you, you know? At least when you're with someone you can distract yourself long enough for those thoughts to go away. I like being able to laugh along with my friends or have someone to gossip with. And—"

I need to learn how to control my mouth.

"When you're alone for long enough, you forget what it's like to depend on others to keep those thoughts away," he says.

"Maybe that's true, until you find someone to remind you that you're not alone. See? Some of my rambles can lead to helpful ideas," I joke.

But Elijah's response keeps things away from small talk. "Do you ramble with me because your other friends don't let you talk very much?"

I can't think of a quippy comeback.

"I notice things too," he says.

Elijah opens the door for us as we walk outside, and I'm hit with a wave of crisp fall freshness full of the scent of crushed leaves.

"They were talking about the party, so I just wasn't all that interested." I feel the need to defend my friends.

Elijah stays quiet and keeps looking ahead, but I know he's listening to me with his full attention.

"It's this Friday, actually. Do you want to come?"

Elijah frowns at me. "You're really inviting me to a party?"

"Yeah, why not?"

Well, Scarlet, there are plenty of reasons not to. But the reason to ask him seems to put the others to rest. You want him there.

Elijah stares at me for a few seconds longer before moving his gaze to the sidewalk ahead of us. "I'm busy Friday nights anyway."

"With what?" I ask against my better judgment.

"I have to help my mom pay our bills every Friday." He chooses his words carefully.

"What does she do?"

"She's a waitress at a diner on Tenth Street," he answers hesitantly.

I rack my brain to try and remember the diner, and a memory of Max taking me out for ice cream hits me. A diner on Tenth Street.

"Diner on Tenth," I repeat. "That's the name of the actual diner, isn't it?"

He seems surprised I know of it. "You've been there?"

"A few times," I say vaguely, not wanting to stir unneeded memories of Max right now. When I think of him it's hard to keep my emotions back.

"I didn't think you would have."

"It's good food," I insist.

Elijah walks off to his truck, cutting through the grass, and I'm left standing alone. His hood flops as he walks and the laces on his worn-down shoes almost rub against the grassy ground.

I set my books down on the ground and take the spot next to them to sit while I dial my dad's number and ask if he can come get me. I call twice, and after I'm left with his voice mail both times, I decide to give my mom a ring, but she doesn't answer either.

I lock my phone and throw it into my lap as my shoulders fall. I sit and pick at the grass, debating whether or not I should just walk home or call Jack or Jessica or someone. As my mind wanders through the possibilities, I hear the light crunching of grass and suddenly I see two worn-down sneakers with the laces almost hitting the ground standing right in front of me. I lift my eyes and the sun illuminates Elijah's figure as I squint at his face.

"No one answered, did they?" he asks.

He reaches his hand out to me. "Come on, I can drive you home."

My brain finally connects with what he's saying, and I take his hand, feeling the rough calluses scratch against my equally rough skin, toughened from working on cars my whole life, and Elijah helps me to my feet. This time it's my turn to be silent and stare at him, only I probably look like a fish out of water with my mouth agape. I never could have imagined that Elijah Black would be offering to drive me home.

"If we're friends, then I'm not about to let you walk home by yourself, especially with the rain coming," he adds, eyes momentarily flickering to the clouds in the distance. "Seems Texas is stuck in a cycle of storms."

"Don't feel like you have to, I don't even mind walking, and I doubt it will actually rain," I quickly say as we reach his truck, but I feel a giant raindrop hit my nose and Elijah's eyes crinkle at the sides.

"I may be a freak but I'm not heartless. Come on, I don't want you to get rained on."

I get into his truck, the scent of old leather covering my senses, and I wince at his comment. Jack may think that way, but I've realized that I don't.

"Elijah, I don't think you're a fr—"

"I know."

It would be silent between us if not for the light rain pattering on the windshield only hard enough for him to use the lowest wiper setting on his truck.

"Hopefully, the rain will let up this week," I say. "Otherwise the game Friday may be ruined. Are you going?"

"I'm not much into football. Which way do I turn?"

"Turn right, go toward the auto shop. I live a few minutes from there. Why aren't you into football?"

Elijah shifts gears and his truck lurches onto the main road, sputtering slightly as he shifts to a higher gear and turns up the speed of the wipers.

"It's a lot of students cheering for a guy I don't really like," Elijah says.

We pass Jack's neighborhood, the entrance closed with an extravagant black gate that requires a code to be let in. He lives lakefront on Lake Conroe: boats, Jet Skis, a large dock, etc. No point in living on the lake on rainy days like today.

"Am I turning here?"

He begins to slow the truck, but I stop him before he can shift down.

"No, I don't live in this neighborhood. I live in Summerset."

The slight lift of Elijah's eyebrows emits his surprise, and he keeps driving along, quickly coming up on the hill leading to Tucker Auto.

"This is the part where you tell me where you live," I joke. "You know, I say something about myself, you say something about yourself . . . the formula for a conversation."

He chuckles. "I live downtown."

"By Diner on Tenth?"

He hesitates. Tenth Street is potentially the poorest area in Conroe. The diner is the only business able to stay afloat. It's surrounded by bankrupt buildings with decade-old For Sale signs in the dirt-stained windows. The crowd around there is not one to be messed with—if Conroe was to have high crime rates, they would all be from there.

"Around there," he finally chooses to say.

"Turn up ahead, left. I've never been anywhere downtown other than the diner."

"It's not a popular area."

It's not a safe area.

As he turns onto a smaller street, complete with cottage-style houses on both sides, we come up to my neighborhood turn. I point out where to turn and soon we reach my driveway, bouncing along the cobblestones as my house is revealed beyond the trees.

"Thank you for the ride, Elijah. You should think about maybe going to the game, or even the party."

I get out of his truck, having to push hard on the door since it sticks a little from rust. I step down, mentally preparing for a slight jump like with Jack's truck, but instead my feet instantly rest on the ground. With one more good-bye to Elijah, I run inside to try and avoid getting too soaked, and go to my room to prepare for the rest of the week leading up to Friday night's party.

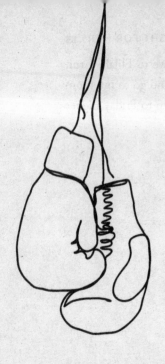

CHAPTER
SEVEN

Friday came quickly, and every day leading up to it Jack and his friends raved about how exciting the party tonight would be. The football game against Midtown's Jaguars just ended, and now I'm headed home.

Minutes ago I was cheering, hollering, and smiling a smile so big I was worried my face would rip in half, but now, as I walk home, I'm shivering, silent, and scowling so deeply I fear my face will stick this way. The football game tonight was one of the most exciting games Jack has played in his entire four years of high school. The news stations were all over this game for the past week.

The media attention didn't bother Jack or intimidate him; it fueled his desire to win. The entire game was one touchdown after the other by both teams; it didn't matter how well the defense was playing on either side, the offense was dominating *everything*.

Jack barely pulled through with a win. At the end of the game, he threw what we all thought was an interception. He let the ball fly out of his hands, and a player from the other team popped his hand up and tipped it. The ball hung in the air for what felt like years and every single player was ready to snatch it, but Jack was quicker than them all and decided he didn't want to wait for the ball to reach him; so he ran, used one of his linemen as a booster, and leaped into the air to catch it, landing easily on his feet.

Because everyone was in shock at what had just happened, Jack had a clear run straight to the end zone and we won the game. He caught his own pass and got the game-winning touch-down. The headlines practically wrote themselves, and I knew this would get a ton of news attention.

Every single student from Royal Eastwood who was on the bleachers stormed the field. And as soon as Jack found me, he pulled me into his arms and swung me around as our ecstatic voices joined those of the roaring crowd. Then he was lifted onto his teammates' shoulders and the roars turned into one unified chant: "Jack! Jack! Jack! Jack!"

Once the hype dissipated, I decided I'd wait for Jack in the parking lot to take me to the after-party at his house. He's been so excited about this party all week, so when he hasn't shown after fifteen minutes, I call him.

Turns out Jack forgot he was supposed to drive me, and is already at his house and *already* tipsy, so he isn't able to pick me up. So, here I am walking home, shivering from the sudden fall chill in the air, sneezing from an oncoming cold, and cursing Jack for being so stupid and forgetful. Finally, I enter my neighbor-hood, my feet dragging on the ground since the walk was so long and strenuous.

My Fitbit progress is going to be phenomenal after that million-mile walk.

At this point, I'm running on the leftover fumes from the short-lived adrenaline rush right after the win tonight, and my oncoming cold is creeping up on me at an amazing speed. I've sneezed and coughed ten times in the past minute.

I tiredly throw my front door open, the warmth of our house hitting me at full blast, and it warms my chilled skin. I close my eyes and let the warm air blanket my body, quickly shutting out the cold by slamming the door.

"Scar?" my dad calls from the den, so I kick off my shoes and follow his voice.

I come upon my dad and mom snuggled under a blanket with a giant bowl of popcorn between them, the only light in the room coming from the movie on the TV that is now paused.

"Hey, where were you guys tonight? Y'all weren't at the game."

"That would be because of me," my mom says in a regretful, stuffed-up voice.

Dad kisses her forehead. "Your mom wasn't feeling well so I thought we would stay inside and watch some movies rather than risking her getting worse by going to the game. How'd it go?"

I wish I had done that. But Jack would be offended if I missed one of his games, and he's always been there for me during important moments of my life. Plus, since I'm a senior, I don't have many more Friday Night Lights left; I need to soak up the last of my high school years.

"We won." The exhaustion is clear in my voice.

My mom picks up on how tired I am, and her lips tug down into a worried frown. "Are you feeling okay, sweetheart?"

"I've never felt better. Just a little tired from all that cheering."

"You can finish this movie with us and pick the next one," Dad says and pats the spot next to him.

I stare longingly at the open cushion and regretfully shake my head, trying my best to cover up a sudden sneeze. "I wish I could, but I promised Jack I'd go to the after-party."

I don't shy away from telling them exactly where I will be. My parents are very understanding people, and they are far from naive. I'm dating the most famous high school quarterback in perhaps all of Texas, so it's to be expected I would go to some crazy after-parties with him, and they trust me enough to stay safe.

Besides, I'm not much of a drinker.

"Why don't you take my truck? I don't want you to rely on anyone there for a ride and then get into any dangerous situations. I know Jack can take care of you, but take it just in case."

I walk over and kiss his cheek. "Thanks, Dad. I'll stay safe."

"And you know you can call us if you feel uncomfortable at any time," Mom adds.

"I know."

The familiar sting in my chest happens as I pass my brother's room. I'll never get over his death—how sudden and unexpected it was left a hole in my heart that will never fully be healed. The house isn't the same without his sarcastic conversations with my dad or his unbreakable bond with my mom, or even the responsibility he felt to make me smile.

Once in my room, I change into high-waisted shorts and a crop top—probably not the smartest outfit choice since it's getting quite cold outside in the fall months, but I've got to play the part, right?

I get lucky and park in an empty space in Jack's driveway. I make my way to the front door, hearing the sounds from the party all around me. A shiver runs through my body as the cold air once again hits my skin. I go inside, trying to hold back my coughing and sneezing, and I'm met with chaos. It's what anyone who has heard rumors of raging parties would assume—it doesn't break a single stereotype. Hell, there's even someone swinging from Jack's chandelier.

And it's Bryce.

Of course.

"Scar! Baby!" Jack slurs, sauntering over to me with his arms thrown out to the sides. "I was wondering when you'd make it! Come on, beautiful, let me get you a drink." He takes my hand and we stumble through the crowd.

"Jack, you know I drove," I say, but he doesn't hear me, and we continue toward the mound of kegs in the kitchen. He pours me a beer and practically shoves it in my hand. May as well just hold it to appease his drunk self.

"You look fucking hot, Scar. I am *so* lucky."

"You're not so bad yourself when you're not a drunken mess," I mutter, but he takes my semiserious words as a complete joke and barks out a laugh, then tugs us toward the dancing bodies.

"Come on, let's dance!"

Halfway through the party, my cough gets too strong to hold off, and being in a crowded room with hot bodies constantly bumping into me and bass so loud my ribs are shaking isn't helping my already throbbing head. I must be coming down with some sort of fever, too, because I'm sweating yet shivering at the same time.

It doesn't help that Bryce fell off of the chandelier he'd decided to make into a jungle gym. He fell onto the floor, surprisingly without the chandelier following, and scraped his entire arm. Since I was the only sober one on scene, I ran to the bathroom to get what I could to fix the problem for the time being—disinfectant and bandages.

Jack could barely let me go for long enough for me to fix Bryce up, and then it was right back to dancing.

"Jack, I'm going to go outside for a little!" I yell over the music, but I don't check to see if he heard or understood me in his drunken state, and I weave in and out of the crowd as the heat from all the bodies makes me feel worse.

I start coughing right after I yell to Jack, and suddenly my throat begins to burn and I swallow hard. I make a stop in the kitchen for a bottle of water, then go sit on the corner of Jack's backyard patio, looking beyond the pool and to the lake. Moonlight glistens off the calm water, disturbed with every gust of wind.

You and me both, water.

I forgot my jacket because I am an idiot, and I have a bottle of cold water as my only companion. At least I'm not sweating anymore.

I get used to the deep bass echoing from inside the house, and soon it becomes background noise to the sound of the leaves in the trees and gentle lapping of the lake against the cobblestone barrier that Jack's property has in place of a sandy beach. However, when I hear the foreign sound of a stick breaking, I turn around to see who caused the noise, expecting Jack to have come outside to check on me.

I perk up when I see Elijah of all people walking toward me.

Per usual, his hands are in his pockets and his ripped hoodie—unzipped to show the T-shirt underneath—is snug on his tall, broad frame. He looks slightly disheveled but not like the drunken mess that everyone inside is becoming. Behind him, back on the road, I barely make out his light-blue truck parked alongside the curb.

"You came?" I ask, not bothering to hide my surprise.

"My other thing ended early."

"Yeah?"

He rocks on his feet and looks out over the lake. "I was driving by and remembered how beautiful the views in this neighborhood are. You're sitting alone."

All of my friends are inside having the time of their life, and I'm outside on the patio all alone. I'm sure I look pathetic. Suddenly, the patterns in the patio are very interesting to me.

"It's not often you see the girlfriend of the host sitting outside by herself," Elijah says.

I scoot over as a gesture for him to sit with me, and he does.

"There, now I'm not by myself."

"No, I guess not."

A lone boat zooms across the lake with nothing but a pinpoint light guiding its way, gaining our attention. We fall into a small silence, and I swallow away the dryness and scratchiness that has lodged itself in my throat from this cold.

"Thanks for coming," I say.

"I had nothing better to do."

My shoulders slump at such a blunt and rather rude answer, and I don't bother to respond, and he seems to notice and tries to lighten the tense mood.

"Plus, I didn't want to disappoint you. I saw how bad you wanted me here."

I snap my head over to him and I can feel my jaw drop slightly. "You just made a joke."

I sense him take on a defensive posture, and I realize I spoke rather rudely, as if he wasn't *allowed* to make jokes.

"Yeah, and?"

"I don't think I've ever heard you make a joke," I admit truthfully and lightheartedly, and it results in a chuckle from him.

"I'm not exactly the class clown, no."

"I like it."

"When I joke?"

I smile. "Yeah. It's something that one may not expect from Elijah Black."

"Well, get to know me and you'll learn I'm full of surprises."

I think of my response, but something irritates my throat and I start to cough profusely, which makes it burn even more. I try to clear the cough, but it just gets worse, and my cheeks heat up from pain and embarrassment.

Elijah watches me as I swallow hard to try and get some sort of relief from the pain, and he furrows his brow, our previous banter suddenly a thing of the past.

"Why are you here if you're sick?"

Perceptive. Not that it's hard to pick up on.

"It's just a small cold." I whisper because it doesn't hurt my throat as much as talking does. "And I have to take care of Jack," I add, and then I sneeze, and exhaustion reenters my body from all of this strain.

"Scarlet, you sound terrible; you shouldn't be out."

I reach for the forgotten water next to me, downing a few gulps that soothe the pain for a second or two. "I have to take care of Jack," I repeat.

Elijah seems annoyed at that response, and I quickly continue, "I know it shouldn't be my job to take care of him, but what if he does something stupid because I wasn't here to watch him?"

"You should be doing what you want." I suddenly sneeze again and Elijah frowns. "And what's good for your health."

"It's not that easy."

"Why?"

Such a simple question, yet it has me sweating to find an answer. Because deep down I know why I strive to help Jack, why I worry every time he gets drunk or goes to some party.

"He needs my help," I say, hoping that will be enough to suffice. But even I know that isn't all there is to it.

But Elijah continues to stare at me, waiting for more because he can tell there's more to it than that.

"I don't want to see anything bad happen to him and know that there was something I could have done."

Because maybe if I had been there for Max, he would still be with us today.

"I lost someone already." I continue to fill the silence but feel tears burning the back of my throat. "I don't want to lose anyone again."

"Your brother," he finally says, putting two and two together as recognition flashes across his expression. "Max, right?"

"How do you know his name?"

For a split second Elijah's eyes widen as though he said something he shouldn't have, but it's gone so quickly that I realize I must have imagined it.

"It's not a huge town, and his death made headlines."

I nod and try to hold back the depressing weight of sorrow

from falling back onto my shoulders. Max was six years older than me, and not many people make the connection that we were related. I'm surprised Elijah of all people was able to.

The papers didn't talk about the distress his passing had on his family; they only morphed his tragic accident into a debate about the need for a law to make all motorcyclists wear a helmet.

Max had jet-black hair that always looked rugged atop his head and striking blue eyes that not a single girl failed to notice. Max was the stereotypical bad boy of Royal Eastwood in his time there. He drove that damn motorcycle, wore a leather jacket, and always smelled faintly of smoke from the cigarettes he kept on hand. I used to beg him to stop smoking, threatening him with the thought of lung cancer taking his life when he was older.

He always assured me he'd be all right.

But the one part of Max that just did not fit his bad-boy reputation was that Max was one of the nicest people anyone could ever meet. He was caring, compassionate, and faithful. Take away the leather jacket, cigarettes, and motorcycle, and he wouldn't have had any reputation aside from being a saint.

"Not a day goes by that it doesn't hurt," I admit.

Elijah focuses on the light shining on Jack's dock, illuminating parts of the water beneath.

"I know what you mean."

"You mean . . . ?"

It suddenly strikes me that I'm not the only one who has lost a brother.

"My brother too."

He lost his brother in one of the most tragic ways anyone could imagine—his brother was taken from him by a drug overdose.

News of what happened spread through the school and the town like wildfire, and that was one of the rumors that was hardest for me to hear.

"Oliver, right?" I ask gently.

Elijah seems taken aback that I remember, or even know, his brother's name, and he nods.

"I'm sorry," I say, because what else is there to say? I missed my chance at comforting him nearly three years ago.

"Me too."

The first few months of losing Max were the hardest. I had to wake up every day remembering that his death wasn't just a nightmare but was a harsh and cruel reality that I had to face. It tore me apart, and I can't imagine having to face that pain all alone.

"When Max died, it left a heartache that not even Jack can fill. No one can."

"Losing someone that close to you is the hardest thing to handle," Elijah admits. "You never know how strong you actually are until strong is the only thing you can be."

His words create goose bumps over my skin.

It's true. You don't know the definition of strength until you've had to deal with the death of a loved one and have come out on the other end still functioning in your day-to-day life as if it hadn't happened. But no matter how you act, you know that it *did*.

I catch sight of something red and put my attention on that instead. I gasp at what it is and where it's coming from: blood-soaked bandages wrapped around Elijah's knuckles. Given, the blood is dried by now, but the crimson brown is hard to miss.

Without a moment's hesitation I reach forward and grab

his poor hands, our conversation a thing of the past. "What happened?!"

Elijah pulls his hands away. "It's nothing," he says dismissively.

I slowly move my gaze from his guarded face and back to his knuckles, and I see that the blood has literally turned the bandages completely red.

"Give me your hands," I say sternly, barely holding back a sneeze that would have ruined my authoritative tone.

"Scarlet, it's noth—"

"Give me your hands."

We stay there for a few tense seconds, his eyes unreadable, and then he silently puts his hands back in my own. I pull out the disinfectant and bandages from my pocket and am instantly met with a question.

"Why do you just have this stuff on hand?"

I realize it is rather odd for me to suddenly whip out first aid supplies, and I smile sheepishly.

"One of Jack's friends got scraped up earlier and I fixed him up. I just kind of kept the stuff on me in case something else happened."

I'm actually surprised nothing more serious than a few scrapes happened to Bryce earlier.

I gently begin to remove the bandages on Elijah's left hand first. They are completely covered in dried blood, and a deep frown takes over my face.

How could this have happened? Who did he punch? Could cuts like this even come from another person's flesh or had he been punching something else?

The questions are on my lips but quickly drift away at his expression. He clearly does not want me asking any questions. So I don't.

Instead, I tend to his cuts. I plaster them in ointment after wiping away all of the dried blood with an unused tissue in my pocket, dampening with the swallow of water left in the bottle. Elijah stays silent as I work on him. I feel his eyes boring into me but I refuse to look at him. He clearly did not want me doing this, and I don't see why. I suppose he didn't want me to ask questions, but I haven't. And maybe that's why he's allowing me to help him.

"All fixed."

Elijah flexes his hands to test the new bandages, and then his analytical eyes shift to me and they soften in appreciation.

"Thank you, Scarlet."

"You're welcome. Also, I'd prefer it if you called me Dr. Tucker."

Elijah quirks an amused brow. "Would you?"

We laugh at my silly comment. "No, not now that I hear it out loud."

Suddenly, a huge gust of wind goes past and freezes me to the bone, and then three sneezes rack my body.

"Did Jack at least give you a jacket?"

"He did. Then he spilled beer on it."

I sense Elijah's body stiffen at my words, and he looks off at the line of cars out front. "I have one in the truck."

We hear a loud crash echo from the house, and I cringe deeply and glance behind us.

"I should probably go make sure that wasn't Jack," I say quietly; regretfully.

Sitting out here with Elijah is the most fun I've had at this party. I stand up with Elijah and dust off my shorts, but then I think about going into the party alone and I realize I'd much rather have another sober friend to stand with.

"Would you want to come with me?"

He looks at me for a moment or two before he shakes his head and starts toward his truck. "I think I'll head home now."

I can't ignore the disappointment that drops into my stomach, but I nod and offer him a smile as I stand and walk to the front with him. "I'm glad you decided to stop by, Elijah."

"Me too, *Dr. Tucker*."

He grins at my dumbstruck reaction, reaching his truck and getting in before I say anything else. I can't keep away one question from plaguing my mind: Where did he get those cuts from?

Back inside the chaotic house, the chandelier looks like it is barely hanging from the ceiling, courtesy of Bryce swinging from it. It's hard to tell how secure it is since the lights bouncing off of it are changing colors every few seconds in time with the music. I wander around the dancing students, finally spotting Jack wandering blindly and drunkenly, seeming lost in his own house.

"Babe!" he exclaims, rushing toward me. "I've been looking all over for you, beautiful. Where did you run off to?" He pulls me against his body as though I'd been missing for years.

He tends to get overly cute when he's drunk.

"I just went outside for some air."

A cough tickles the back of my throat but I manage to keep it away.

"Well, I missed you and your sexy dancing," he slurs with a suggestive wink, ending with a not so sexy hiccup/burp. "Oops, 'scuse me."

"You know, that would have been a lot cuter if you weren't wasted."

"You're the"—he pauses to hiccup—"sexiest girl I've ever met."

"Is that so?"

He nods vigorously. "Definitely. I'm sorry if I don't tell you that enough."

So, despite my entire body aching with exhaustion, I go back out onto the dance floor with Jack as he downs another cup of some sort of alcohol.

Five minutes after he downs two more cups of beer or jungle juice or whatever the concoction is, I'm quickly rushing him to the bathroom before he spews his entire day's meals all over the dance floor. I throw the door open and rush him straight to the toilet, and not a second later he pukes into it, loud moans of pain following. I kneel next to him, rubbing his back soothingly as he continues to basically die.

"It's okay, Jack. You're okay."

You did this to yourself, I can't help but think.

His heaves subside, and I fill up a cup resting on the counter with water. I lift it to his lips. "Drink this." He does as he's told and tries to gulp the whole thing down. "Not too fast. I don't want you to upset your stomach any more."

"How did I get so lucky with you, Scar?"

I stay quiet and he slumps back against the wall, his forehead drenched in sweat. I brush back his hair gently while he closes his eyes.

"You're so amazing, beautiful, and perfect," he mumbles, still drunk. "You always take care of me when I need it," he adds, and then he blinks his eyes open and smiles at me. "I love you."

I lean forward to kiss his forehead. "Are you getting tired? Maybe it's time the party ended."

He nods, so I get up and walk to the makeshift DJ and shut off the music. Everyone almost instantly gets the message that

the party is over, and within ten minutes the entire place is basically cleared out. I just hope people didn't drive home drunk.
That's always my worry when these parties end, and usually I
announce in some sort of way that anyone who isn't fit to drive
home is welcome to stay here, but my voice isn't strong enough
to yell it out tonight.

Once the last of the guests leave, I walk back to the bathroom
where Jack is still lying on the floor.

"Everyone left. Take these," I say softly, handing him two
Tylenol.

"Thank you, beautiful."

I take his hand, my own hands clammy from the returning
fever. "Let's get you to bed, yeah?"

We stumble up the stairs and finally into his room, and I peel
his gross clothes off of him and leave him in his boxers since that's
how he sleeps anyway. Then I tuck him under his covers and crack
the window open to let some of the cold in, just how he likes it.

After I finish getting him all settled down, I sit down on the
edge of his bed. I sneeze from the cold air coming in the open
window and it burns my throat, so I wince and swallow hard.

Suddenly, I feel a hand on my forehead, and I snap my gaze
down to Jack's worried eyes, more sober than before since he
threw up most of the alcohol in his system.

"Scar, babe, you're burning up. Are you sick?"

At least he finally noticed.

"I'm okay. You need to get some sleep."

"No, beautiful, what hurts? Let me make you some chicken
noodle soup or something," he insists. But as he starts to get up,
he groans deeply and lies back down, shutting his eyes tight.
"The world is fucking spinning, I feel sick."

I brush some more sweaty hair from his forehead then rest my hand on his cheek. "You'll feel better once you sleep." My voice has finally turned raspy from all of the strain.

"What about you? I don't want you to be sick."

"Go to sleep, Jack. I'll be okay."

"Only if you stay with me so I can make sure you get better," he insists.

"No, I don't want to get you sick."

"So, you *are* sick."

"And I can't let you catch whatever I have."

He studies my face for a few moments and then lets his head rest back down on the pillow. "I guess you're right. I have a big game next Friday."

"That's right. A game you need to rest up for, so get some sleep and feel better in the morning."

"Only if you do."

"I will."

"Promise?"

"Promise."

"Thank you for taking care of me, Scar. I love you. Good night beautiful, get home safely."

Moments later sleep takes over his body and I silently slip out of his room and out of the house, and I go home to where I can finally sleep off this fever. The whole ride home I'm a coughing and sneezing mess, swerving on the road with every sneeze that takes over my body. My throat feels like sandpaper.

I pull into my driveway, carefully parking my dad's truck where it was before, and I go inside as quietly as possible so as not to wake my family. But when I see light coming from the kitchen, I'm drawn to it like a moth. My mom is leaning against the counter in her nightgown, two warm cups of tea resting in front of her.

"Hey, sweetheart."

"Hey, Mom," I say quietly, with a tired smile to mirror hers.

She nods at the tea. "That should help your throat."

"How'd you know I was sick?" The mug is warm in my hands and I breathe in the beautiful aroma before lifting it to my lips and letting the honey-laced contents soothe my throat.

"Scarlet, I'm your mother, I know everything."

I chuckle and lift the tea back to my lips. "Everything?"

She smirks. "More than you want me to."

I hum in response; she doesn't know as much as she thinks.

"Who's that boy you've been hanging out with—Elijah, is it?"

I just about choke on my tea.

How . . .

She smirks at me over her own tea mug. "I told you. I know everything, sweetheart."

I shake my head at her in impressed disbelief. Never under-estimate a mother.

"Why are you up anyway, Mom? It's two a.m."

"I couldn't sleep," she says quietly.

Ever since my brother died, my mom has been slightly different. She fell into a depression that my dad and I were barely able to get her out of. She woke up every night, screaming for Max to "get away" and "run." I used to cry with her and try to softly remind her he couldn't outrun the truck that killed him, but it never helped. If anything, I think those words only made things worse.

Thankfully, her love for me and my father was more powerful than the sickening disease and she's been doing much better. She's finally come to terms with what happened, and that proves how strong she is. It proves how strong we all are to wake up every day and continue to smile despite the hardships we've faced.

But it still hurts her to know that Max is no longer here with us.

She doesn't get nearly enough sleep. She quit her job because she became unreliable because of the depression, and she never went to get it back even when she got better. Instead, she helps my dad with the company, but she's technically unemployed.

Although she's not as happy as she once was, she's still a loving mother, and is just as selfless and sweet as ever; there's just a big piece of her heart missing that no one but my brother can fill.

"I'm sorry, Mom."

She smiles sadly at me and quickly diverts the conversation, as she usually does when I bring him up.

"How was the party?"

I think of how I babysat Jack for most of the night and sigh, but then Elijah comes to mind. He sat with me and kept my company, and that time with him felt priceless since moments with my newfound friend are rather rare.

"Is this smile for Jack or Elijah?"

"What?" I ask, cheeks hot and red.

"And there's my answer," she says, setting her mug in the sink before she walks past me. "Get some sleep, Scar. I put some NyQuil in your tea—you should feel better tomorrow morning."

I gape and turn to face her retreating figure. I *hate* NyQuil.

My mother just drugged me.

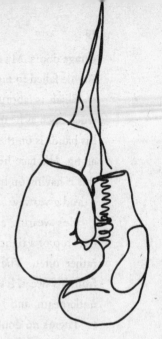

CHAPTER
EIGHT

Thankfully, my cold didn't turn into mono or the flu or anything else, and it went away after a day of rest. Jack felt beyond guilty that he didn't do more to help me feel better and came over to take care of me yesterday. And wore a doctor's mask so that he wouldn't get sick.

Archie was relieved that I was able to come back to work so soon. Turns out there was a backup of orders here at the garage without my help, so I'm swamped today, working on car after car. It's not a bad way to spend my Sunday; I was able to do most of my homework yesterday since I was practically bedridden. After my third car of the day, Archie calls over to me from where he's putting an old pickup on a lift.

"Darlin', that Eli boy is here to see you."

I grab a rag to wipe off my oily hands and walk to the open

garage doors. My feet stick on random sections of the floor that Archie failed to mop when he closed last night, and I cringe.

Elijah is laboring down the road with the front door of his truck open as he uses all of his strength to push it ahead. One of his hands is on the door and the other is steering his poor truck along. His face holds no emotion and barely shows the strain this is having on him, but the sweat glistening on his forehead is a dead giveaway.

He's wearing a dark-red and black flannel shirt kept open over top of a tight white shirt beneath, a shirt he seems to wear rather often. The shirt is discolored and almost see-through from his sweat. It's splotchy in places, almost revealing what lays underneath, and I find myself imagining what does.

There's no doubt that Elijah is fit. I wasn't surprised to learn that he goes to the gym, but it did spark my imagination further as to what muscles he's hiding.

As I run over to help him, he comes to a stop. His breathing is only slightly labored from the exertion of pushing his truck, vastly different from how out of breath I am from the short jog over.

"I'm surprised to see you here," he says once I reach him, and wipes his forehead free of sweat.

"At the shop where I work?"

He smirks. "I meant because you were sick the last time I saw you, and that was just two days ago. Are you feeling better?"

"I rested all day yesterday. At first I felt really sick, but then the more I slept the better I felt. But I think the NyQuil that my mom *drugged* me with brought on some crazy dreams, because I had this one where I had a pet crab. Weird, I know. But it gets worse, the crab started talking to me and . . ."

"Yeah, you're definitely feeling better."

A blush snakes up my neck.

"So, I'm curious, what'd the crab say?"

Light laughter bubbles up from me, and I divert our conversation to his truck. "What happened here?"

"Stopped working. Stalled a few times and then just completely stopped." He pauses and looks at me with sudden confusion. "Wait, your mom drugged you?"

I realize I did mention that absurd and exaggerated fact and smile sheepishly. "She snuck NyQuil into my tea."

He lifts the back of his hand to his forehead, wiping away some more sweat.

"How far did you push this thing?"

He glances at the long road behind us and rests his forearms on the open door. "A few miles."

"A few miles?! And you haven't passed out and died?"

His expression fills with humor but he doesn't answer.

"Here, let's get it into the shop."

Elijah hesitates as I begin to push his truck forward with all of my might. My feet dig into the pavement as I attempt to use gravity to push against the door and propel the truck forward. I get nowhere. Widening my stance to get better traction, I take another big breath and push forward with every ounce of strength I have. Once again, the truck barely moves.

Heaving a few heavy breaths, I turn my attention to Elijah and give an incredulous look upon realizing he's not helping.

"You weren't . . ."—I trail off to catch my breath—"helping?"

He sighs before addressing me. "Scarlet, I don't know how much this is going to cost, and I don't have that much money to spend."

"Elijah, don't worry about the money side of this."

He doesn't answer, the barrier between rich and poor turning him silent.

"You're my friend, I'm going to help you no matter if you can pay for it or not," I add.

"Really?" he asks, and I'm shocked at the surprise in his tone.

"Of course."

I feel my stomach clench, because from the way he looked at me, I have a sad feeling no one has ever done something like this for him.

"Thank you, Scarlet."

Archie walks toward us, throwing a cowboy hat upon his head to shield his face from the sun.

"Nice to see you again, Eli. I don't think we had a proper introduction at the shop last week. I'm Archie."

Elijah takes Archie's beyond-dirty outstretched hand with no hesitation. "It's nice to meet you."

"Archie, since I'm your most favorite worker in the entire world and you love me so dearly, do you think we could keep Elijah's truck in the shop so I can figure out what happened to it?"

It's time for my puppy dog eyes to shine, I think.

"Darlin', I don't see why you're begging me; you know I'd never turn down a customer."

Elijah quickly intervenes. "She forgot to add the part where I don't have a lot to spend on this. I understand if you don't have the space or if it's too much of an inconvenience—"

"Son, I'll stop you right there. I won't have you walking around town with no truck just because of a money issue. Roll your truck on around back. As long as y'all work on it in your own time, y'all are welcome to use the shop and any materials you need from here. Just keep the truck out of the shop during our hours, all right, darlin'?"

"Thank you, Archie!" I exclaim. Then to Elijah, "Told you it'd be fine."

"This means a lot," Elijah says, appreciation flooding his voice. They shake hands once more, a firm, respectful grip on both sides, and then Archie saunters back to the garage.

"Is it bad I'm kind of happy your car broke down?" I ask. "I mean, I told you last week it's like every mechanic's dream, and now I get to really get under this hood," I say, tapping it with my knuckles. "I wonder what even happened. It ran beautifully for such an old engine."

"Why are you so keen on helping me, Scarlet?"

"Oh come on. You knew I'd help."

He crosses his arms as he replies. "I did?"

"If you didn't think I'd help, then why'd you come to the shop?"

He analyzes me for a few moments, and his silence allows me to hear the way my heart speeds up. I try my hardest to read his expression and figure out what thoughts are running through his mind, but he's still too tough of a code for me to crack. Despite us becoming friends, his walls are still up. Just when I think of something to say, Elijah relaxes and begins to push the truck forward with ease. I follow silently, the question that I know he won't answer still hanging in the air.

~

Elijah and I decide that we'll start working on his truck tonight and that I'll try and diagnose what's wrong with it. For the sake of the truck, maybe not much will be wrong, but hopefully, for the sake of spending time with him, it won't be an easy fix.

Elijah is the first friend in a long time that I don't have because of Jack. I like spending time with him.

He stays at the shop until closing time since he doesn't have a mode of transportation to get anywhere else. Archie finally turns off the neon Open sign my dad requires every shop to buy. The colors stop dancing across the sign and instead the light goes off, turning away any late-night customers.

"All right you two, make sure y'all lock up once you've finished working on the truck. I don't want to have to tell your dad we got robbed in the middle of the night," Archie says, tossing me the keys.

"Thanks again, Archie."

"Just get to working on the truck, darlin'. It'll be fixed in no time with you under the hood." He winks kindly before grabbing his hat and his own keys and walking off.

Elijah goes to the back lot to get his truck since I'd had so many failed attempts at moving the million-ton vehicle.

I walk out into the sudden twilight, a cool fall breeze blowing the wind chimes Archie hung out front. I can smell the crispness of the chilly air; it seems like a cold front is coming in.

Elijah pushes the truck from around the back, steering with one hand and pushing with the other.

"Now you're just showing off," I mutter as he easily glides it into the garage.

"By pushing the truck into the shop like you asked?"

"By doing it so effortlessly."

Elijah isn't even out of breath from pushing his truck, and silently walks over to a bench sitting against the back of the garage to watch me work.

I ignore his electrifying gaze burning into me and try to place all of my focus on the truck as I lift the hood, making sure to remind myself to prop it up securely in order to avoid having it slam on my head. That would hurt both my head and my pride.

I check every single wiring system I can reach, as well as the oil levels and all of the other important liquids. I forget about Elijah sitting off to the side, watching me as I work. I eventually stop noticing his stare on me altogether and am able to relax in my own skin again.

"I have a question," he says.

I jump from the suddenness of the question and nearly slam my head into the top of the hood. My arms fly out to the sides and hit the rod holding the hood up and knock said rod down, causing the hood to fall. I place my hands above my head just *barely* before the hood cuts my head off.

"What's up?" I ask as I spin to face Elijah, trying to act cool even though I just about concussed myself.

"Do you want me to pretend that didn't happen?"

"That would be preferable, yeah."

He smirks for a moment or two, but as he asks his question that smile in his eyes disappears.

"How come you haven't once asked me about the rumors?"

I know I don't hide my shock very well. "I told you, I don't think they're true."

"Fair."

"That answer isn't what you wanted, was it?"

"You may be different from other girls, Scarlet, but everyone has a curious bone in their body. I just have a hard time believing you don't."

"I guess I am curious."

But not about the rumors.

Elijah seems satisfied with that answer and nods, settling back into his comfortable silence.

I shuffle my feet along the floor. He may be the type of person who is fine with such a simple answer, but I feel the need to exhaust the topic until I'm satisfied that we've covered everything. Plus, I was aiming for him to question this further so I could hit him with an ominous response.

"But I'm not curious about the rumors," I speak up.

That sparks his attention.

"I pointed out that you're mysterious, that your knuckles are scraped up, that you always wear a hoodie large enough to cover your face the days you need it to. That's what I'm curious about, not whether you smoke or do drugs. I never asked before because you aren't exactly the type of person to tell everyone about yourself," I say, feeling some sort of need to explain myself.

When our eyes meet, I suck in a breath.

"No one ever asks."

"I'm asking now."

"Curiosity killed the cat," Elijah muses, much to my confusion.

"Good thing they have nine lives."

Despite the witty comeback, all I get from Elijah is a chuckle. He still doesn't answer. He stays silent, and I choose not to press the topic again. But asking about the rumors made me all the more curious. To distract my wandering mind, I start back on his truck. Maybe he needs time to answer the real questions I have, not the silly rumors he assumed I cared about.

Elijah stands up, but with my focus solely on diagnosing the truck's issue, I don't fully register his movement. So I jump when I hear his voice suddenly right next to me.

"How bad is it? Be honest."

My whole body flinches from shock. He leans his arms on the truck, clearly humored by my reaction.

"The truck, how bad is the damage?"

I shake my head clear of the surprise I was just thrown into and get my bearings back. But it's not easy to focus on clear thoughts with Elijah standing less than an arm's length away.

"It's going to take me a while to figure out what's wrong with it. I'm not used to working on engines from before the '90s."

He smiles. "Okay."

My face heats up, and thankfully my hair falls in front, shielding my reddening skin from his view. Who would have thought I'd be the one to get to know Elijah Black? I realize our conversation earlier didn't satisfy any thoughts in my mind, and though the rumors don't excite me nearly as much as the mystery behind him (which he clearly does not want to discuss) there are other things about him I want to know.

"You talked about your mom the other day." I notice the hardening of his face as he predicts where I am going with this. "But nothing about your dad. What's he like?"

Elijah's body stiffens and he backs away from the truck, eyes stuck off in the distance. "Not much to say there. He works for the Houston PD. I haven't seen him in over two years, not since Oliver passed."

My heart tugs painfully for him. I had no idea. I figured Elijah had faced hardships, but it seems things for him only got worse and worse when fate should have made them better.

"I'm sorry."

He has to deal with a father he hasn't seen in years as well as losing a brother to drugs, and to top it all off he has to deal with Jack and his friends picking on him every second they get. I don't think my definition of strength compares to his.

Elijah sighs. "Life happens."

I offer Elijah a ride home after I finish working, since my dad let me take his truck to work, but he says he already has a ride on the way. I wait with him, hoping to catch a glimpse into his life, but the car stays far back in the parking lot and Elijah jogs out to greet it. With one final wave to me, he gets inside, and they drive off.

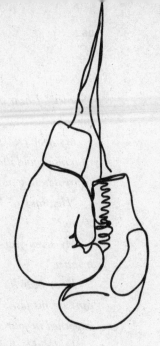

CHAPTER
NINE

I gasp as my eyes shoot open and my body jolts up, wide awake after a nightmare about Max. The dreams have been happening less and less since he passed away, but I still get them every now and then. And each seems worse than the last.

With a deep breath, I blink a few times so that my eyes can adjust to the darkness of my room. There's a small stream of light coming from the clock on my nightstand, whose digits are much too neon for the dead of the night: 3:06 a.m.

When I was younger and would have nightmares, Max would hear me sobbing in my room from whatever scary thing I had dreamt. So he would come to my room, take me downstairs, pop us some popcorn, and have me tell him about my dream as we munched on the snack. By the time we ate the last piece of popcorn, I would be laughing with him and would have completely forgotten about what it was that woke me up in a fright.

~

"Scarlet?" I hear a voice call from the doorway, instantly hushing my tears.

My door creaks open, allowing the light from the stairway to rush inside and illuminate my face. It creates a glow around the tall figure standing in my doorway, almost like an angel.

"Hey, squirt," Max says softly, stepping all the way inside. "Bad dream?"

My seven-year-old self whimpers her response. "There was a monster."

I can hear his throaty chuckle, although with the glow I still can't see his face. "How about some popcorn, yeah? Tell me what happened in your dream."

I childishly shake my head, too afraid to get off of my bed because I know the monster is waiting for me underneath it.

"Come on, you know talking about it will help you not be scared of him anymore."

Max walks to my side and I hold out my arms for him to lift and carry me, pretending to be too tired to walk down myself.

"You're seven years old now, squirt. How much longer are you going to have me pick you up?"

"Until I turn eight."

He lifts me onto his back. "Last year you said until you turned seven."

Already, I can feel the memory of the monster fading away. Max sets me down on one of the kitchen chairs and walks over to the pantry. He's wearing his Batman pajama pants. I got them for him for Christmas last year; he said they were his favorite gift.

He stays by the fridge, pouring a glass of milk as the popcorn *pops, then grabs a second glass for me before bringing our midnight snack to the table.*

"Okay, now. Tell me all about this big bad monster that dares mess with my little sis."

I reach to the back of the pantry, sifting through bags of chips, boxes of random types of pasta, and clearly outdated boxes of cooking supplies, and grab the almost abandoned package to place in the microwave. I smile as I recall those memories of Max.

If only he could be here today to tell me that his death was nothing but a scary nightmare, that the tractor trailer that killed him was just a silly monster and I dreamt the whole thing. He's okay. He's invincible. He's my big brother who promised to never let the monster get to us.

The microwave beeps in the silence of the night, filling the air with the scent of slightly burnt popcorn. Nearly burning myself from the steam, I empty the bag into Max's favorite bowl and sit down at the kitchen table, the sound of my crunching echoing in my ears.

"Hey, sweetheart."

My body tenses, taking a few seconds to recognize the voice as my father's. He's standing in the doorway with a sad smile on his face.

"Hey, Dad. Did I wake you?"

He shakes his head and walks into the room, sitting down next to me.

"I wasn't fully asleep."

I tilt the bowl of popcorn toward him, and he reaches over to take a handful for himself.

"What's wrong?" he asks after a few minutes of silence.

"I'm okay."

"Scarlet, normally you're talking a mile a minute and you haven't said more than a few words. What's wrong?"

I finally tear my eyes away from the emptying bowl of popcorn, allowing him to see the sadness brewing in me.

"I had a dream about Max," I admit.

"What was it about?"

I don't want to answer. I always have nearly the same nightmare, just different variations. My mind makes me imagine what the crash was like, what his last few moments were like, and sometimes I'm there with him but am unable to do anything to help. Tears burn the back of my throat, and I try my hardest to swallow them down.

My silence gives me away and I feel Dad's callused hands on my own.

"I miss him, too, more than anything in this world." He continues, "Your brother loved you so much."

I nod, unable to keep a tear from dripping down my cheek. "I know he did."

"We're lucky to have had his love. It makes this grief ten times harder, but don't you think it was worth it?"

"I'd rather have him here with me."

"Me, too, Scar. But I still have an amazing daughter to look after. I always think of you and your mother and remember I didn't lose everything."

I get a flush of admiration for the strength my dad has. "I love you, Dad."

Now tears spring to his eyes. "I love you, too, Scarlet. Don't ever forget that."

"I won't. Promise."

He reaches over, scooting his chair closer to mine as he pulls me into his arms. I cling to him tightly, wishing to be as strong as him. We head to bed shortly after, and I follow him back up the stairs. I walk past Max's room and keep my eyes straight ahead.

I don't want my heart to sting anymore tonight.

I mount the stairs to my room but I know I won't be able to sleep. I want someone to talk to, to keep my mind off of this reality of not having Max here anymore. Once I sit on my bed, I reach for my phone and dial Jack's number.

It rings.

And rings some more.

Then goes to his voice mail.

"Hey, this is Jack, leave a message."

I set my phone down and sigh heavily. I shouldn't be surprised, it's the middle of the night. But I guess talking is out of the question.

I don't know if it's from the fact I was able to open up to him about Max, or maybe the fact I just need someone to talk to, but I find myself calling Elijah when Jack doesn't answer his phone. I don't expect Elijah to answer. I expect him to be fast asleep at his house, ignoring a call from some girl who is fixing his truck. So when he does answer, I don't know what to say and stay silent on the other end.

"Scarlet? What are you doing up this late?" Elijah asks as he answers, and I'm surprised that he doesn't sound groggy at all.

I finally find my voice and clear my throat. "I could ask you the same question." I chuckle.

He pauses on the other end. "I couldn't sleep. I get the sense you didn't just call to talk about the truck?"

I use my free hand to hug my body, once again feeling cold without Max here.

"No, I didn't . . . just . . . I had a dream about Max, and I guess I just wanted to talk to someone who knows . . .

"I'm sorry," I say quickly. "I shouldn't be bothering you with—"

"You aren't bothering me, Scarlet."

I let out a small sigh of relief and pull my knees up to my chest, switching the phone to my other ear. "Why are you up, anyway?"

"Similar reasons."

"You had a dream about Oliver?"

"Something like that. So, are you going to keep me waiting in suspense, or do I get to hear about another talking crab?"

"I wish this one was just about a talking crab."

"Talking lobster this time?"

Snorting, I reply, "No talking animals, that only comes when I'm drugged. And I don't think my dad drugged me with the popcorn, so no talking sea animals for me."

"Should I be worried, or . . . ?"

I realize I probably sound a little crazy.

"No, no. I went downstairs to make popcorn after I woke up, something Max and I used to do . . . and my dad came downstairs, I guess I woke him or something."

Nothing but the static on the line.

"Pretzels," Elijah says, then clears his throat. "Oliver and I used to stay up late a lot, our go-to snack was pretzels."

"Really?"

"Nearly every night."

"I pegged you as a potato chip kind of guy."

"Only if they're barbeque."

"Sour cream and onion, that's my vice," I say, rolling my bottom lip between my teeth when I find myself smiling.

Elijah begins to respond but suddenly his words are cut off by another call coming in. Jack's face appears on the screen; a picture of us on the lake together. He's wearing American flag swim trunks and driving a speed boat, and I'm sitting in his lap, wearing a matching bikini. It's my favorite picture of us, and I knew it had to be his contact picture.

The silent vibrations linger as I stare down at the picture.

Why am I not answering?

"Hold on, Elijah," I finally say. "I have another call coming in."

"I should probably get some sleep, anyway."

"Yeah . . . thanks for talking to me for a bit. It was a nice little distraction."

"Good night, Scarlet."

"Good night, Elijah."

Answering Jack's call, I hear his groggy voice through my phone speakers.

"Baby? I woke up to go to the bathroom and saw the missed call. Why so late?" Jack moans.

"It was nothing. I had a bad dream, but I'm okay now."

"You sure?"

"Yes, I'm okay. Promise."

"Okay, I'm glad. Good night, babe, get some sleep."

"I'll try, good night."

When I finally do fall asleep, for the first time in a long time my mind feels at peace and I don't fear the monster coming back.

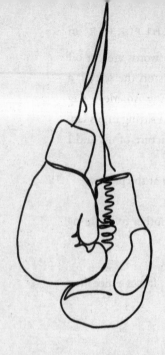

CHAPTER TEN

I wake up groggy this morning, practically falling back to sleep as I pick out my outfit for the day before choosing to stay in my pajamas instead of changing because that requires too much effort for a Saturday morning. The coffee pot downstairs is calling my name, the aroma blanketing the entire house. Walking into the kitchen, I beeline for the pantry and choose my favorite mug: white with a black diagram of an old truck with parts of the engine labeled. The warmth of the coffee spreads over my body, effectively waking me up.

"Scar! Jack's here," my mom calls from the living room.

I set my coffee down on the kitchen island and furrow my brow. Jack didn't tell me he was coming over, and it's only nine, which is awfully early for him on a Saturday. He rarely wakes up before twelve unless he has practice. And on a day like today, when it's pouring rain outside, a thunderstorm well on its way yet again, I'm surprised he got out of bed at all.

"You sure it's Jack?" I call back.

"Do you think I could mistake that truck for anyone else's?"

She's got a point there.

I stand from the barstool I was occupying and leave the last swallow of my now-cold coffee in my mug. Then I exit the kitchen and walk down the hallway, complete with pictures of me throughout the years, and go to the front door. The way the front of my house is set up is breathtaking—when you come inside you walk into a room with a vaulted ceiling with a chandelier hanging above a winding, wooden staircase.

"Hey, beautiful." Jack grins as I open the door, and hands me a bouquet of flowers with water droplets dancing around the petals.

My eyes widen as he thrusts the bright-red roses into my hands and swoops down for a chaste kiss. Well, this is an awfully nice gesture so early in the morning.

He eyes my pajamas—spandex shorts and an oversized T-shirt—and he chuckles. "Did you just roll out of bed, Scar?"

I take in *his* attire; he's wearing khakis and a light-blue dress shirt. And he brought me roses unannounced. At nine in the morning.

He smirks at me and leans against the door frame, crossing his arms over his perfectly toned chest.

"You forgot today's our anniversary, didn't you?"

Oh shit.

My face flushes as today's date comes flooding back into my mind and I shove the flowers in front of my embarrassed face.

"No?" I squeak out.

When Jack and I first began dating, I dreamt of our one-year anniversary, and I've been looking forward to it every month since. But since I've started working with Elijah on his truck, my mind hasn't been occupied with much else.

Jack moves the flowers to the side so that he can see me. "Don't worry about it, beautiful. I don't have anything planned until dinner tonight. I thought you could come over and we could spend the day together until our reservations."

"That sounds perfect, let me go change."

"I think we both know you don't have to worry about what you're wearing; it won't stay on for long," he says suggestively.

"My mom's right there in the living room," I hiss, playfully slapping his chest.

"She was young and in love once."

⌒

Thirty minutes later we're in his room and he's attacking my sides with the only pleasurable form of torture: tickling.

"Jack!" I yell through laughter that's so strong it's hurting my stomach.

He laughs with me and continues to attack my sides, and tears spring to my eyes.

"You've got to get free, beautiful," he says, and I squirm against him but get nowhere.

"Jack, stop!" I laugh.

"What do I get if I stop?"

I narrow my eyes at him as I try to catch my breath. "I won't kick you in the nuts."

His eyes widen at my blunt response. "You wouldn't."

"Try me."

He stares at me for a few seconds and then swallows, shifting so that he's lying next to me on his bed instead of keeping me trapped under his body.

I sit up and smile down at him, patting his chest. "Good choice, babe."

He reaches up to me, intertwining his fingers in mine and pulling me down gently. I twist so that I'm lying comfortably in his arms.

"You know what a good choice was?" he asks.

I hum my response, drawing circles on his chest.

"Deciding to ask you to be mine a year ago."

"You're so cheesy, you know that?"

He chuckles and rolls us so that he's back to hovering over me, arms bent on each side of my head as he stares softly at me.

"Only for you, Scar."

I smirk and lift my hand to tap his nose. "Now why don't I believe that? Prince Charming is charming to everyone."

"Oh, so I'm your Prince Charming then?"

"You did come at the perfect time," I say quietly.

Sadness sparks across his eyes as I allude to Max's death. Jack asking me out was the first thing I had to look forward to after Max died.

He leans down and brushes his nose against mine, avoiding the pit of sadness the conversation could have easily fallen into.

"Well, that makes you my princess then, doesn't it?"

"I wouldn't call myself a princess."

"I would."

"Yeah?"

"You're beautiful enough to be a queen, Scar," he whispers before crashing his lips onto mine.

I lift one hand and rest it on his chest while the other plays with his hair, pulling him closer, which he gladly obliges with. He softly bites my bottom lip, seeking entrance and I open to let his tongue explore. He moans into my mouth and presses himself into me and I wind my legs around him.

But all too soon we hear a knock at the door and Jack is forced to pull away. He groans in annoyance and lifts his head from mine, sending a glare over his shoulder at the door.

"Maybe you should get that?" I suggest.

"I'd much rather continue this."

Another knock takes our attention away again and he throws his head back with a heavy sigh.

"Fine, I'll get the stupid door."

He mutters something under his breath as he twists the knob and opens the door, and I can see his dad standing in the doorway with an annoyed expression on his face.

Jack's dad is a big man. He's well over six feet tall, has a full head of strikingly brown hair and icy-blue eyes, as well as the build of a football player; not entirely muscled but not nearly fat. He radiates business authority, and I've always been intimidated by him. As owner of the Houston Texans, he's a big name around here. And he's not humble about it. Jack's parents own potentially the biggest house on Lake Conroe; and that's saying a lot. This is the most pristine real estate in our town, and even in neighboring towns.

I sit up on Jack's bed and fix my clothes and hair to try and hide the fact his son and I were doing unholy things, but I'm sure his dad already knows.

"Hey, Dad."

I smile sheepishly over at him. "Hi, Mr. Dallas."

He offers me a curt smile and eyes me with a judgmental tinge to his expression.

"Hi, Scarlet. Having fun, I see."

I swallow and my eyes fall to the dark-blue comforter on Jack's bed.

"What's up, Dad?" Jack asks.

Mr. Dallas's lips twitch into a proud smile as he looks at Jack and claps him on the shoulder.

"I called O'Brien and he organized the team to scrimmage today against Baylor as a big promotion for them—playing against the Texans is a huge honor for them. I pulled some strings to have you as the QB for the entire first half! We need to leave here shortly, but we should be home by seven tonight."

"Are you being serious!"

"Of course I am, and I haven't even told you the best part. Since this is such big news for Baylor, they have buses taking loads of students to the stadium to come watch, so you should have a crowd." Mr. Dallas smirks.

Jack's jaw practically drops, and I swear he jumps up from his enthusiasm. I feel the elation coursing through my own veins; this is an amazing opportunity for him, and I know it's something that is going to help his football career tremendously.

"Be ready to leave in fifteen minutes," Mr. Dallas says before he walks away.

Jack whirls around and darts across his room to his closet to pack his things for the game, and I push myself to the edge of his bed.

"I would ask if you're excited, but something tells me you are."

Jack grins and runs over to me, taking my face in his hands as he places a big kiss on my lips.

"Excited is an understatement, Scar. I'm about to play with professional players against a very impressive college team. I'll drop you off back at home really quick before I go."

"That's amazing, Jack." I smile, but then it sinks in that he's about to leave and won't be home until seven tonight.

He's spontaneously leaving on our anniversary, after he said he wanted to spend the whole day with me. But I guess I can't necessarily be upset; an opportunity like this is something he can't pass up. To do so would make him a fool, and to be mad at him would make me a bad girlfriend.

So I keep the smile on my lips and don't show my disappointment when he drags me to his truck to take me home, promising to be home in time for our dinner reservations at eight.

Once Jack drops me off at home, the rain starts pouring even harder, and the storm that every weatherman has been excited about really sets in. Distant thunder comes closer and closer, and the off-and-on drizzle turns into a constant downpour.

Even so, I didn't want to be stuck inside. So I decide to drive to the garage, even though Archie closed up shop due to the weather. It was too difficult for him to drive here since he lives close to a creek running off of Lake Conroe—his street was flooded and he couldn't make it, so he shut the shop down for the day.

I throw the shop's dark-red garage doors open, but even with my efforts to fling them all the way up, they come tumbling back down to the ground and smack down on the concrete. I huff and try a few times before I'm able to toss them up with enough velocity that they catch the rest of the tracks and open all the way. The rain outside is still pouring down, but there is an overhang in front of the garage that prevents the water from flooding the inside or soaking me to the bone.

The sound of each droplet slamming against the pavement fills my ears and I walk farther into the garage, brushing the water that accumulated in the short run from where I parked my dad's truck to here off of my arms. But then I hear another noise that barely hovers over the rain and I turn around to see headlights illuminating the downpour around them. Elijah steps out of the passenger side of a car and tosses a duffel bag over his shoulder, then jogs to the safety of the garage as the car drives off.

He shakes the water from his soaked hair and I take in his appearance. He's sporting a ratty black T-shirt with basketball shorts and ragged tennis shoes. Beads of rain dot his exposed skin, but it looks like sweat is mixed in as well because his hair is beyond soaked, and I know it's not just from that quick jog to the garage.

He sets his duffel bag down and lifts the bottom half of his shirt to wipe his face off. I gasp at the sculpted *V* that he reveals above his low-hanging shorts.

Oh my *lord*.

Scarlet. Look. Away.

After he situates himself, Elijah's striking eyes lift to mine and a microscopic grin hits the corners of his lips.

"Hey," I squeak.

Elijah bends down to grab his bag from the floor, and I watch wide-eyed as the muscles in his arm ripple as he tosses it effort-lessly over his shoulder. The veins that dance across his arms are prominent, bulging from whatever he was doing before he came here.

"Hey, Scarlet." He greets me curtly as he walks to the back of the garage, setting his bag down on the bench. "I'll go get the truck?"

"Unless you'd rather not get a shower."

He answers me by walking straight into the rain and to the back lot. To each his own, I guess.

I walk over to the radio sitting on Archie's desk and scan through the stations until I find one that hasn't been ruined by the storm. Of course, living in the heart of Texas, it's a country music station. But, since I'm a Texas girl, I'm by default a coun-try music fan. I turn the volume up slightly to hear the music over the rain, and country tunes fill the garage.

I dance slightly to the music, but suddenly my phone buzzes, and I slip it out of my pocket to see Jack's name and picture flash across the screen. I slide the shining bar across the bottom to answer him and lift it to my ear, praying he speaks loudly enough to be heard over the patter of the rain and hum of the music.

"Hey, beautiful."

"Hey, yourself. Did you get there safely?"

"Yeah, we just got here. The drive that was supposed to be an hour took well over two because of this storm. They had to delay the game."

I feel my chest clench as I foreshadow his next sentence.

"Scar, the game hasn't started yet and won't start for a while. I won't be back in time for dinner."

A sting of disappointment flutters across my chest and I clench my jaw. It was one thing for him to leave me today out of the blue, but he promised me he'd be home for dinner.

I take a deep, silent breath and allow myself to think rationally. The storm was out of his control and there's no way he could have changed this aside from not going, which I would never have asked him to do. This is such an amazing thing for him, and I should be happy for him.

I *am* happy for him. He deserves this, and I don't want to be the girlfriend who holds him back. And I know how much a moment like this means to him. The last thing he needs is an angry girlfriend weighing on his mind. But this isn't the first time something like this has happened.

"It's not your fault. Just have fun at the game and play your heart out, okay?"

"You know I will. I promise I'll take you out tomorrow to make up for this, okay? I love you, babe." Voices in the background call his name. "I've got to go, I'll see you soon. Happy anniversary!"

I'm relieved he can't see me but can only hear my voice, which I make sound cheerful rather than laced with disappointment. "Happy anniversary, have fun."

He hangs up and I slide my phone into my back pocket with a little more force than needed. That call just completely dampened my mood. I'm not angry. I have no right to be. I'm disappointed that I can't be with him tonight, and that dinner won't work out.

Turning around, I see Elijah pushing his truck into the shop. The light-blue paint that coats it is illuminated in the garage lights, and it also accentuates the small areas of rust that dot the exterior of such an old truck.

I rush to help him get the truck situated where it needs to go, and then I look at Elijah. He's drenched from head to toe. His hair is a dripping mess, falling around his forehead, and his shorts are dripping onto the garage floor. His black shirt is sticking to his body in all the right places and suddenly everything that I imagined lays beneath is revealed. The shirt is so stuck to him that it outlines the pattern of muscles across his stomach, lifting to his defined chest and broad shoulders.

Scarlet, you literally *just* got off of the phone with your boyfriend of one year. Look away.

"So, how was your shower?" I ask.

"Cold," he quips, walking past me and to his duffel bag, unzipping it and digging around, leading me to assume he was at the gym before this.

"Did you bring an extra set of clothes?"

He stands straight up and pulls them out as his response, and I direct him to the bathroom inside the shop so that he can change. My phone buzzes and I see an Instagram update from Jack; he's already posted a picture with the Houston Texans coach, a smirk on his dazzling features, his helmet resting in his hand and pads fully on. My earlier annoyance comes back full force, and I lock my phone, trying to will away unfair thoughts. This opportunity is perfect for his career. So why am I a mix of upset and something that feels like more than just disappointment?

"You're mad."

Elijah stands at the connecting door from the shop to the garage in his new set of clothes. His arms are crossed against his broad chest and his eyes are locked on me.

"What?"

"I'd have to be blind to miss the fact you're upset. What's wrong?"

I look away as I answer. "Jack."

Elijah nods and walks farther into the garage, but he doesn't look surprised.

"Today is our anniversary."

"And you're here with me?"

"Not that I don't like working on your truck, but this wasn't my first choice of events today."

Elijah doesn't get offended by my words, and instead cocks his head. "What happened, then?"

I walk to the garage doors and stare out at the rain.

"He's living out his dream."

Elijah watches me silently.

"He got called to go play a big game after promising to spend the day with me. To be fair, I'm the one who forgot today was our twelve-month . . ." I begin, turning around to face Elijah and putting my back to the rain.

"I'm sorry," Elijah says.

"I guess I can't be mad. This is an amazing opportunity for him, and I can see him any other day of the week. It just makes me a little irritated, you know? I mean, it's our one-year anniversary and he just ditched me for football."

I divert my gaze to the truck and smile, giving Elijah a side glance.

"I thought you were going to stop me when I rambled?"

"It looked like you needed to this time."

I move my attention to the pouring rain. "I'm just being selfish. This is his dream."

"There's nothing selfish about wanting to be someone's first choice."

My heart stutters from the intensity of his gaze.

"I sense this feeling isn't just from today?" he asks.

He's right. This isn't the first time Jack has chosen football over me. A large part of me knows it's important to choose your future over a girl or a guy, but there's still that voice reminding me how lonely it feels to be someone's second choice when you've made them your first. Of all the people to complain about Jack to, Elijah is the one person who should be biased against him and not want to listen. Because of the things Jack does to him, maybe ranting to Elijah is unfair.

But he's here to listen.

I turn my head to look at Elijah with regret-tinged eyes. "I don't like what he does to you, you know. I don't like how mean he is."

Elijah sits up, body tensing slightly. "Is he ever mean to you?"

"No." Then I pause. "Not in the way he is to you."

Elijah quickly scans all of my open skin, and I realize that I just made it sound like Jack is abusive toward me.

"How then?" he says tensely.

I instantly shake my head and rid that thought from his mind. "Oh no! He doesn't hit me or anything like that! He's not a bad guy, it's just"—I pause and search for the proper way to explain it—"he can be late to things. He can be too much of a showboat. He can leave me in a second for his friends or football. . . . So, I guess he's not mean to me at all, just rude at times. I love him, though, so it truly doesn't matter. We love each other. He's been there for me with Max being gone."

Elijah visibly relaxes to his normal posture but doesn't seem to have a response.

"I shouldn't let him say what he does to you," I admit.

"I can hold my own."

He shouldn't have to hold his own. He should live the regular high school life like everyone else instead of having to worry about Jack and his friends.

"Always so deep in thought," Elijah muses, walking to the bench situated at the back of the garage.

I sit down next to him. "Me?"

"When you're not rambling to me, you're rambling in your head."

I laugh and don't bother to deny it. It's the truth.

"It's nice to have someone here to listen."

He tilts his head and I see his face soften.

"Same for me."

In the background, past the rain and the hum of the lights, the radio that I had forgotten was even on switches to one of my favorite country songs and my face lights up. As I jump from the bench, Elijah's eyes widen slightly at my sudden movement, and I rush to the radio to turn it up.

"Why Don't We Just Dance" by Josh Turner fills the garage and I laugh, spinning around. I tap on the hood of Elijah's truck to the fast beat as I move to the open portion of the garage, which is conveniently the space in front of Elijah, and dance to the music without a care in the world. There's something about music that can bring a whole different side out of someone. A side that they either have trouble pulling out or always have on hand. In my case, it's a side I always have on hand and that comes out when I hear a song I can dance to.

"This used to be my favorite song!" I exclaim over Josh Turner's voice.

Elijah stares back at me in slight shock, clearly amused by the events that just unfolded.

"Do you know it?" I ask, running up to him in a bit of a rush to get to him before the chorus starts.

"I live in Texas, Scarlet. I would know this song even if I didn't want to, which I don't," he says with a small chuckle.

"Perfect." I lock my hands on his and tug him to come with me. "Come on, Elijah! Dance!" I exclaim, turning and dancing back to the open section with my hands in the air and jumping to the beat as the chorus hits for the first time. I sing along, closing my eyes and belting out the words.

Elijah is still standing there, looking uncomfortable but humored by my rather terrible skills, and I roll my eyes playfully. He's too rugged to know how to let loose and dance, so I suppose I'll just have to teach him. I take his hands in mine, moving my arms to the beat and ultimately forcing his to move as well. I throw my head back and dance around, and slowly Elijah comes out of his rigid stance and appeases me by moving his feet, albeit completely off tempo.

"There you go!"

He looks at me and smiles as we dance. Well, more so as *I* dance and he stiffly moves his arms and feet to the best of his ability. I laugh along with him and encourage him by continuing to sing, which causes his smile to widen. As the lyrics hit their climax, he even lifts one arm to spin me.

I laugh as I spin around, landing back closer to him than I was before, but barely noticing from the excitement of this moment. Goose bumps take over my skin, but his touch is warm and inviting. I hold his hand tighter, reveling in the rough texture of his skin, which matches mine. The scent of the garage is masked by the gentle cologne he's wearing, and I drink it in. We continue to move our hips, arms, and feet, probably unattractively, to the beat while the rain pours outside, forgetting that we're meant to be working on the truck but also forgetting any troubles in our lives.

After the song finishes and I spend more time working on the truck, I decide it's time to head home.

"Are you sure you don't need a ride home?" I ask Elijah.

"My ride is almost here."

Moments later, headlights sweep into the garage as the same car from before comes to take Elijah home.

"I'll see you around, Scarlet."

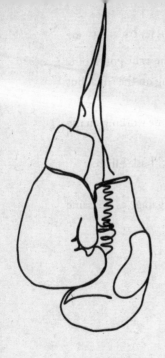

CHAPTER
ELEVEN

So, this morning at school, I'm exhausted because Jack made new reservations last night to make up for missing Saturday's dinner, and we pretended as though that was our anniversary instead. He talked about his game the whole dinner, pausing here and there to let me pose a question. We were out until late—the only reservation time that was open was at nine o'clock, so we ate late, and he took me back to his house for a while after. Mondays are hard anyway, but Mondays with little sleep are exhausting.

"Thank you for dinner last night," I say as Jack interlocks our fingers.

He opens the door for me to enter school and I walk through, sending him a smile of gratitude, and we walk inside to the chaotic hallways.

"Of course, babe. Thank you for the post-dinner activities," he whispers quietly.

"Shut up." I giggle and smack his chest.

"I love you, and especially your body."

As we walk through the hall, a familiar black hoodie walks past us in the other direction. Elijah. My heart rate speeds up upon seeing him, and our dance session from the other night shimmers in my mind. Today he's buried inside the hoodie, hiding from the world again.

"Keep walking, freak," Jack spits. "You may as well disappear like your crackhead brother and sorry excuse for a father. You may as well not even exist at this school."

My face falls at his words, but Elijah ignores him and keeps his eyes locked on mine. I see his shoulders tense at Jack's cruelty, but he doesn't offer any other reaction. Jack's words do send a question into my mind: *How does he know about Elijah's father?*

I suddenly have an even stronger sense of respect for Elijah. How he can ignore Jack is beyond me. But I guess, if you're looking at it from his perspective, I'm ignoring Jack, too, by not speaking up for Elijah.

Suddenly, Jack spins me and gently pins me against the lockers with a possessive smirk.

"What are you doing?" I ask.

He trails his hands down to my waist and his eyes flit down to my lips. He doesn't answer me and instead crashes his lips into mine and makes out with me in the crowded hallway. Squeezing my waist, he somehow pushes himself closer to me as he deepens the already very intense kiss.

When he pulls away, he has a cocky grin, and I take a few moments to get my bearings back. I lightly push Jack back, and Elijah stalks away. He discreetly pulls his hoodie higher on his head for more coverage of whatever it is that he doesn't want me to see.

"That was nice, but why the random make-out session in the middle of the hallway?"

"What? I can't kiss my girlfriend?"

"You can kiss me whenever, but don't you think that was a little heated for school? I mean, I've heard you complain about PDA before."

"Yeah, when band geeks do it."

"I'm just saying that it felt like more than just a way to show your love for me this time around," I reason.

Jack suddenly narrows his eyes. "Meaning what?"

I choose my next words carefully, aware that the hallway is becoming more and more crowded as this conversation becomes heated. "Meaning it feels like there was a vendetta behind it."

"I want everyone here to know you're *mine*, because it seems some people have forgotten. Especially that freak."

"You're worried about Elijah?" I ask in disbelief.

"Dancing in the garage, really, Scar?"

Our watching classmates are all around, not even trying to be discreet. There's no use in getting even more into an argument here at school that everyone can witness and then talk about for the next week.

"How did you hear about that?"

"Bryce was driving by and he saw *my girlfriend* dancing with some freak! He told me this morning!"

I hear a gasp from somewhere in the mass of students listening to us, trying and failing to be quiet. There's one kid in an orange sweatshirt who seems to think I haven't noticed him walk back and forth in the hallway four different times during the course of this conversation.

"I was just working on his truck," I say quietly, looking down at the floor.

"Not from what I heard."

"You left, on our anniversary—otherwise I would have been dancing with you."

"I didn't have much of a choice, Scar. You know I would have stayed back to be with you, but that game had Baylor looking at me for a scholarship, and many other colleges that I didn't already have scouting me sure as hell are now. But while I'm playing football, my girlfriend is off with the school freak! As if I need something else to worry about while on the field."

"Jack, I liked the song, that's it." I place my hands on his chest reassuringly, but he scoffs.

"Dancing seems pretty personal to me."

I know everyone in the hallway is listening, because it is never this quiet. Now, there's only a murmur here and there, the main commotion being Jack and me.

"It wasn't. I'd have done it with Jessica or Katie if they'd been there. Hell, I'd have even done it with Bryce." I lie. "I'm sorry, Jack. I love *you*, it meant nothing."

"I don't like hearing about you off with another guy," he says, anger subsiding. "Eli better watch his back. If he thinks he can dance with you, he needs to get put in his place. A freak like him doesn't deserve to even talk to you."

Panic spreads across my chest; I don't want more pain to come to Elijah because of this. "No, Jack, just leave Elijah alone. It was all me, and we're friends. Let's just forget about it. Move on, okay?"

"Whatever, Scar."

I flinch from the coldness in his tone and swallow back sudden tears as he walks away. He should believe me when I say I love him and that the dancing meant nothing. I should believe myself when I say it meant nothing.

As he walks farther away, my mind shifts from that argument to the hoodie Elijah had covering his face expertly, and a different kind of panic fills my chest. Jack may be on a warpath, his sights set on Elijah to relieve his anger. Elijah doesn't deserve any of that; we shouldn't have to feel guilty for having fun together.

Walking in the opposite direction of Jack, I start on my way to find Elijah. I run up some steps, scanning the emptying hallway for him.

"Elijah!" I call when I finally spot him.

He strategically moves to the side enough for me to only see the side of his hoodie and I huff.

"Hey," I say a little more forcefully than intended.

He refuses to look at me.

"Elijah, why aren't you looking at me?"

He stays quiet.

"Elijah."

He still doesn't say anything.

"Ignoring people is considered rude, you know."

No answer.

"Am I so ugly that you don't want to look at me?"

"You know you're not ugly," he *finally* replies. "I need to get to class," he says, turning to walk away from me.

As he goes, I reach out and grab his hood, fed up with his attempts to keep hidden. His entire body stiffens as I pull his hood down, and once it falls, a part of me wishes I never had. He has a huge, purplish-blue bruise on his jaw that looks beyond painful, and stitches running for about an inch above his left eye.

I gasp at the wounds on his face and instantly step forward to inspect them. I was wishing my assumptions were wrong and the only reason he was hiding his face was actually because he had a runny nose that was embarrassing him.

"Elijah, what happened?" I ask quietly, ghosting my fingers across the raw, dark bruise on his jaw.

He closes his eyes for a moment or two, and then turns his head away from me so that my hand falls. "It was nothing."

"That definitely doesn't look like nothing."

"Scarlet, drop it. Please. We have to get to class, anyway."

He walks away, pulling the hood back over his beaten face.

I stomp my way back to him, stepping in front of him. "We have another five minutes before the bell rings, and I won't just drop it. I'm tired of seeing your hands scraped up or how you sometimes have your hood up. And now that I know why it's up? You're insane to think I could just forget about this."

"Why do you care?"

"*Why do I care?*"

"You don't have to care so much just because you feel guilty about your boyfriend."

He thinks I only care to be his friend because I'm feeling guilty about what Jack does to him.

"I don't like what he does, I've told you that, but I'm not friends with you because I'm trying to undo his wrongs. I'm friends with you because I like you, is that so hard to believe?"

His body stiffens in shock.

"I like you because you listen to me a lot more than any of Jack's friends do. Especially Bryce. I don't know what his problem is but Bryce, *freaking* Bryce, seems to have this weird thing against me. I'm convinced he thinks I'm always taking away from bro time and—"

I cut myself off when Elijah's lips curve up at the corners. There was more I could have said. How I may have started my friendship with Elijah because I was feeling guilty about what Jack did to him. How I felt like I had to. But also, how it's already blossomed into actual feelings and how I see Elijah as someone I can open up to.

"I'm just going to stop talking now."

The warning bell sounds as he responds and starts to walk away. "We'll see how long that lasts."

"Wait!" I call, and he instantly stops walking. "You never told me what happened. You avoided the question altogether at the garage last week, and now you're just going to walk away. I told you I'm asking because I care—don't leave me in the dark, Elijah."

He turns around with an excuse already on his lips, but something in my eyes must change his mind. He furrows his brow as he looks at me, thoughts racing through his head, and then responds differently from what I was expecting.

"I'll explain everything tonight when we work on the truck."

~

Since I have work after school anyway, I wait for Elijah to come to the auto shop after Archie leaves. I take the liberty of pushing Elijah's truck into the garage, practically throwing out my back and exerting way too much energy. I slipped on at least twenty leaves as I pushed it—the autumn weather is taking hold around here. However, now I'm a sweaty mess. I just hope I cool off before Elijah comes, because these dark-gray jumpsuits we have to wear in the shop are already quite unattractive. Add being a sweaty monster onto that and I really will be a sight for sore eyes.

I haven't been able to take my mind off of the injuries on Elijah's face all day. The bruise on his jaw was no doubt from someone else's vengeful fist, and I'm terrified that fist belonged to someone in his family. Elijah speaks very little about his home life, and though his father is gone, there could be a stepfather in this equation, or his mother could pack a mighty punch. I can't see him fighting back against someone he's meant to love either.

I know I'm jumping to conclusions, but after what I saw the conclusions are jumping to themselves. I know instantly assuming it's his home life may be assuming too much, but there was a moment I was afraid the injuries stemmed from Jack.

I can't think my boyfriend would do such a terrible thing. Because if I do believe that then there are other questions I should be asking myself.

"What's got you rambling in your head this time?"

Elijah's hoodie is gone, replaced with a ratty long-sleeved shirt I've seen him wear before. Without the hood, the bruise and cut on his face are all too noticeable. He's not wearing them with pride but he's not trying to keep them from me anymore. The fact he trusts me this much—enough to know he doesn't have to hide his bruises from me—causes my heart to melt.

"I figured if you'd already seen them then there was no use in hiding them," Elijah says, picking up on my exact thoughts.

"Elijah, I think I know what you've been hiding."

His face fills with silent surprise and he crosses his arms as he waits for me to expand my statement.

"Look, I know you're being abused," I begin, and his eyes

widen, so I continue. "I'm so sorry I never noticed earlier. I know talking isn't really your strong suit, but I'm here for you to talk to about this. I know it's going to be hard to do and I'm no therapist, but I'm here for you. And—" He opens his mouth but I lift my hand to stop his excuse.

"No. Don't tell me some excuse about falling down the steps or whatever, I'm not dumb. That bruise was definitely from someone hitting you, and that cut . . . well, I don't know where that came from, but I doubt it was from whatever excuse you've thought of! But, Elijah, I won't stand here and see my friend get abused so I've decided—"

I stop my structured rambling when Elijah tilts his head and watches my dumbfounded expression with a chuckle.

"You're laughing," I deadpan.

"Scarlet, I'm not abused."

Oh.

My eyes widen and I feel heat take over my entire neck, crawling up to my cheeks so clearly that I have to look away. This is why jumping to conclusions is *not* a good thing.

"I can't tell if I should be flattered or offended you thought that," he muses.

"Let's go with flattered. If not abuse, then where did the bruise and cut come from?"

Please don't tell me what I've tried so hard to convince myself is impossible. Don't tell me it was Jack.

I clear my throat when he doesn't reply. "It . . . it wasn't—"

"Scarlet, Jack didn't hit me," Elijah says, putting an end to my cruel thoughts before I can even speak them.

Relief floods over me and I nod. My heart rate slows back down to its normal speed, and Elijah continues.

"I'm a boxer."

I blink at him and say the first thing that comes to mind.

"I assume you don't mean the dog breed."

Elijah snorts and drops his head.

"You said you would explain, and right now I really think you need to before I make any more of a fool out of myself."

The humor in his eyes stays for a second or two longer, but all too soon it melts away.

"I fight every week," he explains seriously. "Sometimes the fights don't go my way and I try to hide the consequences. I've gotten pretty good at that part, and no one at school knows. Except for you, now."

Elijah Black is a boxer. And not the dog kind.

"When you say you are at the gym—it's like a boxing gym?" I ask, slowly piecing it together. "How long?"

"At least a year," he admits.

"Where? I don't even know of any boxing places."

Elijah studies my face with a glimmer of shock, almost waiting to see if I will take my statement back. When I don't, he continues.

"It's in downtown Houston. Not many people who aren't actively involved in it know about it," he says, gauging my reaction in an odd way.

I wonder how the hell I didn't pick up on this. It explains all the cuts I saw on his hands after the party, the tape I often see on his knuckles, and the random days of the month when he covers his face like he did today. It's been going on for an entire year, and somehow, I'm the only one who knows.

"Is it safe?" I ask, eyeing his bruises.

His next answer isn't as confident as the others. "It's fighting. There are times it can be dangerous."

I stare at him and push off of where I'm leaning on his truck to walk closer. He stiffens as I stand in front of him, only a few inches of room between us, but I keep my eyes glued to the injuries on his face. I lift my hand and touch his bruise with featherlight fingers. I can feel his penetrating gaze stuck to my every movement, but it doesn't deter me. I notice a small scar running just under the bruise and trace it with my thumb.

"Why do you do it?"

He seems unable to speak, either from not wanting to or not knowing what to say. Then he clears his throat and takes a small step back, looking outside the garage and at the fallen leaves covering the ground.

"I first started to do it as a release. I needed something to take my mind off of . . . well, everything. At that point it was just for the hell of it, but it's changed since then. I had originally heard about the ring from my brother. Nearly three years ago. He had friends who knew about it, friends who turned him into what he became. Friends who sold him what ultimately killed him."

I want to reach out and offer a comforting hand, but my curiosity gets the better of me. "You said your reason changed, why?"

He moves his eyes back to mine. "When Oliver passed away, he passed away with debt still attached to his name. Since I was fighting at the ring, his so-called friends decided to turn on me to get back all of the money Oliver owed them for the drugs he bought."

I hitch my breath from his explanation, which seems all too fictional yet all too real in the same breath.

Elijah is standing tall even with the weight of the world on his shoulders.

"How much do you need?"

He turns his head to the side. "Ten thousand."

"*What did your brother*—" I start to ask, and then stop myself.

"He had an addiction, he got into bigger and more expensive doses. He didn't realize how deep in his debt he was—I guess he was very persuasive with convincing his dealer he'd get him the money, but he overdosed before he could ever figure it out, leaving me to clean up the damage."

My heart lurches for him, for the anger hidden beneath his tone.

"How much do you have?"

He's quiet for a moment or two and then turns to me. "Five thousand."

How often does he fight in order to have made that much? And if he does fight often, how skilled is he to only have these injuries once or twice a month?

"I know his debt sounds like a lot. Oliver . . . he was into a lot of bad and expensive stuff. The debt originally was only about five thousand, but now that I'm the one getting the dealers the money owed, they've decided to charge some major interest. The longer it takes me to get the money, the more I actually owe them before the final deadline."

"When is the final deadline?"

Elijah pauses, seemingly debating whether or not to tell me. "I only have about a month to get the rest. It's okay, though," he adds, and I glance at him. "I sort of like it there. Fighting is a nice release. Why do you look guilty?"

I look away. "Because of how easy it would be for me to get that money if I was in the same situation."

"You aren't spoiled if that's what you're getting at."

I offer him a troubled smile in return. I may not be spoiled, but that doesn't take away from the guilt that eats at my stomach for having such an excess of money when families like his are struggling. I would offer to help pay off this debt, but *I* don't have that money. It's all my parent's money, and I don't like asking them to even buy me candy from the store, much less for drug money for someone I never met.

"How serious is this? The fighting?"

"Serious enough."

"Vague," I mumble. "How does it work?"

"It's simple, really. I set up a fight and if I win, I get money for it. If I lose, I owe that money. The ring isn't necessarily illegal itself. Will, the owner, runs a clean business. I can't say the cops know everything that goes on there, however."

"If it's clean, how are drug dealers involved?"

"Like I said, the cops don't know everything that goes on. The place is mostly safe, most of the fights are just for bets and a business profit for Will, but the dealers were able to worm their way in. Most of the people who attend the fights don't know about the dealers unless they are actively using. Mostly they're just there to attend some late-night violence."

"What does your mom say about all of this?"

"She doesn't like it, but she of all people understands that sometimes it's not easy to crawl out of the hole life throws you into. Sometimes you have to do undesirable things to fix problems."

For once, I stay silent.

"You aren't scared or anything now, are you?" Elijah suddenly asks, apparently taking my silence in the wrong way.

"Worried, yes, but not scared."

"There's nothing to worry about, Scarlet."

However, I watch as his eyes flash with guilt for a few moments until he pushes that to the side.

"I guess I'm not just mysterious anymore, but a mysterious street fighter paying off his brother's drug debt."

"No, you're becoming less and less mysterious by the minute, Elijah Black. But I have a feeling there's a lot more to learn."

"Is that a good thing or a bad thing?"

"Good."

With a smile, he walks past me to the front of the garage. He leans his chiseled body against the wall and stares contentedly outside. I take the hint that our conversation is over, so I decide that now's the time for me to actually work on his truck.

Though I know I should focus my mind on my mechanic training, my thoughts are consumed by the mystery that is Elijah. Yeah, I told him he's becoming less and less mysterious the more I get to know him, but now I'm not so sure that's true. Unraveling facts about him just creates more questions that have yet to be answered.

His personality has a depth so deep that I don't know how long it will take me to reach the bottom.

"Who taught you to fight, Elijah?"

He turns his head back to me and narrows his eyes in curiosity.

"Why do you call me that?"

I laugh at the question. "What? Elijah?"

He nods.

"Well, I was pretty sure it was your name . . . ?"

He chuckles. "I just mean that everyone else calls me Eli, but you have always said Elijah."

"I didn't think you liked to be called Eli."

Because whenever someone addresses him as Eli, it's normally followed by the cruel label of "the freak."

"Who gave you the nickname anyway?"

"Your boyfriend, a long time ago."

I furrow my brow at his answer but move past it for the time being. "I don't want to call you the same thing as everyone else," I add. "Friends grant nicknames, and in this case it's kind of like the reverse of that, you know? You have one that I know you're not fond of, so I'll call you something unique to us, which is the whole point of a nickname in the first place," I muse, forming my thoughts as I go along. "Almost like an antinickname."

"I don't have one for you."

This time I stay quiet. Everyone else seems to have one for me. My parents address me as Scar or sweetheart, and Jack always calls me beautiful.

Elijah's eyes focus back on me and he shakes his head decisively.

"But I don't think you need one."

"No?"

He smiles as he responds, watching the world outside the garage.

"Your name is too pretty to be changed."

Looking at his muscled back, I try to picture him in a boxing ring going up against someone like Mike Tyson, but I can't seem to imagine it. I want to see him fight. I want to be able to put some action to what he's saying, because as real as it all is, I want to know just how serious the fighting gets. He said there was no reason to worry, but I want to be able to come to that conclusion myself.

"So, when do I get to come see you fight?"

He seems surprised as he turns around. "You want to come?"

I grin and start punching the air against an invisible opponent.

I bounce around on my feet, trying to mimic a boxer, and jab at the air in front of me.

"I want to see your moves. You can talk a big talk, but I want to see if you play a big game."

"Calm down, Ali." He chuckles.

I beam at him, utterly satisfied I was able to make him laugh enough to put his smile on display. I don't know how he isn't swarmed by the girls at school. Elijah is more than attractive, and with such a radiant smile? I would think he'd be any girl's full package, aside from one untruthful fact: that he's a freak.

"Is that a yes, then?" I ask.

He mulls it over for a moment or two, thoughtfully staring at me as he decides what he wants to do. For some reason, the internal fight between letting me come or not seems much more complicated than it should be. That same guilty look I saw on his face moments ago is roaring back, and it makes questions shoot across my thoughts.

Before I can ask any of them, he makes up his mind.

"I have a match tomorrow tonight."

I can't help myself, I actually squeak. I even jump up and down while clapping my hands delightedly.

"One condition," he adds.

I calm my racing, excited heart and try to stand still and look as serious as he does right now while I nod.

"Your parents have to say yes."

"Done," I say, my cheeks sore from smiling.

"Now, back to work?"

Nodding, I grab the proper tools for tonight's examination of his truck.

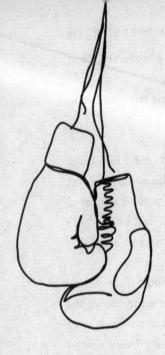

CHAPTER
TWELVE

Rocketing up from my place on the couch, I practically spring to the front door when I see a foreign car roll into our driveway. I know it's Elijah. He told me he'd be driving his mom's car when I asked how we would get to Houston. The ancient Trailblazer looks out of place next to my mom's Escalade. It has much more character, with dents and scratches dotting the exterior.

When I asked my parents if I could go out with Elijah tonight, I didn't give much detail.

"How does Jack feel about you going out with Elijah tonight?" my mom asks now.

"He—well, he doesn't really know."

She sets her glasses down on the cookbook she was going through.

"Jack doesn't know?"

"He doesn't really like Elijah all that much and I just thought it would help us both if I didn't say anything."

I hear her sigh. "Scarlet, Jack is your boyfriend. He has the right to know."

"I know that, Mom. But when I say he doesn't like Elijah I mean he *doesn't like Elijah*. This is just easier."

She studies me for a few moments, the only sound coming from outside as Elijah shuts his car door, and her tough exterior cracks.

"It's been a while since I've seen you so excited to see someone. So, whatever you think is best."

"I love Jack," I instantly say.

"You don't have to prove anything to me, sweetheart. It's okay to get excited for a friend."

I don't have many people come to my door aside from Jack, and Jessica on occasion. Even then half the time I'd rather sit in bed and watch Netflix.

"Have fun, sweetheart," she says.

The doorbell cuts through my small Thank you in response.

"Is that Jack?" My dad yells from his home office, deeper in the house.

"No, Dad! I told you, this is my friend Elijah! He and I are hanging out tonight."

"Oh. Is this the boy with the truck?"

I roll my eyes, leave it to dads to forget things you've repeated over and over again. "Yeah, this is the boy with the truck."

"Well, it's about time I meet this kid," he says, walking down the hall, trying to make himself look taller and more intimidating. He puffs his tiny chest out and tries to raise his arms in order to be the scary father archetype.

My father just is *not* an intimidating man. A lovable, laughable one most definitely, but scary? Not even close.

"Dad, if that didn't work on Jack, I doubt it will work on Elijah."

His entire poster deflates at my cruel, yet true, statement and a scowl takes over his wrinkled features.

"Who says it didn't work on Jack?"

"Everyone."

"Well, why wouldn't it work on Eli?"

Why does *everyone* grant him that nickname?

I debate giving him my actual explanation: that Elijah is bigger and stronger than Jack. I don't know if he is any taller than Jack, but his broadness adds to the illusion.

"Just a hunch," I decide to say, worried that the door is too thin and Elijah will hear my creepily in-depth description of his body compared to my boyfriend's.

I open the door, and Elijah's standing on the other side, his usual, silent confidence radiating off of him in waves. He's standing tall with normal perfect posture, the flannel over top of his large frame open to reveal the white shirt underneath. I greet him, and not a second later my dad nudges my back so that I'll invite him inside.

Calm down, Dad. I have manners.

"You must be Elijah," my dad says, and I cringe when I notice his "subtle" attempt to deepen his voice. "I'm Kurt Tucker, Scarlet's father."

"Very nice to meet you, sir."

"So, what are you two doing tonight?"

I was *so* close to getting away without an explanation.

Elijah still holds my father's hand in their handshake, intense eye contact suddenly stirring up from both of them.

"I'm taking her to the boxing ring in downtown Houston."

Confusion fills my entire system as my dad's expression floods in recognition of a place Elijah told me not many people know about unless they're actively involved.

"I see," my dad says, breaking the shake. Then he turns to me with a smile. "Scarlet, mind if I have a small chat with Eli?"

I shrug my approval. He did the same thing with Jack when I first introduced them, so I figured he'd so something like this with Elijah. He likes to know the guys I hang out with; it's understandable. Of course, I'm curious as to what they're discussing, but I don't let myself think too much of it. A few minutes later, Elijah and my father come out of the office and they both seem calmer than before.

"Ready?" Elijah asks.

"He gave the okay?" I ask, glancing hesitantly at my dad.

"Eli and I had a nice talk; I think it's okay for you to go. Have a good time and stay safe," he says, metaphorically pushing us out the door. "Call if you need to."

I instinctively check my back pocket for my phone before he shuts the door behind us, and I realize that it's not there. I whirl around and stop the door from closing, pushing it back with a sheepish smile.

"Nearly forgot my phone. You can come, Elijah, I'll be just a second."

I run upstairs and grab my phone off of my bedside table. I turn around, expecting to see Elijah, but instead nobody is there. Confused, I start on my way back downstairs to see if my parents stopped him. But instead, I find him on the second floor inside a room that we try to forget about: Max's room.

Elijah's broad back is turned to me, but I can tell he's holding something. I tentatively walk into Max's room, and as Elijah hears the scuff of my feet his head snaps slightly to the side. I stop in the doorway and he turns around to face me, and my eyes automatically go to his hands. He's holding a picture of Max but sets it back down on the desk as he clears his throat.

"I'm sorry, I didn't mean to—"

I cut him off with a small wave of my hand, blowing it off.

"That's him?" he asks, nodding slightly at the picture on the desk but keeping his eyes on me.

I shift my sight to the picture of Max on his high school graduation day. He has his arms around me and Mom, one arm holding me close and the other around Mom, cap in hand, while dad takes the picture.

I close my eyes and look away from a day that seems as though it was a lifetime ago. "Yeah. He always drove his motorcycle to his friend's place, every week. But that curve on Boundary Lane, you know the one with the blind spot? That's where . . ." I have to pause to keep my voice steady. ". . . where the eighteen-wheeler hit him."

We fall into silence, Elijah seemingly not knowing what to say.

"Heroin," Elijah finally says. "It . . . it was heroin that he got into toward the end."

We don't hear of many drug-related deaths in our town, but they mostly all come from the area where Elijah lives. From how separated this side of town is from his, the news of these deaths doesn't affect us in the way it should. But that doesn't make the heartbreak any less real for the families.

"I'm so sorry, Elijah."

"He did it to himself."

"It doesn't matter how it happens." I frown. "Death still sucks."

My eyes travel around the room and down to Max's blankets, and I run my hands over the faded fabric.

"Sometimes, when I'm feeling down, I come in here to feel closer to him. He always had a way of helping whenever I had a problem, so somehow coming in here just makes me feel safer. He was my overprotective older brother who never wanted to see his little sister cry—mainly because he was terrible at handling a crying child," I say with a sad laugh, sitting down on his bed. "He learned the hard way that ice cream doesn't fix everything.

"I've been told that those we love don't leave us when they die. I know Max is still here with me every day, but I want the real thing, you know? I don't want his imaginary footprint next to mine. I want to jump from one of his real footprints to the other, like when I used to chase him through the mud on a rainy day because staying inside was too boring for me. When I used to see how small my feet were compared to his and wish I could someday fill his shoes," I say quietly, keeping my mournful gaze on the floor. "I just want him back."

I would have said more, but for once I feel like there's no more to say. I don't talk about Max that often, but somehow becoming friends with Elijah over these past couple of weeks has made me talk about him more than I have in the past year. Sniffling, I hastily wipe away the first tear as I feel it fall, and suddenly the bed dips next to me as Elijah sits down. "I must sound crazy."

Elijah shakes his head and eyes me sadly, a silent sense of understanding between us, as well as the same guilt I've been noticing lately.

"You aren't crazy, Scarlet."

I give an unbelieving nod as another tear slips down my

cheek. Elijah reaches out and wipes it away with the pad of his thumb before his hand drops back into his lap.

"You're stronger than you think."

"I wish I didn't have to be. I wish Max had never gotten on that motorcycle that night. I wish he could have met Jack, met you."

Suddenly Elijah's expression becomes guarded, his eyes heavy.

"Is everything okay?" I ask.

"Your dad asked me not to do this," he starts almost to himself. "But this isn't fair to you, Scarlet."

"What are you talking about, Elijah?"

"I haven't been completely honest with you."

I feel my heart drop in my chest at his words.

"What do you mean?"

"Come on," he says, standing up. "We need to get going. I'll explain on the way."

CHAPTER THIRTEEN

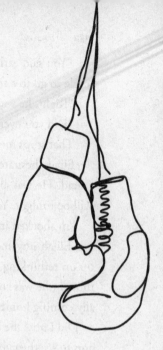

Despite my insisting he tell me right that second and not wait until we get to his car, Elijah doesn't say any more until we're on the road. My knee will not stop bouncing as he pulls out of my driveway and starts down the road, when he finally speaks up.

"I . . ." He stops for a moment, clenching his jaw as he tries to decide what to say. "I don't know Max's name from the newspaper articles like I said. I know more about him than you think."

I feel like someone just punched me straight in the gut.

"Excuse me?" I cough out.

"I shouldn't have kept this from you for so long. No one should have. I didn't know that you didn't know until that night at Jack's, when we were sitting out back during the party—the way you talked about Max and never once mentioned the boxing ring . . ."

"What about the ring?"

"You said earlier that your brother was always on his motor-cycle to go to a friend's place in Houston."

"Right, he was there every week."

"Did you ever meet this friend?"

That stops me in my tracks. "Where are you going with this?"

Elijah hesitates. "He wasn't just driving out there to see a friend. He was always driving out there to go where you and I will be tonight. Your brother was a boxer like me, Scarlet."

I'm shocked into silence for the rest of the drive. I can't even ask Elijah any more questions about it because I'm too hung up on rethinking my entire childhood with Max. Every night I thought he was coming home from a friend's house he was actually coming home from a fight.

Did I miss the bruises on him? Did I never pay enough attention to see the cuts?

"We're almost there," Elijah says into the silence, hands shifting on the steering wheel.

I slowly nod, trying to figure out how I should be reacting right now. We drove through miles and miles of cornfields and small waterways just to reach Houston, but we quickly drive out of the tall buildings and dazzling lights of the city and toward the poorer district of the city. We turn down a narrow, darkened street with only a few working streetlights, graffiti on the passing buildings. He turns down an alleyway and parks the car in a small yet crowded lot filled with a mix of expensive and cheap cars.

"Scarlet, I'm sorry that you didn't know about Max. I don't know why your parents never told you, that much is their story to tell, but you're going to be meeting someone tonight who may have known Max better than even your parents. He can answer whatever questions I know are stirring up in your mind."

"Why was my dad okay with me coming if he knew the possibility of me finding out?"

"I think he came to the conclusion that your finding out was inevitable, and when I mentioned Kevin, he seemed to give in to the fact this was finally out of his hands."

"I just don't get it."

"Let's go inside, you may find out more."

The building is covered with graffiti, and has bricks chipping away at certain ends and a shattered window up top, yet cars are lined up in the parking lot. Living where I do, I've never ventured to a part of town like this, aside from the few times I went to Diner on Tenth with Max.

I have to remind myself that this is where Max used to be every week. He came from the same family as mine, had the same upbringing, yet he felt comfortable enough here. So, I have to trust that this book is not properly judged by its cover. Besides, the only way for me to get the answers I want seems to be for me to go inside that uninviting building.

"Okay," I say, reaching for the door handle with a shaking hand. "Let's go."

We walk to the metal door, and images of Max doing the same fill my head. I try to imagine the life he had that I never knew about. I try to picture him coming here with the intent to battle someone, his mind-set, what got him to do this. Max was always a sweet, gentle guy. I rarely saw him get angry. I rarely saw him get stressed. I can't imagine him actually fighting someone for money. I don't think I ever saw him throw a punch in his life.

Everything I knew about him seems to be the opposite of the lifestyle here.

"Scarlet?" Elijah says, and I realize I've stopped in front of the door.

"I'm okay."

He studies me for a moment or two and then opens the door, and I stay close to him as we enter a smoky reception-like room. It's just as run down as the building, with cracks in the paint on the walls and a desk nearing retirement. I take a small step closer to Elijah. There are a bunch of men in ripped tank tops and with scraggly facial hair, their eyes filled with pent-up anger they've collected through the years.

Focused on the men, I don't register Elijah leaving my side. They each eye me hungrily and stand up, and fear enters my bloodstream; those looks definitely aren't for fashion advice. Suddenly, their gaze goes to something behind me, and their smirks disappear. Like dogs being scolded, they go back to their seats and act like nothing ever happened. Relief floods my racing heart and calms it down. I turn around to see just what got them so spooked, and I see Elijah standing there.

"I'm sorry, Scarlet. I thought you were behind me."

"I got stage fright," I joke to calm myself.

"This place isn't a walk in the park, Scarlet. Stay close to me, okay?"

I glance back at the sketchy characters and instinctively wrap my arm around Elijah's arm, feeling the muscles of his bicep.

"If you can make them run away with their tails tucked between their legs, then deal. There's no way I'm letting you out of my sight."

He moves his whole arm around me to keep me against his protective side as a silent form of reassurance, and I realize just how tall he is.

I wasn't sure if he was taller than Jack, but being this close to him makes me realize Elijah has an inch or so on him, and that inch or so seems like much more due to the difference in stature between the two of them. Elijah has a broad and sturdy build. Even without his muscles he would still be a force to reckon with because of his large shoulders. Jack, on the other hand, is more of a skinny type of muscle. He has a lean physique that's perfect for a quarterback, but without his workout routine he would be more like a twig.

Not that I'm comparing them. That would be wrong.

I slowly begin to feel at ease with Elijah here with me as we walk farther, distant noise becoming louder. Yes, I'm still on my guard and would never walk off on my own, but his lack of worry has mine slowly dissipating.

"Believe it or not, this place is less sketchy than it was a few years back. Back when your brother fought here."

"What do you mean?"

The buzz of shouting suddenly gets more prominent as we come upon a large room and Elijah has to speak louder for me to hear.

"Some things happened years ago that brought in dealers who were part of some gang. The gang itself has since thinned out, only pockets of dealers hang around anymore. But, since it appears the gang atmosphere is gone, it's not as dangerous as it once was."

"Why did they thin out?"

"Something happened, I guess, that freaked them out enough to scatter, and they've since left, for the most part. Aside from the few drug dealers who . . . well, that Oliver hung around."

I start to ask what happened, but he stops me.

"Before you ask, I have no clue what happened. But don't worry about any of that, you're not in danger."

We come upon a packed crowd of people where the majority of the roar I heard from outside is coming from; the room is dimly lit and a haze hovers in the air. Bodies are packed tightly together, everyone hooting and hollering for the only lit thing in the entire room, the boxing ring. The room smells of sweat and cigarettes, a foul combination. Two fighters are up there now, beating the crap out of each other while the crowd cheers and screams for more blood to be shed. The bigger of the two lands a harsh punch to his opponent's gut, and when he hunches over from the pain, the bigger fighter slams his knee right into the same wound and the beaten fighter falls to the floor in a groaning mess.

My brother once did . . . *this*?

Elijah looks down at me and bends down so that I can hear him over the crowd, having to lean quite far since I'm at least a foot shorter than he is.

"You doing okay? We can leave if you want."

"I'm okay!"

Though this isn't a walk in the park, I still have questions I need to get answered.

"Come on, there's someone you need to meet." He offers me a smile, and it calms even more of my nerves and allows me to relax into my surroundings.

And somehow, I feel closer to Max.

We walk into the cheering bodies, and Elijah's large frame shields me from being bumped into, taking away my fear.

"Who am I meeting?"

"My trainer, Kevin."

"Trainer?"

"He used to fight here a few years ago."

"Why did he switch to training?"

I watch as Elijah's eyes shift, darkening at the question, though he hides it well.

"Sometimes," he says carefully, "things happen that make you realize what is actually the path for you. I guess he figured boxing wasn't for him . . . but there's another reason I want you to meet him, Scarlet."

"Which is?"

Elijah sighs, almost as though questioning if he should be saying anything.

"Just meet him, you'll understand."

We reach a small break in the crowd, right next to the ring, and Elijah points Kevin out to me. Had he not said that was Kevin, I would have pinned him to be a scary bouncer for some exclusive club.

Kevin has short, dark-brown, almost black, hair and an even darker goatee dotting his chin, a faded shave on the rest of his jawline. He's definitely just as tall as Elijah, which has to be a whopping six-four and looks to be just one step short of a bodybuilder, with jacked arms filling out his black V-neck shirt. I see a tattoo on the bulging muscles of his left arm. His stance is guarded and unforgiving, and his expression holds stern anger as he watches the rest of the fight in front of him. He doesn't even flinch at every hit like I know I've been doing.

"Kevin!" Elijah calls as we get closer.

Kevin turns his head to us, and his calculating gaze lands on me.

My heart rate starts accelerating, silence falling between the three of us. Kevin's expression is guarded but I can tell he has a million things racing through his mind as he analyzes me. But then his eyes lighten.

"You look just like him, you know," he says.

"How do you . . ."

"Know who you are?"

"Know my brother."

"Max was my best friend."

Once again, it feels like the breath is knocked out of me. I have never seen this guy before, never even heard of boxing in Houston, and here I am standing next to the ring where my brother used to fight, talking to his supposed best friend.

"You look beyond confused," Kevin says into my silence.

"Can you blame me? This is a lot to learn in one night."

Kevin suddenly becomes sympathetic. "Max never wanted you to find out . . . I was wondering if I'd ever meet you."

"But *why?*"

"Max was worried you'd think of him differently. He wanted to keep that part of his life to himself. He didn't even tell your parents until they started asking questions."

"He of all people should have known my opinion of him could never have changed."

"Your brother thought that you would somehow think less of him or worry. He didn't want to put you through anything like that. From what I heard, you really looked up to him."

"I did. I do."

"He'd turn over in his grave if I explained all of this to you."

"I'm not ten anymore and I already know this much. May as well keep going."

"When my time comes, he's going to be waiting up there with his fist ready," he mutters, then louder, "Your brother was the best fighter here, Scarlet."

Max lived a double life and I had no clue, and apparently that was the way he wanted it. I thought he and I told each other everything.

"The best?"

"Enough to where you never saw any bruises on him. He and I were sort of like the dynamic duo here. Everyone knew us, and everyone respected him."

I try to calm my racing thoughts and choose the questions I need answered.

"How did he find this place?"

"Though Max and I quickly became best friends, there was a time we hated each other. He ran into my car with his bike—that was the first time I ever met him. We started duking it out right there on the side of the road because the hothead said it was my fault for slamming on my brakes too late. Then Will, the owner of this place, saw us and ran over, scolding us for fighting over something so stupid."

His eyes get a faraway look as he recalls the story, and I find myself getting lost in it with him.

"He told us he had a place for us to settle our anger, said we could go in that night for all he cared. Boys being boys, we accepted. Max was the first guy I ever fought here, and we nearly beat one another to a pulp."

As my mind wanders to memories of Max, a distant memory comes back piece by piece the more Kevin explains. Max coming home late one night, looking tired and sweaty but not grease stained, so not from the shop, and with a dent in his motorcycle.

I can't remember his excuse; I can't remember what he told us, but that's not important.

Turns out that story was just another lie he told. Another truth he withheld from me.

"But Will saw potential in us, he offered for us to start fighting for money. Said he needed young blood to get the crowds excited again. Through fighting and training together, Max and I quickly became best friends. It started out as a fierce rivalry to see who the best between us was, but the more we trained the closer we became and, well, the rest is history," he ends with a small chuckle.

I want to smile along with him since I've just met someone who seems to have known my brother just as well as I did, but instead I frown. I can't seem to wrap my head around why Max would keep all of this from me. I hug my arms to my body since I suddenly feel cold and alone without Max.

"I was devastated when he passed away," Kevin says.

"I always wished he hadn't decided to buy a motorcycle."

He masks his confusion before I can fully register it. "When I got the news, I couldn't believe what had happened."

Neither could I. No one could.

No one can fully comprehend the idea that someone can be smiling and laughing with you one second and be permanently gone from your life the next. The cold feeling sinks farther into my skin as I look around the rowdy boxing club.

Kevin smiles softly at me and the terrifyingly intimidating brute I saw earlier disappears. "You know how I recognized you?"

I shake my head, wishing to be ten again with a big brother to take me to get ice cream when I skinned my knee from tripping on the sidewalk.

"He talked about you all the time and would always show me pictures of his little sister. You look older now, but still like the girl he constantly bragged about. Even though I never met you, I felt like I knew you just as well as Max did. He loved you more than anything."

"I loved him too."

Kevin frowns and does something I can already tell is very out of character for him—he hugs me. There's something about sharing the devastating feeling of loss that can bring two people closer together. It's a slight silver lining to such a severe storm.

"It's nice to finally meet you, Scarlet."

"I never knew you existed until now, but it's nice to meet you too."

I could think of this as a betrayal of my brother's trust, and a part of me does, but the other part is spinning it around to see it as an opportunity to relearn about Max. Finding out so much about him keeps him alive.

Elijah being called into the ring directs my attention to him. He was discreetly watching Kevin and me, trying not to step in on a conversation that didn't involve him. But I know he listened. He is gauging my mood, trying to decipher how I'm feeling after getting some of my questions answered, so I send him a smile and he relaxes.

"That was my ten-minute warning. I need to go get ready."

I follow the two of them to a small set of rooms along a hallway on the far side of the room. I stay close to them among the many bodies mingling as they await the next match, and Kevin stays with me right outside of Elijah's changing room while he gets ready. A few minutes later, Elijah emerges in nothing but a white tank top and a pair of black shorts. His hands are taped up, the white fabric covering everything but his fingers, to ensure his hands' safety. He said this was boxing, so I assumed gloves would be involved, but he seems to have no intentions of putting any on.

"You ready?" Elijah asks me.

Looking between him and the ring, my body begins to buzz with adrenaline.

"Don't get your ass kicked."

His chuckle resonates through the narrow hallway. "I'll do my best."

It suddenly hits me that I'm about to watch my new friend either get his ass kicked or kick someone else's ass. And either way, he's going to look like a god. The white shirt he's wearing covers only a portion of his shoulders, allowing me to see all of the muscles and veins on his arms. If I was his opponent, I would be terrified.

Minutes later Elijah climbs into the ring. He looks completely comfortable up there as at least a hundred voices chant unintelligible words while he waits for his challenger to enter the ring. He doesn't acknowledge the crowd at all, and it seems as if he barely notices them. Then the fighter he's to go against squeezes through the ropes and I hold my breath when I don't see a scrawny man like a part of me was hoping to. Instead, I'm staring at a man who is definitely Elijah's height, and has only a *slightly* skinnier stature than Elijah. He has long blond hair, parted in the middle, which he didn't bother to tie back, and a smirk on his face as he jumps around to get the crowd excited.

Elijah shows no reaction to his challenger's actions. Then I look at Kevin, who is leaning against the ring, calculating what's to come. Elijah's challenger is still jumping around to get the crowd hyped when the bell sounds, and I feel my heart just about burst from my chest out of worried anticipation. Elijah steps forward but the other guy is playing the crowd. Elijah slowly stalks up to his challenger, and I'm in disbelief that he could be so dumb as to still be focused on the crowd instead of Elijah.

The crowd suddenly yells for him to turn around, and the second he does Elijah's fist flies across his face. He spins around and falls against the ropes, and I swear my jaw drops all the way to the floor. Even though Elijah caught him off guard, that punch held a monstrous amount of power behind it.

"That was called a cross. It's his best punch," Kevin explains.

Elijah's challenger takes the next few seconds to get situated again, blinking to either shake off the pain or remember where he is as blood pours from his nose. Elijah steps back and waits for him to stand straight up instead of using the ropes to support himself, and my eyes widen when I realize that was only a *warning* shot. The two of us dancing in the garage the other night pops into my mind; I'm amazed that someone with so much power could have been so delicate while he held me.

His opponent wipes the blood from his nose and rage fills his face as he charges at Elijah for a counterpunch. Even after having such a perfect hit and getting the crowd to go wild, Elijah stays focused. However, when his challenger runs at him, I see the slightest smirk form on the corner of his lips and all he does is side step and then slam his fist into the other guy's back. He goes flying forward with the added momentum from Elijah's punch and slams face-first into the corner pole of the ring.

"That was a parry. Another great move."

Elijah walks to his opponent and lifts him up by the scruff of his tank top and spins him around so that his back is against the pole, his broken nose visible to the crowd. He grits his teeth and sends an uncoordinated punch at Elijah, who swipes the arm to the side and punches his opponent's now fully exposed face. The crowd somehow gets even louder as Elijah dominates the fight and his challenger drops to the ground, unable to get up. They scream and chant for Elijah, and I can't seem to contain myself from doing the same. I jump up and down and throw my fists into the air as I holler his name and copy sayings from people around me.

Who knew I was so into violence?

Elijah barely breaks a sweat as he stares down at his opponent lying on the ground after tapping three times to signal that he's done. The referee comes over to Elijah and lifts his hand high in the air to announce his victory.

"Eli Black takes yet another victory!" he shouts into a crackling microphone.

Elijah keeps a stoic, humbled expression until he looks at me, then smiles while I cheer with the rest of the screaming crowd. As the referee drops his hand, Elijah walks back over to me and Kevin and everyone chants his name. Before he can fully reach us, his name is yelled into the microphone again as the announcer gets the crowd excited again.

"Not so fast, Eli! That was only your first challenger of the night! Up next to try and take tonight's title is Percyyyyy Fisher!"

I turn to Kevin. "He has two fights?"

"Once you win one fight, people tend to step up to the plate and want to challenge you. They scope you out during your scheduled fight to see if they can take you down."

"Does this happen often?"

"Against Elijah? Every once in a while some idiot thinks he

can take him down, assuming he's tired from his previous fight."

"And does their strategy work?"

Kevin chuckles and nods at the ring. "Watch and find out."

This fight doesn't go as easily as the first. Elijah's opponent is bigger than his last and clearly more skilled, and he even lands a few hits to Elijah. Kevin leans over to me and nods up at Elijah as he shields his face from his opponent, blocking Percy's hits.

"He practices how to duck day in and day out. He'll make his challenger think he's only going to play this match defensively, but watch. As soon as it's believed he's going down, Elijah will lead right, which just means an unsuspecting and powerful punch. His challenger is just a shoe shiner right now, making his punches look good but they aren't actually doing any damage. Elijah will throw an uppercut when the time is right to win the match."

"You seem to be a good trainer."

"Elijah has natural talent, anyone could train him."

"If you were such a good fighter," I find myself asking, "then why switch to training?"

Kevin's eyes harden and his jaw sets. "Story for another time."

Note to self: don't ask about that.

"Right! Back to the fight!" I say with an overly done smile as I direct my attention to Elijah.

I look just in time to see him deliver the final blow needed for his opponent to hit the floor. This time he falls unconscious instead of tapping out and Elijah comes out victorious yet again. The ref raises Elijah's hands to show that he's won for the second time tonight, and he walks back to me and Kevin. Once again, every single person in this place is chanting his name, a loud roar of excitement for who seems to be the favorite fighter. Elijah is popular here.

I run up to him with excitement coursing through my veins. It ignites my senses and I wonder why I never got into boxing before this. If Max thought I'd think differently of him, he couldn't have been more wrong.

"You were amazing! You were in a pinch, just ducking is what Kevin said. But he said that was just a ruse and that you were fine. But I got worried that you were going to lose, and then you threw another punch and he blocked it, but you would come right back and land a hit and—"

"So, you enjoyed yourself?"

I playfully shove him, feeling his muscles beneath my hand. "That was badass."

"You continue to surprise me, Scarlet."

I smile up at him but his expression drops to one of concern and he lowers his voice. "But enough about the fights, are you okay?"

"I'm okay."

"Your dad was right."

I crease my brow in question.

"You are a terrible liar."

I look away and blow a light amount of frustrated air from my lips. "It's just a lot to process, but I'll be okay."

"It's okay to not be okay."

"I have to try and reason with why Max did what he did. Easier said than done, but I'll get there."

Before Elijah can respond, Kevin pulls him aside to discuss the fight. He goes into what I assume is his training mode as he points out the weak spots of Elijah's performance. I didn't even notice a single flaw in his fight. Every move seemed fluid and perfect, but Kevin found small things for him to work on.

As the two of them talk, I suddenly feel eyes burning into me, and I become very uncomfortable. There's a group of shady characters staring me down. They are around Kevin's age, early twenties, but their looks are definitely not nice. However, when they smirk maniacally upon getting my attention, I shuffle closer to Elijah. I accidentally bump into him and he stops his conversation with Kevin to glance down at me and my frightened form. He subtly steps more in front of me to shield me.

Kevin notices as well and stands up straight rather than leaning against the ropes. He crosses his jacked arms over his equally jacked chest and narrows his own skeptical eyes.

The group all smirk and cryptically walk off, sending one final look at me with threats in their eyes and I gulp. I instinctively step closer to Elijah and Kevin turns to us.

"Looks like I'm not the only one who recognizes you."

With Elijah's second match finished and the creepy group of gangsters or whatever are gone, he drives me home. We talk about the fight, but I do most of the talking per usual and he does most of the listening. I talk a lot about Max. I haven't spoken so much about him to anyone before aside from possibly my father, but there are things I don't say to him that I find myself relaying to Elijah. Now, however, I'm trotting up to my front door to head inside.

"How was your night with Eli?" my dad asks.

The grandfather clock my mom insisted we keep in the living room, despite the way it clashes with all of our furniture, dings and signals that it's eleven o'clock.

"I had an . . . interesting time."

I was able to put away my feelings of betrayal and anger for the latter half of my night. Seeing Elijah fight and being hopped up on adrenaline from the crowd altered my sour feelings, but being home now with the two who have lied to me the most has put those sour feelings back into my mind.

"Why didn't you tell me?" I instantly ask, unable to keep back any of my anger.

He stands there like a deer caught in headlights, eyes wide and guilty.

"Can I pretend to not know what you're talking about?"

I don't laugh at his lame attempt to lighten the mood. My mom walks into the room, and I direct my question to the both of them.

"Why did neither of you tell me?"

"I asked Elijah not to tell you . . ."

"This isn't Elijah's fault. If you didn't want me finding out, then why let me go in the first place? Especially if you knew I'd be meeting Kevin."

My dad shakes his head. "I don't know, Scar. I guess a part of us did want you to finally know the truth."

"That he was a boxer? *Why* is that something so important not to tell me? I don't get it!"

For a moment, my dad seems confused that that's all I say. He gets a puzzled look in his eye and glances over at my mom, but she shakes her head and looks over at me.

"It was important to Max, sweetheart."

"Is there anything else I should know?"

They share a look, and once again my mom speaks up before my dad can say anything.

"No, Scarlet. That's all we kept from you, that he was a fighter. He even kept it from us for the first year."

I can hear the strain in her voice from talking about Max. It's never been easy for her since he died, and most of my anger dissipates. They were just keeping up what Max wanted—for me to never find out.

"Oh, sweetheart, come here," my mom says as tears spring into my eyes.

Both she and my dad pull me closer to them for a hug, and I melt into their arms like I did when I was a little girl.

"I wish he was still here." I sniffle.

"I know, honey."

"We do too."

As we pull apart, they each offer me a small smile and though I'm still a little angry, I push that down and smile back.

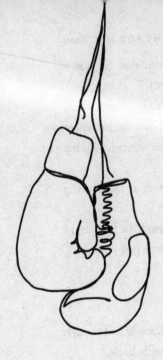

CHAPTER FOURTEEN

As I finish my last bite of cereal, Jack's truck roars into my drive-way. The diesel engine hums loud enough to shake my house and I quickly toss my bowl into the sink, dousing it with water to make it look clean.

"Bye, Mom!"

The last thing I want is for Jack to beep, because he came to the shop months ago to modify his horn into some loud, blaring siren. He's leaning against his truck as I walk outside; it's so lifted that the tires nearly reach his waist.

"Hey, beautiful," he greets me, opening my side of the truck and helping me hoist myself in. "You look just as gorgeous as ever," he flirts, slowly eyeing my light-blue dress matched with an off-white cardigan.

"Hey, yourself."

The ride to school is short, no more than five minutes, and

soon his truck roars into the parking lot. His football buddies run over to us as we get out and one of them helps me step down from the raised seat. I notice Jack sending him a hard glare for touching me. I internally roll my eyes; Jack has always been on the jealous side of the boyfriend spectrum, and I often don't know how to handle it. It's even worse with Elijah coming into the picture, which is part of the reason I've been so secretive about hanging out with him. I wish I didn't have to be. I don't want to feel like I have to hide Elijah.

But to Jack, it's one thing for me to be hanging out or talking to another guy, but for that guy to be Elijah? To him, I'm basically committing relationship treason.

As they all talk about the upcoming game, I notice Elijah walking on the sidewalk, his torn backpack hauled over his shoulder. He's wearing a worn shirt that I've seen him wear countless times before. As a matter of fact, I'm pretty sure he wore it yesterday. My mind is drawn to how he looked that night we worked on the truck while it poured outside, when his shirt was stuck to his skin, revealing all of his abs underneath. And last night, with nothing but a tank top on as he fought, the muscles in his arms rippled through every punch. Now, I can't seem to stop staring at them.

Unconsciously, I grin when he looks over at me, and I mouth a Hey. His lips twitch up into a smile and he gives a nod as his own form of silent greeting. But then his expression drops as his eyes flit to Jack behind me, and he walks past us and avoids catching Jack's attention.

He's unable to avoid it all day, though. By lunch, Elijah and I cross paths again and unfortunately so does Jack. Jack walks me to my locker to retrieve my books for my AP European History class just before lunch and as I work on getting my things from my locker, he talks about some crazy play he conducted at football practice yesterday.

"Mm," I hum.

"It was something I've seen Aaron Rodgers do before, but amateur quarterbacks only dream of doing."

Suddenly a few of his friends show up and chime into the story, and he starts to direct his words toward them rather than me. I close my locker, leaning my back against it as I listen to them all talk and Bryce gush over Jack. But then he abruptly stops talking and narrows his eyes at something behind me.

Elijah's down the long stretch of hall, adjusting his backpack with a passive expression stuck to his features. Jack's face lights up as he nods to his friends and tells them to watch.

"Hey, freak!" he yells, and I notice the subtle stiffening of Elijah's jaw.

"Not only are you a crackhead, but you don't even know hygiene! Tell me, freak, how many times have you worn that shirt *this* week? Three, four?"

Elijah doesn't pay attention to Jack's bullying, but I do.

"How does it feel to get your clothes from a dumpster?"

I'm torn. Jack is a jerk for what he says to Elijah, but he's my boyfriend and I should love him for every part of him. But Elijah is becoming a really good friend and it hurts me to hear the things Jack says about him. If I stand up to Jack and tell him to stop, we are only going to argue, and I know I don't want that. But I don't want to stand back and watch him belittle the one friend I think genuinely cares.

So I do the only thing I can think of.

I scream.

I shut my eyes and scream as loudly as I can and cut off Jack's next rip at Elijah, and I freak out the entire hallway and quite possibly the entire school.

Why do I do it? I have no clue. But it works.

Jack instantly lifts his hands to his ears and cringes, as do all of his friends. Elijah looks at me with confused shock and he takes a step toward me. My screaming dims until the hallway is silent, and Jack slowly takes his hands off of his ears.

"*What the fuck,* babe?"

I feel every single pair of eyes in the hallway stuck on me, and I realize what exactly I just did; I screamed bloody murder for seemingly no reason.

My face heats up and I fumble for a good enough excuse. A lame excuse hits me a few seconds later, but it's all I have to work with.

"I saw a rat."

I see Bryce's eyes widen in fear as he takes a not so subtle step closer to Jack. Jack blinks at me, still slightly irritated from my bloodcurdling scream, but relaxes his tensed features.

"That's it?"

I nod a little too quickly, almost a perfect giveaway to show that I'm lying, but he doesn't pick up on it.

"Well, it's gone now, so come on, let's get to class," he says, taking my hand in his.

I force a smile at him and nod, and follow him and Bryce down the silent hallway—people are still quite shocked from my scream—and to class. I glance behind me and catch Elijah's gaze. He has a smirk on his lips and his arms crossed over his broad chest, and I barely hold back my blush. He knows there was no rat.

Word must have gotten to Principal Meyers that the screamer was me, because she stops the three of us in the hallway to "chat."

"Yeah, Principal Meyers, she saw a *rat*!" Bryce exclaims in disgust to our outdated pantsuit–wearing principal.

"I just don't see how that's possible, Bryce," she says strictly, with an old southern twang to her sharp words. "We have exterminators come every weekend to be certain our school is not infested by anything. There is a reason we are number one in Texas's Cleanest High Schools."

Jack tugs my hand. "Tell her, babe."

"About what?"

"The rat."

"Oh! Right, it was *really* big, too, and just kind of scurried across the floor and then behind a set of lockers."

"Tell me, Scarlet, how come you are the *only* student who saw it?"

I swear she has it out for me. Principal Meyers gushes over Jack every time she sees him, praising him on the morning announcements every Monday morning for his Friday night wins.

"Everyone else seemed focused on their friends, and my eyes happened to be in the right place at the right time . . ."

She stares at me for a few moments, debating whether or not she wants to buy my answer.

"It's true, Principal Meyers." Jack speaks up, and her hard expression melts away at his voice. "She has a keen eye for the oddest things."

I nod quickly with a fake smile. If I were to tell her the truth, that I did it to stop my boyfriend from being an asshole, she would probably not be too pleased with that either. So I speak up again before she can argue with me.

"I'm sorry for causing a disruption and screaming, but it won't happen again! Now, the three of us should get to class before we're late!"

~

Jack insists on coming over for an hour or two after school, but for the first time in our relationship I don't want to spend time with him. How he treats Elijah is cutting deeper into my feelings for him. It's always bothered me, Jack's bullying of random people, but lately it's going beyond dislike—it's changing the way I feel about him. It's making me ashamed to be with him.

I tell Jack that I'm not feeling well, but that doesn't deter him, and he comes over anyway to make sure I'm okay. I didn't lie by saying I didn't feel well—I am exhausted—so Jack and I end up taking a nap. However, I don't get to sleep for as long as I want because Jack wakes me up, insisting we have some "fun."

He leaves afterward, and I get myself ready for the fight that Elijah invited me to tonight. Elijah picks me up in his mom's car, since his truck refuses to run, and we're on our way. Though this is only my third time going to the fights, I've already started memorizing the way. The differences in the cornfields, the ponds and streams we pass, the random sharp turns along the road, and almost every corner once we enter the city.

"Do you know who you're fighting?" I ask.

He simply calls the location the Arena, but I prefer the nickname Sketchy Underground Street-Fighting Building.

"Not sure. Kevin lines up most of my fights. You're staring," he teases.

I blush and look away. "Was not."

His lips twitch up at my childish response and he stays quiet. He's good at that; staying quiet.

"How much money did the fights from last week earn you?"

"Not enough."

"How much more do you need?"

"A couple thousand."

Hopelessness settles into my stomach, and I wonder why he doesn't have the same feeling. He only has three weeks to get the rest.

"Stop worrying, Scarlet," he says, cutting into my thoughts.

Was it that obvious?

"I just don't see how—"

"I'll figure it out, but you don't need to worry about it," he says firmly but in a gentler tone.

"Too late."

He looks over at me with a scowl, but I sense the gratitude beyond it.

"I still have three weeks, there's a possibility I can still make enough in time." But then part of his brave facade crumbles. "The problem is that there aren't enough fighters for me to go against."

"You don't know that."

"I know most of the fighters there. And their rank dictates how much the fight is worth—there aren't enough highly ranked fighters for me to go against in order to get the money."

"Ranked? How?"

"Every fighter for the club is ranked one through five. A one's fight is worth one hundred and a five is worth five hundred, and then the respective numbers in between," he explains. "So, if I was to fight a one and lose, I'd owe them five hundred, but if they lost, they owe me only one hundred."

"Can you not line up a lot of fights against fives? Then you could fight maybe a few more nights a week, like four, and that way you don't always have to fight a five. You can just fight a wide variety, that way you will still be getting money without the risk involved, and if there's more you need I'm sure my dad could lend you the remaining two thousand if you worked in the shop to pay it off and—"

"People tend to not want to fight me."

"Why?"

He gives me a side-glance. "I'm one step below your brother's record. Your brother was the best boxer there in years."

"So, you're, like . . . really good."

I mean, I knew he was good. I saw him fight. I saw how effortlessly he threw his punches and calculated every move before it even happened; fighting seems to be his element.

"You could say that."

"Then ask the arena to pay you!" I exclaim, as if it's the answer to all of our problems. "If you're the best fighter there, then I'm sure they'd pay you more!"

He smiles at my attempts to help but shakes his head.

"The arena is barely hanging on as it is. Will can't lend me anything."

"What do you mean it's barely hanging on?"

Elijah sighs deeply. "I know I told you it's not as bad as it was a few years ago, and that's true. The gang that used to reside there has thinned out, only pockets of drug dealers remain, as I've said. However, those small pockets seem to slowly be expanding. They've taken over a lot of the fights, fixing them out of Will's control, despite the fact they were dormant for so long."

That's the only explanation he offers me, and I stay quiet for once as I ponder it.

"There *is* one way I could get the money . . ." he says but ends his statement almost instantly after.

As Elijah turns down the dark alleyway taking us to the lot squeezed between two run-down buildings, I notice his fists tense on the steering wheel. He suddenly seems on edge, and I notice his eyes scanning the packed lot.

"Everything okay?" I ask.

He parks the car farther from where we usually park and it makes more confusion pass through me.

"I'm good."

"Something is bothering you."

"The fights you see tonight may get bloody. Not mine, but the others. The illegal fighters are here tonight, which also means it may be more crowded since people pay a lot more to see them."

Illegal fighting.

That's all that sticks in my head.

"What kind of illegal fighting?" I'm almost afraid of the answer.

Elijah's voice comes out wary. "Knives sometimes. Mostly brass knuckles, sometimes with spikes, for a more expensive fight."

His words scare me so much that I can feel my pulse in my mouth. Our earlier conversation pops into my brain, causing my heart rate to quicken. He said there was one way for him to get the money in time, and I think I now know what that option would be.

"You said earlier you didn't have any way to get the rest of the money in time, but you thought of one. If you fought against them . . ."

"I'll be okay."

"That didn't answer my question," I say, scanning his face.

He looks at me with no response and I sense the wall going up behind his eyes since I'm cracking the code to this whole fighting scene.

"Don't worry."

As we walk inside, I take special interest in the subtle changes in his behavior. He has a straight posture to begin with, but now he's completely rigid. We walk past the reception area, and from the shift in his mood, I stay as close to Elijah as possible.

I don't see anyone out of the ordinary as we walk inside, so I'm not sure why he's so on edge. There is the same mix of classes per usual, but Elijah most definitely sees someone or something he doesn't like. I can't help but wonder if maybe it has to do with that bad crowd that he's hinted at so many times.

"Hey, Eli, Little Tucker." Kevin greets us before we reach the door, and even he seems to be glancing around more than usual.

"Little Tucker?"

"You're Max's little sister, I felt like it suits you," Kevin says with a friendly wink.

My heart swells. Little Tucker. Max's little sister. Finally, a nickname I like.

"It's good."

He smiles at me, but all too soon that smile vanishes into a scowl as he scans the crowd. He and Elijah share a not-so-secret look and I begin to wonder what I'm walking into tonight.

Though Kevin is sweet to me, I never fail to notice the cold, intimidating brute I first met. Every time I see him before he notices me or Elijah, he has a stone-cold glare stuck to his hard-ened features that wards off any unwanted visitors. I wonder if he was like that with Max.

My phone buzzes in my pocket, and I pull it out to see a text from Jack flashing across the screen asking me to come over.

Me: Hey, babe, I'm so sorry but I'm crammed studying for my history test tomorrow . . . I don't think I can hang tonight.

Better to not tell him that I'm with Elijah. My phone buzzes again.

Jack: Damn, okay. I'll see you tomorrow. Good luck studying, be thinking of me.

I let out a breath I didn't realize I had been holding. Jack bought the lie, and I'm rewarded with guilt. Rule #1 of dating: if you can't tell your partner what you're doing, you probably shouldn't be doing it. My problem with that rule, though, is how badly I *want* to be doing it.

I've never felt so much adrenaline than I do when watching Elijah in his element. Every punch, every person cheering, every fist flying . . . it's all doused with excitement and it's contagious. And knowing that Max used to do the same thing, well, it makes me feel closer to him in a way.

I used to have the same feeling watching Jack play football. The first few games I watched during the beginning of our relationship were euphoric. I didn't think life could get any better; I was dat-ing the star player. Over time, however, that euphoric feeling has dimmed.

The three of us walk to the board that lists the fights for tonight. Elijah reaches for my hand as we walk ahead so that I stay close to him in such a packed crowd, and I take it. But with the bodies being so close together, I first lose my grip on his hand, and then I lose sight of him altogether. I get pushed along in the crowd until I'm on the outskirts, staring in at the raging bodies watching the current fight. It doesn't help that most of the people here are big men who have no problem pushing around an eighteen-year-old high school student. I try to go back into the crowd and find Elijah, but I get shoved right back out and tumble to the ground.

However, before I hit the ground, I stumble into a muscled body that steadies me. My heart leaps out of my chest from first the shock of almost hitting the ground, and then the shock of *not*. I turn around to thank my savior, but my words get caught in my throat from the beautiful brown eyes that stare back at me. Their owner has dark-brown hair styled with a decent amount of gel and a dusting of facial hair across his jawline.

However, as attractive as he is, something about him seems slightly off. Especially the way he's eyeing me.

"Well, thanks so much for being in the right place at the right time and saving me from falling on my ass, but I better get going!" I exclaim awkwardly, turning on my heel and toward the crowd.

My attempts to get into the crowd fail once more, and I find myself leaning against a dark corner of the building with my creepy hero standing in front of me.

"What's your name, beautiful?" he asks, and his brown eyes practically undress me by the second.

Oh, well, that was sweet but also slightly creepy.

"Scarlet," I rush out. "But as nice as this introduction was, I really do need to go—"

He steps closer to me. "What's the rush? *Scarlet.*"

Something about the way my name rolls off of his tongue

makes me more than uncomfortable, and I look around for someone in the crowd to notice the small and scared girl being cornered by a rather large and intimidating guy. Out of nowhere, my prayers are answered and a familiar, even larger and more intimidating guy steps protectively in front of me.

Elijah.

The muscles in his back are tense as he stands tall and faces the mystery man who caught me before I fell. He's taken off his hoodie to reveal his ratty white V-neck, showing off beautifully buff arms that are flexed by his sides and ready to fight.

"Come to join the party, Eli?" the guy asks with a sinister smile.

Not so surprising that he knows Elijah; everyone here seems to.

"Get out of here, Alejandro."

Shock sparks into me when Elijah reveals his name. He knows him. The guy, Alejandro as I've now learned, smirks at Elijah.

"Oh, she's *your* girl?"

Elijah doesn't respond. My heart jolts from the rather flattering accusation, but I can sense he didn't say it in a congratulatory manner. Alejandro's eyes snake around Elijah and he looks at me, slowly down my body and back up again.

"You better make it known, Eli. People here are starting to say things about her," he says slowly, practically licking his lips as his gaze lingers where it definitely shouldn't be.

"Don't look at her like that, Alejandro," Elijah snaps. "She's a Tucker."

Alejandro's eyes widen, a million emotions crossing his face for a fleeting moment, and he directs his attention back to me.

"A Tucker? As in, Max's sister?" he asks, and all of his previous flirtatious nature disappearing for the moment.

"Yeah, Max is my brother."

"Was," he corrects.

Anger courses through me from such a small, snarky comment. My brother's death is not something to joke about.

"Watch what you say, Alejandro, and get out of here," Elijah says, his voice low.

Alejandro rolls his eyes and starts on his way away, but not before glancing back at us. "For the record, I wouldn't tell people she's a Tucker. Just some advice."

And then he walks away without another word.

"Who the hell was that guy?"

Elijah stares after Alejandro, a cold look in his eye, before directing his attention back to me. "He's a part of the gang that sold my brother the drugs."

I feel a chill go through my body. "The gang?"

"He's the reason I have to keep fighting. Remember I told you they have some crazy sort of interest on Oliver's debt?"

"Yeah, you were supposed to have paid it off by now."

"He's the reason why. I give him the money, and he tells me if I owe more or not. Are you okay? You seem a little shaken up."

I nod that I'm okay, not trusting my voice, but Elijah doesn't seem entirely convinced.

"Nothing bad is going to happen to you while you're here, Scarlet. I promise," he reassures me, and I instantly believe him. I trust him.

I reach for his hand without even realizing, and he takes it without any question as we walk back to Kevin. This time, he's sure to hold on tighter, and thankfully, I don't have any more dangerous encounters the rest of the night.

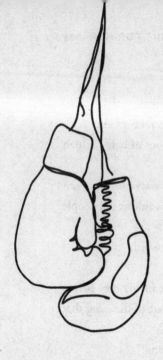

CHAPTER
FIFTEEN

Jack comes over today to make up for missing me last night, though that was my doing and not his.

"I feel like I haven't seen you in forever," Jack breathes.

"You've been a busy guy lately."

"I know, football has been crazy."

He hugs me and I melt into his familiar embrace. Twelve months with someone and everything about them becomes so comfortable to you.

"I'm glad we get to spend some alone time together," he whispers in my ear, taking keen interest in the fact that both of my parents are out tonight.

He lifts me up so that I'm straddling him and heads upstairs while I giggle like a little girl. When we reach my room, he lays me down on the bed and plops down right next to me.

"So, what have you been up to this week?" he asks.

Images of Elijah's fights flash through my mind, and guilt gnaws at my stomach. This shouldn't be something I have to hide from Jack. The trust should be there.

"Actually, um, I've been hanging out with Elijah a little," I admit, wringing my hands as I await his response.

In an instant, Jack lifts himself off of my bed and stands in front of me. "You've been hanging out with that *freak*?"

"Yes, I have, but, Jack, it shouldn't matter—"

"Oh great!" he yells sarcastically. "My girlfriend is hanging out with some low-life creep without me knowing."

"He's not a creep, Jack."

"Now you're defending him! Really?!"

"I just don't think it's fair of you to call him things that he isn't! He doesn't do drugs either!"

"He's a freak, Scar!"

"He's a good guy!"

"If you think that sorry excuse of a person is a *good guy*, then I don't know who you are," Jack spits.

I try to calm myself down despite the fact every hair on my body is standing straight up with anger. "I think you should leave."

"So he gets to spend time with *my girlfriend*, and I can't? What the fuck, Scar?"

"You literally said earlier you've been busy lately! Do you expect me just to sit around alone and wait for you to be free?" I push back.

"You're getting *close* with the school's freak," he snaps out, and from the way he says close I know he's suggesting a certain amount of intimacy that just isn't true.

"Jack," I say firmly, standing up so that I'm only inches from him. "Don't you dare insinuate I'm cheating on you. I would never do something like that." I don't let his hard stare deter me.

Finally, he lets go of his tough-boy facade and I see his anger flicker into vulnerability.

"I'm sorry. I just don't like seeing you get close with another guy, Scar. I can't help but be jealous."

I try to keep myself calm. But how come he gets to snap at me and let his emotions out over *one* guy when I constantly see him dance with other girls and flirt with them? I knew when I started dating a player that those things would happen. What has always been most important to me is just that he ends up in my arms at the end of the day, and he always has. He should trust me to do the same.

"I still think it's best if you leave for now," I say quietly, stepping back from him.

His posture deflates; I never ask him to leave. Even when we argue I find myself still wanting to be around him. And the fact that I don't want to see him right now tells me something. It may be time to move on from Jack.

He covers up his hurt with a cool, nonchalant expression and turns to walk out. "I'll call you later."

But later that night I'm not sitting by the phone waiting for Jack's call. Instead I'm texting Elijah to come to the shop so we can work on the truck, and so that I can vent about a relationship that is slowly falling apart. I show up before he does and unlock the shop, throwing the heavy garage doors up on my first attempt. They catch the gears and continue to open, and I wheel his truck into the garage since I've gotten used to the weight of it.

I guess I've gotten stronger since meeting Elijah.

In more ways than one.

A few minutes after I get here, familiar headlights bounce into the parking lot and Elijah finds a suitable spot for his mother's Trailblazer. The parking lot is engulfed in darkness again as he shuts the lights off. The wind picks up a small bit as he gets out of the car and it lifts up the corners of his jean jacket; one that he's worn for the past few years and has come to be too small for him.

"Hey." I greet him tiredly.

He leans on the wall opposite me and nods his response. My eyes wander to the world outside the shop and I listen to the wind blow through the trees and throw some of the loose gravel around the ground. Elijah is staring at me, and he eventually breaks the silence.

"I'm guessing this is more to talk than for the truck?"

"How'd you know?"

He pushes off of the wall and takes his hands from his pockets as he walks to the back of his truck, which is conveniently facing the open garage doors. He lets the tailgate down and sits atop it and then gestures to the open garage as if to say Ramble away.

"Jack came over today, and we got into an argument. We haven't seen one another all week and we got into a fight as soon as he showed up. He accused me of cheating on him! *Me* cheating on *him*! The player of all players; the best-known high school quarterback in all of Texas, and he thinks *I* would be the one to cheat! I'm not saying he would, but between the two of us, it would most definitely be him if it ever happened."

"I've never heard you say one nice thing about him."

It sinks in that he's right. I've barely said anything nice about

Jack to Elijah, but I've always blamed it on the fact I don't want to waste my breath on justifying his actions to the person he bullies the most.

After a few moments of silence, Elijah adds, "This would be the place where you defend him and start saying nice things."

"What if I can't?"

"Then I think there's another question you can ask yourself."

I sit on the truck next to Elijah. "I thought it was love for the longest time. In the beginning, I wanted to be by his side at all times because he was new and exciting, and he was more than attracted to me. The star quarterback wanted *me*; how could I ever turn that down? That was enough to make me happy when I'd been sad for the longest time. He was there for me when I needed someone the most, just after Max died."

"You're speaking in past tense a lot," Elijah says softly.

I falter for what to say, staring at the trees outside.

"I love him, right? He's a star, he's attractive, he's funny, he loves me . . . he's everything a girl should want. I don't know, I guess beauty is only skin deep. I used to think he was his true self with me but now I think I'm starting to realize his true self comes out when he *isn't* with me and the way he acts with me is just a facade. I hate how rude he is, I hate how he bullies you. I hate it. I hate it so much that I don't think I want to be in this relationship anymore."

I admit it for the first time out loud, and it causes me to snap my mouth shut.

I tentatively continue, "Suddenly our spark is gone, and I find that I don't want to spend time with him. I don't feel the same way when he kisses me. I barely think about Jack anymore, and he used to be the only thing on my mind."

Elijah asks me the question I've been trying to avoid asking myself.

"So why stay with him then?"

"I guess I feel like I'd be an idiot to break up with someone that popular."

"That's what you've been telling yourself, but that's not it."

I look away. He's right.

"I'm afraid that if I let him go, I let my happiness go. He was the only thing that made me happy after Max passed away. I can't feel that way again, Elijah. I can't."

"Does he still make you happy?"

I don't answer, because I truly don't know. If that was all there was to it, though, wouldn't I have figured it out and ended things already?

"There's more, isn't there?"

Though I'm talking to Elijah, I don't register what I'm saying or who I'm saying it to. I'm just venting and speaking whatever comes to mind.

"If I broke up with the most popular guy in school, not only could I lose my happiness, but I'd suddenly be treated like a freak. Everyone would turn on me. I can't have that happen to me."

My breath gets caught in my throat when I think back through what I said. I just admitted I don't want to be a freak; I don't want to be like what the school claims Elijah is. I sense his anger, but he refuses to look away from me.

"You're afraid to end up like me. A freak."

"Elijah, I don't think you're a—"

"It doesn't matter, Scarlet. Everyone else does, and you're afraid that they'll think you're one too. Especially if you broke up with him to spend more time with me—that'd really hurt your reputation, wouldn't it?"

Something in the way he's talking doesn't sound accusatory. As always, his words are well thought out and hold a purpose.

I don't think he's accusing me. I think he's testing me.

I don't answer him, because a part of him is right. There are a lot of reasons I don't know if or how to end things with Jack and being afraid of what would happen at school is one of them. I know that makes me shallow and I shouldn't care, but I'm afraid to get bullied. I don't want to wind up on the bottom after living so long on the top. I don't want to give up the lifestyle that's distracted me from the sadness in my life.

Elijah is beyond strong for being able to deal with all that Jack puts him through. I don't know if I could.

I have to look away from him.

"I get it, Scarlet," he says tightly with the remnants of a scoff.

Then he pushes himself off of the truck, throws his hands into his jacket pockets, and stalks away without so much as a single look back.

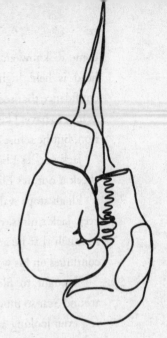

CHAPTER SIXTEEN

Elijah has been passive with me lately. He hasn't asked me to go to any fights with him in the past few days, and he doesn't even really acknowledge me in the halls. Jack's noticed the lack of communication between Elijah and myself, so he's beyond happy to see that I'm not hanging out with him. Apparently, he doesn't notice that I'm sad about not talking to Elijah.

Now he's ranting to Bryce about a stupid play that the Texans pulled last night. I'm attached to his hip per usual, but he doesn't direct the story to me at all. I'm stuck in my own thoughts about Elijah and Jack.

I did love Jack. This entire relationship has been real; my feelings for him were seemingly unbreakable, but that doesn't mean I'm unable to fall out of love with him. And I think that's what it has come to. The loss of feelings for him is taking a toll on me.

My heart skips a beat when I see a black hoodie that I've

come to know all too well walking down the hallway. Elijah's head is held high as always, his posture radiating the self-confidence that seems almost impossible for someone as bullied as him to have. I keep my gaze on Elijah, trying to gain his attention, but he refuses to glance my way.

Jack notices Elijah and instantly stops his story. "Hey, Bryce, check it out, it's Eli the freak!"

Elijah stops walking and stiffly turns to face Jack with hard eyes. Jack smirks, clearly pleased with gaining Elijah's attention so much that he actually stopped. He usually ignores him and continues on his way.

"I ought to file a stalker charge against you for hanging around Scar so much. You really think she wants some freak like you even looking at her, much less hanging out with her, when she's got a star quarterback for a boyfriend?"

Elijah shifts his attention to me and my breath gets caught in my throat. He's challenging me because he knows the answer to that question; he knows I prefer my time with him over Jack. He stares at me; his dark eyes luring me in as he watches to see if I'm going to make a move or not.

I don't. I don't say anything to stop Jack or tell him how wrong he actually is.

"Guess not," Elijah says, then walks away again, and I sense the betrayal hidden in his words.

I made a mistake. He was giving me the chance to make it all okay—the chance to finally stand up for him. The chance to finally stand up for myself to no longer be the girl attached to Jack's hip. I'm so tired of Jack constantly being a jerk. I'm tired of being ashamed of his attitude toward Elijah. I'm tired of relying on him for my happiness.

Jack barks out a laugh. "Oh, and the freak actually speaks! Ladies and gentlemen, the freak—"

"Elijah, wait!" I call out, and he instantly stops walking. Then I direct my words to Jack as I step away from his side. "I do want him to hang out with me. He's my friend, Jack."

"Excuse me? Did you just say that sorry excuse for a life is your—"

"Friend." I end his sentence firmly, anger seeping into me. "Yes, Jack. I did. Elijah is not a freak, he's not a sorry excuse for anything, and he's my friend."

Jack doesn't seem to know what to say. Everyone in the hall has stopped to watch the scene unfolding, but Jack is just standing there dumbfounded. I step closer to him and place my hands on his tense arms to plead with him.

"Please stop. I know you, and I know you know he doesn't deserve all of this hatred, Jack. Please stop being so mean to him."

"Stop being so mean to a freak of nature?"

"Why do you think that? What could he have possibly done to make you hate him so much?"

Jack moves his eyes from me to Elijah as he replies darkly.

"He may have nothing, but he got the one thing I ever wanted."

"What do you mean by that?"

He shoves me away in anger. I stumble slightly back from surprise, and I feel large, calloused hands land gently on the back of my arms to make sure I'm all right. I tilt my head to see Elijah standing behind me, focused on Jack.

"You have a decision to make, Scarlet," Jack says.

"Jack, please don't do this."

Because I know I won't pick him. I know I'll pick my friendship with Elijah over Jack. But I don't want to have to make that choice.

"I don't see why it's so hard, you're clearly choosing me. Now just come on and let's get to class, you've made enough of a scene."

I realize I really do have to make this choice and I drop my eyes to the ground as tears come to them.

"Jack, I can't choose you," I whisper.

For the first time in this argument, his voice is quiet and confused. "*Why?*"

"I—I just can't."

"Scarlet, don't you love me? I thought we would always choose one another."

I don't answer him, and his tone changes on a dime.

"Fine. Be a freak like him. See if I give a fuck, why would I want to be with you anyway?"

I offer no reaction to his words despite this being exactly what I was afraid of.

He keeps pushing to get some sort of a response. "You're really going to walk away from me for this scum? I can't believe I just wasted a year of my life on you."

The tears I was somehow able to keep back start to fall down my cheeks, and something in Jack twists upon seeing that he just made me cry.

"Don't do this, Jack. Don't make things end like this. Just stop," I say.

"You know what? At least you were always there for a good fu—"

"Stop," Elijah says in a low and demanding voice, stepping forward. "You don't mean any of that."

His voice startles me; I've only ever heard him sound this angry when he was facing Alejandro, and I can tell it surprises Jack too. He never thought Elijah would actually speak out against him. But isn't this exactly what Jack wanted? A reaction?

"What makes you think that?" Jack boils.

"Because despite how much of a dick you are, it's obvious you care about her and I know you would never want to hurt her," Elijah says.

"You don't know shit, freak."

"I know what a big mistake you're making. And you know it too."

"What a big mistake *I'm* making?" Jack says incredulously. "You're the one dangerously close to making a mistake, Eli."

"I suggest you walk away and cool off before you say more things about her you regret," Elijah advises darkly.

"You're in no place to make demands, Eli," Jack spits, shoving his finger into Elijah's chest.

Elijah doesn't react. He glares at Jack, letting the intimidation on his face do the talking for him. Jack, upon having no one responding to him, glances around and sees the shocked faces watching him and backs off.

"Whatever," he says, fixing his letterman jacket as he spins and walks away. My so-called friends throw themselves at him as he goes.

As Jack disappears down the hallway with his friends, I stand still as a statue. That just happened. Elijah wraps his arm around my shoulders to protect me from everyone's judgmental stares and leads me outside, forcing students to move out of our way. I'm thankful for it; this school suddenly seems like it's closing in on me.

"Are you okay?" he asks once we make it outside.

I stand there numbly. I just broke up with Jack Dallas. The guy I gave a year of my life to. The guy who made me happy at a time when nothing else could. The guy who gave me a fairy-tale romance and made my high school life one where I lived on the top. The guy who was my first for everything. First kiss, first love, first everything.

And I don't regret it. But that doesn't take away from the fact there's going to be a lot I miss. But there's so much more that I won't miss. His demands, the way he bullies Elijah, his posses-siveness, the player within him that came out every time he saw another girl.

"You may not be saying it out loud, but I can tell you're ram-bling in your head," Elijah says.

"I'm okay."

He studies me for a few silent moments. "You can cry."

"He doesn't deserve my tears."

"You deserve to feel how you want."

I wait for tears to make an appearance, but they never do. I realize I don't want to cry. Knowing Elijah is here for me makes me feel better. If it wasn't for him, I wouldn't have even broken up with Jack. If it wasn't for him, I wouldn't have realized there's more to happiness than a boyfriend.

But now I know that I can be okay without Jack. My happi-ness doesn't derive from him; it comes from my own actions. It comes from the way I treat myself, from the people I surround myself with.

"Thank you, for being there for me. I wouldn't have done that if it wasn't for you," I admit.

"You would have."

"No, I think I always knew the stuff about Jack. But having someone to talk to about it made me realize it, and this actually forced me to think about it. Without you this wouldn't have happened. So, thanks."

Elijah chuckles. "I think you give me too much credit."

"I don't think you give yourself enough."

He looks down and smiles, but he doesn't reply. I let my mind go back through the entire breakup and I recall everything we said, and I get stuck on something Jack said to Elijah.

"What did Jack mean when he said that you had the one thing he always wanted?"

"I was wondering how long it would be before you found out."

"Well, that wasn't mysterious at all," I mutter. "What is with you and knowing more about things in my life than me?"

He lets out a small breath of air that could be considered a chuckle but gets serious all too soon.

"There's a reason Jack hates me so much. When we were kids, Jack and I were best friends. I lived in the house next door to him."

My jaw drops all the way to the ground. Jack and Elijah were best friends? I was just thrown a curveball and missed it by a mile. I never suspected that.

"Our parents even owned a business together," he continues. "We grew up together and did everything together. We were on the same little league teams, and it was clear that we were both extraordinarily talented at sports. But as good as we both were, I was always a little bit better.

"Coaches always gave me the MVP award, and I always made the better plays no matter the sport. Then we became quarterbacks.

Jack has an amazing arm, there's no doubt, but mine was just a little bit better and everyone noticed. I was bigger than he was at every age and it made a difference when we played. He was benched in every league we played in together up until junior high."

I had no clue.

"I guess Jack was always jealous because everyone noticed me instead of him. It seemed like I had it perfect; even Jack's dad seemed to like me a little more than he did Jack. Once we got put on separate teams, his dad would come to more of my games than Jack's, and when we played against one another, he cheered for me instead of his own son," Elijah admits guiltily.

I piece it all together. "So that's what he meant; that you took everything from him, he meant his father's approval and sports?"

"That's why he hates me. I was always a little bit better than him, and despite never bragging about it, he knew I was better, and it bothered him. But then stuff in my life started falling apart and I fell behind in sports, and Jack took that as his chance to rise to the top, which he felt needed to involve beating me down lower and lower so I could never reach him again. So he started making fun of me for everything in my life—my brother getting arrested for drugs numerous times, my brother overdosing, and my dad leaving us. He was finally better than me, and he never wanted me to forget that."

Sensing the end of his story, I take a step closer to him. I see the sadness hidden deep beneath the rough exterior he's been forced to build over the years.

"Why don't you stand up to him?" I ask gently.

"What good would it do? I don't care about the rumors; I just want to keep a low profile and get out of school. But the way he spoke to you just now? I wanted to throw him into the ring and have at him."

I smile. "That'd be an interesting fight."

The warning bell blares into the school grounds outside. Elijah and I share a look, upset to have to go face our peers' faces again, but we head back inside together.

"Are you going to be okay today?"

I want to be able to say yes, but will I be?

"I think so. I can't just put my life on pause because I broke up with Jack."

"No, but no one would blame you for needing time to yourself."

I feel gratitude toward Elijah for being so caring. "Thanks, but I think it's best to keep myself busy rather than be alone with my thoughts."

We walk inside and I try to go about my day. I hear through the grapevine that Jack has left school for the day, giving me a huge sense of relief. Now I don't have to worry about running into him while the wounds are so fresh. I try to focus on my lectures, but all I can do is replay my breakup over and over again in my mind. As the day ends and I go home, I do my best to keep my mind off of Jack.

The best way to do that? A nap.

I practically dive into my covers when I get home, cuddling into their warmth and stopping myself from recalling the times I used Jack for warmth and comfort late at night. As I snuggle my head into my pillows, I hear my phone buzz from somewhere deep in my sheets.

Elijah: You doing okay? I have a fight tonight—it may take your mind off things to tag along.

Me: Against Jack?

Elijah: Lol, not quite.

I grin at our banter; his text gives me something to immediately look forward to, something to keep my mind on instead of Jack. Because of Elijah, I'm able to drift off to sleep peacefully instead of full of heartache.

~

I leap up from my bed in the least graceful manner possible, tripping over my stray covers and then face-planting on the carpeted floor. My legs are sprawled up, still leaning on my bed while my face is full of shag carpet and my arms are thrown over my body like a rag doll.

Ouch.

I fell asleep right after Elijah texted me asking if I'd like to come to his fight tonight, but I have no clue how long has passed since then. Once I fall asleep, there's no telling when I'll wake up without an alarm.

"Graceful," a voice teases from the doorway.

Instantly, I untangle myself from the heap of a mess I am, and my legs fall with a loud thud to the floor as I adjust myself to stare at my door. Elijah's leaning against the wall with his arms crossed over his broad, jean-jacket covered chest, an amused smile on his face.

"I was just sleeping here, content and in the middle of a fantastic dream about Chris Hemsworth, when my blankets suddenly attacked me and shoved me over the end of my bed! And then they—" I cut myself off after actually listening to the bullshit that's spewing from my mouth. "I told you, I've always sort of been a klutz. Wait . . . how—"

"I came to the door to pick you up and your dad said you were still asleep, so he sent me up here to get you."

He casually pushes himself off of the wall and turns to walk back downstairs. But he pauses and glances at me over his shoulder.

"I'm a little surprised, though—I always pinned you as a Liam Hemsworth type of girl."

My face turns twenty shades darker as I rush after him, grabbing a brush to pull through my hair, knotted from such a restless sleep. I say a quick bye to my mom and dad since they are leaving soon for a business trip that will keep them away overnight. I kiss their cheeks before I jog to the Trailblazer.

"How do you feel?" Elijah asks as he begins to drive.

A jolt of pain reaches my heart and I tilt my head to stare out of my window. I eye the passing fields and let my gaze drift to the headlights in the oncoming lane.

"I don't regret it. I know I made the right decision, what will ultimately keep my happiness alive. But it's going to hurt for a while, I can't just pretend this past year didn't happen. Keeping myself busy . . . that will help. When I think about the fact there are things I miss, things I can't help but to remember and wish back, I know there's more that I won't miss. Jack wasn't a good guy a lot of the time—cute words mean nothing if his actions are as vile as they were every single time he saw you."

Elijah snorts slightly and I chuckle at the sad truth of that statement.

"He had his moments! Just not around you."

"Moments like what?"

"First date, first kiss."

"And the next eleven months and twenty-nine days?"

"Oh hush."

A deep chuckle rumbles from his chest and I instantly smile, and for the rest of the ride we—or rather I—ramble on about random things to keep my mind occupied. Once we reach the ring, however, I notice that there are a few cars I'm not used to seeing. Elijah seems to notice, too, because when we start to walk inside, he stops me. My anxiety grows when I notice the guilty tinge to his expression. He looks off to the side instead of keeping eye contact with me, and it does nothing to calm my worry. If there's one thing Elijah is good at, it's keeping eye contact no matter what; but this time he's not. He opens his mouth to say something, but then stops short and looks away.

I reach out to take his free hand in mine, and his hand engulfs mine. I offer a smile of reassurance to try and convince him that he can tell me whatever is on his mind.

"Tonight's fight may get bloody," he eventually admits.

I swear the blood drains from my face and my expression drops, which is probably what he was afraid of.

"Elijah, don't tell me you actually took on an illegal—"

"I'll be okay."

But he doesn't know that for sure. He can't predict exactly what's going to happen. He doesn't know if his opponent will whip out a knife and stab him. He doesn't know, so how could he reassure me?

Elijah notices my worried silence so he gently squeezes my hand and pulls me closer to him. I'm only inches from him, and being so close, I have to tilt my head up almost all the way to meet stare.

"Don't worry, Scarlet."

"I'm worried."

"Have you seen me lose a fight yet?"

"There's a first time for everything," I mumble.

"You act like you have no faith in me."

I smile at his teasing, but then I divert my eyes to the ground, and he squeezes my hand again.

"I'll be okay."

"Why? Why do you have to do an illegal fight? Did Alejandro raise your debt again?"

"Only by a little, but I was already behind, and now I'm falling farther and farther into Oliver's debt." I feel a small sense of shock from the defeated undertone of his voice. "I don't know what else to do, Scarlet."

This time I squeeze his hand. I know I should be as supportive as possible and try to give him a little bit of hope, but I don't want him to have to resort to this in order to get the money.

"How much is the fight tonight for?" I ask gently.

"Nearly a thousand."

"After this fight, how much more will you need?"

"Still another thousand. And more and more until Alejandro stops raising the amount I owe, but I don't know if that will ever happen."

As much as I don't want to, I'll have to just accept the fact that he's going to do whatever he can to get the money to pay off his brother's debt.

"So, this won't be your last illegal fight, then?"

He looks at me and doesn't respond, but the answer is clear in his eyes.

"Just be careful, Elijah."

"Promise," he says quietly. "I'm not used to this."

"Not used to what?"

"Having someone worry about me."

Suddenly the door to the ring swings open and an angry Kevin storms out; he's wearing a leather jacket over top of a maroon V-neck that's almost as red as his face.

"*There you are!* Elijah, you're on deck. Will was raising a fit wondering where the hell you were. Get your ass in there."

At the severity of his tone, I jump and quickly rush to him but when he sees me, he shuts his eyes and sighs, lifting a hand to pinch the bridge of his nose.

"I wasn't snapping at you, Little Tucker. Wait, you came?"

"Yeah, why wouldn't I?"

He swiftly moves past it.

"No reason. Now come on. You're not about to miss a thousand dollar fight, Elijah."

Elijah snorts and walks inside with Kevin and me following, and when he walks ahead to go get ready for his fight, I stay back with Kevin.

"Are you concerned?" I ask.

"Eli knows what he's doing."

"Does that matter if the guy he's going against is fighting illegally?"

"Like I said, he knows what he's doing."

The announcer calls Elijah's name and then names the illegal fighter he's going up against, Tim or something of the sort, and I pray that he won't come out holding a knife. My prayers are answered when I don't see a knife, but the brass knuckles on both of his hands don't make me feel any better.

Elijah fighting isn't something I can stop. I can't protect him from getting injured. It physically hurts my heart when I think about him getting beaten down and knocked unconscious, but luckily, I haven't had to see that yet because of how talented he is.

The bell signaling the start of the fight cuts through the air and through my thoughts, and his opponent charges Elijah. I watch with worried anticipation as Elijah dodges most of his hits, landing a few of his own perfectly legal punches. But then Tim lands a ferocious blow to Elijah's ribs and he springs back from the force of it.

As I watch, I learn that it's not just the added props that make these fights illegal. There are no rules. Every hit is a legal one. Kicking is allowed, low punches are allowed, and there's no limit to how long the fight will go on for. They still have breaks in between, but they don't stop for a tap-out. It's a fight until one boxer is knocked out, nothing else will end it.

The fight takes a turn and Tim starts landing more hits that affect Elijah more than any of his hits are affecting Tim. As Elijah blocks a few, twisting out of the way and landing a blow to Tim's back, his opponent twirls around and barely misses Elijah's head with a punch that I know would have left him concussed. He was faced away from me, so from my angle it looked like he really did avoid the hit. But when he turns to reveal his face, my blood runs cold when I see a giant gash on his forehead.

I tap Kevin's large bicep. "Should I be worried now?"

He glances back at the fight. "Definitely not. Look."

I follow his gaze and see Elijah putting his opponent away with fatal blow after fatal blow, and eventually Tim hits the ground, out cold. Relief fills every part of me, so much that I forget to even cheer for Elijah. The announcer lifts Elijah's cut-up hand and he tiredly raises it in the air, blood pouring from the gash on his head.

He meets my eyes and once the announcer lets his hand

down, he walks straight toward me. When he reaches me, though I'm filled with relief, I don't hug him or say how relieved I am. No, I slap him. Not in the face, but on the shoulder, and he flinches back.

"Okay, ouch," he mutters, rubbing the spot.

"You promised me you wouldn't get hurt!"

"Elijah, if these fights don't kill you, I think she might," Kevin jokes.

He ignores Kevin and steps closer to me. "I promised you I'd be okay, and I am."

"You have a purple bruise already forming on your cheek. And I don't even want to see how many bruises your stomach is suffering through."

He lifts his hand up to touch his cheek, flinching as he does. "If that's the worst that happened to me, I think I'm okay."

"I'd say that gash on your forehead is a little worse."

He lifts his hand to touch it, but I quickly reach out and stop him. I focus my attention on the wound despite his stare setting my whole body ablaze.

"Come here," I say quietly.

He steps closer to me without hesitation as I gently lower his hand back down to his side. I reach my own hand up to inspect his wound and he stays silent as he watches me.

The blood is making it so that I can't see how bad the gash actually is, so I can't tell if he needs stitches. I take the rag Kevin used earlier to gently wipe away the blood, but it just smears it across his forehead. I frown and wipe my thumb gently along it to clear the cut. My hair falls in my face and I blow some air to try and get it away, but it lands right back, tickling my nose. Suddenly, Elijah lifts his hand to brush it behind my ear, his palm brushing across my cheek, and the gentle action makes me freeze.

My cheeks heat up at the tenderness of his expression, and I clear my throat. "I think you may need stitches."

"Thanks, *Dr. Tucker.*"

"I was hoping you had forgotten about that one."

Before Elijah is able to respond, Alejandro suddenly shows up and my body fills with anger. After Elijah told me that Alejandro is the whole reason that he has to keep fighting, and after his little comment about my brother, I get a particularly sour taste in my mouth if he's ever brought up. To say I don't like him would be the understatement of the century.

"Hello, friends," he drawls with a cocky little smirk on his face.

"You have a lot of nerve, coming over here as though you aren't a twisted little—"

"Eli? Control your girl, would you?" Alejandro asks, easily shifting his bored eyes from a seething me to an equally angered Elijah.

My jaw drops. Did he just—

"What do you want, Alejandro?" Elijah snaps.

"To ask why you're still bringing her here."

"Why does that matter?" Elijah asks.

"Come on, Eli, you're smart. I would have thought you could figure this one out on your own."

"Quit the games and tell me, Alejandro."

Alejandro's cocky look diminishes, and he glances around the ring before settling his eyes right back on us.

"She's *Tucker's* little sister," he says, moving his eyes to me. "And considering the way your brother actually died I'd assume you'd be cautious about throwing out your name."

My mind focuses on one thing.

The way your brother actually died.

"He died in a motorcycle accident . . ."

Alejandro furrows his brow and then glances at Kevin and Elijah.

"She doesn't know?"

My body freezes in shock, and I barely notice Elijah shoving Alejandro away. That same sentence keeps playing over and over again in my mind. Max died in a motorcycle accident. That's what the cops told me, that's what my parents told me, and that's what they said at his funeral.

Somehow, I find it in me to turn to Kevin. "Kevin, what did he mean?"

Kevin doesn't say anything, he just looks at me with an undeniably guilty expression.

"Kevin. Max died in a motorcycle accident. Right?"

He doesn't answer me.

"Kevin," I say, my voice becoming weaker and weaker.

He closes his eyes and shakes his head, and when he opens them, they are swamped with guilt.

"I'm so sorry, Scarlet."

My heart drops to my stomach.

No.

Elijah walks to me and takes my hand, but rather than making sure I'm okay he gently drags me out of the building, dropping my hand to instead place his arm around me to shield me from the watching eyes.

The tears don't even come. I'm too numb to do anything but stare straight ahead and think about the fact my entire knowledge of my brother was a lie.

We get into the car, Elijah gently helping me into the Trailblazer, and then we drive to my house with Kevin hot on our tail. I stay silent the entire ride, though I feel Elijah glancing over at me periodically with troubled eyes. I don't even have time to think about why Elijah rushed us out. My thoughts are too consumed by memories of Max as I try to piece together his secret life and decipher what was real and what wasn't. Frustration racks my brain. Now I can't even understand which memories are the truth, and I'm stuck rethinking my entire relationship with someone I can never ask for the truth from. My entire memory of Max is getting twisted and mangled, and he's the one person in my life that I thought I knew inside and out.

We pull up to my house, and next thing I know Elijah is rolling down his window for Kevin who glances worriedly inside the car.

"Is she all right?"

I don't even look at them, but I finally find my voice.

"How?"

Neither of them speaks up.

"If it wasn't a motorcycle accident, then how did he die?" I ask, this time with a stronger voice.

I'm tired of being kept in the dark. I'm tired of being the only one who doesn't know what happened to her own brother. The only one who doesn't know anything about his secret life.

Kevin frowns deeply and sends another look to Elijah before answering me.

"Scarlet, your brother was murdered."

His words may as well be a bullet piercing my heart.

"No. No, I don't believe you! He died in a motorcycle accident, that's what happened!" I cry, vision blurred and throat closing up.

"Scarlet—"

Throwing the door open, I race out of the car, but Elijah is quick to do the same. He gently grabs my arm, but I shake him off.

"Get away from me!" I yell, but my voice is scratchy with tears.

I run inside while Kevin and Elijah call after me. But I don't want to hear them. I don't want to talk to them. I don't want anything or anyone other than Max.

I end up in Max's room, angrily sifting through all of his things to try and find out more of the story. A story I never even knew existed. A story kept from me for years upon years, and who knows if I ever would have found out if Alejandro hadn't said something? I numbly feel the tears streaming down my cheeks but I don't even bother to wipe them away. Instead, I simply blink them away, and though the tears slowly dissipate, the pounding ache in my chest doesn't.

He's gone. It was hard enough when Max first left me, but now I feel like I'm losing him all over again. Just like before, there's no way for me to talk to him and ask what went wrong, ask why he left me.

But it's different now.

It wasn't some tragic accident. He was sought out and killed in cold blood. Who knows what other secrets he kept from me; what secrets my family kept from me? I want to confront my parents—ask them if they know and why they never told me, but they aren't coming home until tomorrow night from their business trip. I wonder what they would tell me. Do they even know? If they knew, wouldn't I have seen more cops around our house as they conducted their investigation?

I feel like this is just the beginning of me uncovering more and more family secrets.

After frantically searching, I find Max's photo album and flip through every page. I go through baby pictures, every Halloween, Christmas, Easter, high school graduation, and I find it. My eyes zero in on a page toward the end of the thin album: Max at what I now recognize as the ring with Kevin. I slowly take the picture out of the book and look closer at it.

I've seen this picture countless times before, but I never pieced it all together. And now that I'm looking more closely, I see the fighters in the background. I see the ring off to the left side behind Max, the crowd behind them, and even how his knuckles are taped. It was all right there. Every clue that he was a boxer was right here in this picture, and I needed Elijah and Kevin to tell me. I've looked through this album more times than I can count, each time making me feel slightly closer to Max, but this time I couldn't feel further away from him.

I clench my jaw and crumple the picture, tossing it into the trash before throwing the album on the floor and sliding down next to it. I sit with my knees tucked into my chest and my hands in my hair as I start to cry again with sobs that make my whole body shake.

I'm losing him all over again. I thought the hardest part was over, but digging up all of these skeletons is just bringing back the pain. I miss Max every day. I'll always be hurting a little because I lost him, but now it feels stronger than ever before.

The hardest good-byes are the ones never said.

I cover my face with my hands and sob, hating myself for

being so stupid. *Of course* he didn't get into a motorcycle accident. It was believable for my young self; that was why they said the ceremony was closed casket. It could still be believable today. Nothing has changed; he's still gone. Yet everything has changed all in the same breath.

Suddenly I feel hands covering my own, gently forcing them away from my face. Elijah kneels in front of me. I thought he and Kevin would have driven away, leaving me to deal with this on my own and giving me space. Elijah squeezes my hands but I suddenly just feel angry, and I shove him away from me. He never told me.

"You knew?" I seethe.

He knew how my brother died and knew that I had been told a different story. Yet he never saw it as necessary to tell me, Max's own sister. I can see how distraught Elijah is seeing me like this, but it's nothing compared to how I feel.

"I'm so sorry, Scarlet. I promise I didn't know until after you met Kevin. I knew Max fought there, but not that the motorcycle accident was a front until Kevin and I talked about it. The ring kept it on the down low—it isn't something they wanted people finding out about."

"And you never told me?"

"Kevin told me after I introduced you two. We both thought it was best if you didn't know. We sure as hell didn't want you to find out like this."

I sniffle and look away from him.

"Keeping me in the dark shouldn't have been up to either of you."

He pauses and reaches to wipe the tears from my cheeks, his rough skin brushing across mine.

"I'm *so* sorry, Scarlet," he says softly. "You don't deserve this."

I break down again. Elijah moves so that he's sitting next to me and puts his arm around me, allowing me to curl into his side. I rest my head on his chest, feeling the cotton soak up my tears and caress my face. I grasp his shirt as though it's the only thing keeping me afloat while he holds me tight.

I've been dealing with Max's death on my own for so long. Jack was there as a distraction but was never much of a shoulder to cry on or a person to talk to. He kept my mind off of Max when I was with him, but I never faced my emotions when I was alone. I learned to cope. But all of that hard work feels like it's crashing down all around me.

"Why did this have to happen?" I whisper through my tears.

"I don't know, Scarlet. I'm sorry."

"Everything about him is different now."

Elijah gently rubs my back. "It doesn't have to be. He's still the same brother you remember, Scarlet."

"He lied to me."

"He lied to keep you safe," Elijah reasons.

"I can keep myself safe. I'm not some weak girl!"

"I know that, Scarlet. I'm sure he knew that too; he just did what he thought was best. I'm sorry."

I sniffle and try to calm myself down, and finally my tears dissipate but the ache in my heart remains.

"He left me all alone," I whisper.

"You aren't alone. You'll never be alone."

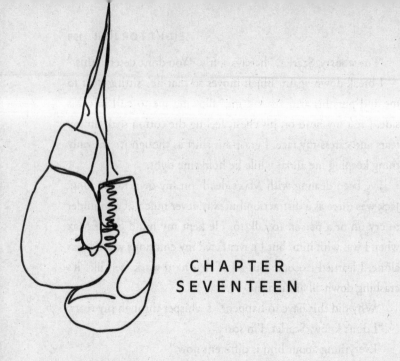

CHAPTER
SEVENTEEN

Confronting my parents is going to be difficult. My pent up anger at this situation doesn't bode well. I have so many questions, and I hope they have the answers. Last night wasn't easy, staying home alone after learning what I did about Max. But my parents are getting back today.

Elijah and Kevin have agreed to be here with me, because as much as I hate to sound weak, I don't know if I can do this on my own. I don't know if I can hear my parents admit that they lied to me for so long without having a support system behind me. Elijah didn't hesitate for a second when I asked him to be here. He even sat with me as I worked through what I want to say a hundred times.

Now the two of them are here with me, awaiting my parent's arrival. They said they would be home tonight, and this is one sunset I am not looking forward to seeing.

I've gone over a thousand times in my head what I want to

say to them. How I want to confront them. But now that the time is getting so close to put those plans into action, I can feel myself retreating. As much as I want answers, I also wish that I had never discovered the truth.

"They're here," Kevin says, drawing me from my thoughts.

I glance out the same window as him and I see my mom's Escalade pull into the driveway, the headlights flashing through the windows, and seconds later I watch my parents step out, confusion crossing their faces as they eye Kevin's Mustang in the driveway. This won't be their first time meeting Kevin. He was my brother's best friend. Another secret kept from me.

"You ready for this?" Elijah asks.

I swallow back the lump in my throat, trying to calm my rapidly beating heart. I wipe my clammy hands on my jeans as I offer him a nod.

"I just want to know why."

Suddenly, the front door opens, and I watch as my parents step inside. They move their eyes to the living room where Kevin, Elijah, and I reside. In a second, their confusion slips into remembrance as they look at Kevin.

"Kevin . . ." my mom says, her voice barely above a whisper as tears slowly spring to her eyes.

He offers a smile, and I see the emotion in his eyes.

"Hey, Mama Tucker, long time no see, eh?" he says, and though he's here for a dire confrontation on my part, I can hear the love in his voice for my family.

But my dad seems slightly more wary, calculating the situation in front of him. He may be piecing together that having the three of us in the living room, clearly waiting to confront them, may mean that I found out their biggest secret.

"You know," is all my dad says as he looks at me.

And just like that, everything I rehearsed with Elijah disappears from my memory.

"Why didn't you ever tell me?" I say, trying to make my voice as strong and angry as I had imagined, but instead I only sound exactly how I feel.

Betrayed.

My mom instantly catches onto our conversation and her face falls.

"Scarlet, sweetheart . . ." she says. "Max never wanted you to know—"

"He's my brother. Lying to me about the way he died was just . . . you should never have lied to me."

"I'm sorry, Scarlet," my dad says.

"*Why?* Why did you lie to me?"

"You had just lost your brother, Scarlet. You didn't even know that he fought at the ring, telling you that he was killed . . . it would have devastated you more than you already were."

My mom chimes in, her eyes pleading with me to understand. "He's right, sweetheart. It killed us to see how hard you took his death. We didn't want to make anything harder on you."

I glare at them, fighting with my craving for their hug, for them to drown out all of the horrors I've discovered in the last day and make it all go away. But I hold that need back. I still need answers.

"How did it not get out that he was killed? Did the police never even get involved?"

"They did, but the officer in charge of his case had to drop it soon after. It went cold. We assume they never got enough evidence to figure out who did it, why, or even what happened,"

my father explains with a heavy heart. "Kevin was the only witness who would talk to them, and his word wasn't enough."

"I tried to get them to listen and find who did this. But the
case went cold and they just moved on to the next one. I'm
sorry," Kevin says.

"We're sorry, too, Scarlet," my mom says, sniffling away her
tears. "We never wanted to hurt you, we thought this would
prevent that."

Somehow, the tears I was able to keep back push forward.
Seeing me cry is all my parents needed to break this face-off
we're having and rush forward to hug me.

"We are so sorry," my dad whispers as I bury my face in his
chest.

"Is there anything else I should know about?"

"No, sweetheart. No more secrets," my mom reassures me.
"No more."

"How did you find out?" Dad asks.

"I found out it wasn't a motorcycle accident from someone
at the ring," I explain. "And I forced Kevin and Elijah to tell me
what happened."

"And we weren't here for you."

"He was," I say, meeting Elijah's gaze.

As my parents and I pull apart, I make my way toward him.
He's been there for me ever since we met.

"Thank you, Elijah," my mom says from behind me, my dad
echoing her.

"I'm just sorry she found out the way she did," he says.

"That's no one's fault but ours. We should have known she
was going to eventually figure this out since she has been going
to the ring so often with you," my mom says.

Relief fills me as I realize the hard conversation has passed. I have the answers I need. And though a small part of me will always be angry about how much my parents have kept from me, I at least know there are no more secrets.

"Elijah. How is your fighting going? Scarlet told us a little bit about your money situation. If there is a way for us to prevent you from fighting at the ring . . ." my dad says.

"I have it all under control."

My dad nods slowly, glancing between me and Elijah for a moment or two.

"Your truck, though. How is that going?"

"Yeah, I've gotten nowhere with that thing. It's never going to run again," I admit.

Elijah isn't surprised like I expected him to be; I guess he kind of already knew, considering the past few times we've gotten together to work on it, we've really only talked.

My dad smiles at Elijah, nodding down the hall. "Come with me, son."

I look over at Kevin, and somehow, he seems to know what's going on. But since I have literally no clue why my dad pulled Elijah off to the side with a weird smirk, I follow them. I walk through the hallway, through the kitchen, and through the mudroom to find them in the garage, and Kevin follows me. We stop in the doorway, and neither of them seems to notice us.

"That Mustang . . ." I breathe, looking at Kevin. "I thought maybe it looked familiar, but he really gave it to you? How could I be so clueless—I don't even remember you ever coming to our house!"

He chuckles at my dumbfounded expression and nods. Whoa. How come my entire life is basically a mystery?

"Whoa," Elijah breathes, voicing my thoughts but for his own reason. He's completely in awe of my dad's collection. "These are all yours?"

"I bought them all as junkers and fixed them up. Scarlet used to help me when she was a little girl. She still helps sometimes."

"That's amazing. She always talks about how you got her into cars."

"The two of you are becoming close, yeah?"

Elijah grins. "We are."

"Thank you for being there for her last night."

"You don't have to thank me for that. She needed me; I wasn't going to turn away."

"That's exactly why I need to extend my gratitude. I haven't seen her so lively in a while, Eli. With everything she's been discovering, I was just afraid her smile would disappear since Max has been brought up so often. But, if anything, it's been the opposite."

"She's strong willed. The thought of Max seems to bring more personality to her."

My dad changes topics as they walk around the cars. "Which one is your favorite?"

Elijah sucks in a breath as he tries to decide, and his eyes wander to the cherry-red 1960 Corvette.

"They're all beautiful, but that Vette has got to be my favorite."

It looks like it's straight out of the movies, with a cherry-red exterior, whitewall tires, a white splash, and red leather interior. Not to mention it's a convertible.

My dad's smile softens, and he leans back against the steps. "It's yours."

My jaw drops. Elijah whirls around to look at him with wide eyes.

"I'm sorry?" he coughs.

My dad walks to the wall, takes the keys from where they hang, and tosses them to Elijah.

"It's yours," he repeats. "Your truck won't run, and you need something to drive, don't you? I'll go get the paperwork; it'll be rightfully yours."

"Mr. Tucker, I can't accept this," Elijah rushes out.

"Of course you can, son. You don't need to be so chivalrous and humble, and I won't take no for an answer. I wouldn't be offering this to you if I didn't want to."

Elijah is beyond floored. "Sir, you have no idea how grateful I am."

My dad walks over to him and pats his shoulder, squeezing it comfortingly. "You're a good kid, Eli. You were dealt a bad hand in life and I can tell you're handling it the best you can, and you've been there for my daughter. You deserve this."

The most surprising part of all of this, though, is Elijah's reaction. He hugs my dad. The second my dad's words sink in, Elijah wraps his arms around my dad's skinnier frame out of gratitude.

"Thank you so much, Mr. Tucker."

In the back of mind, I can't help but wonder if maybe my dad is seeing Elijah as Max in some sort of way. Obviously, no one could ever replace Max in any of our hearts, but I'm sure there is a part of my dad that misses being the father figure to a son, so maybe he's subconsciously stepping into that role for Elijah. I can see why he would. Elijah is close with Kevin, someone Max used to consider his best friend, and Elijah is also getting close to me. He's there for me, in a different way than Max was, and my dad has taken notice.

It's clear that my dad respects Elijah and has welcomed him with open arms, which is much different from his experience with Jack. He liked him, saw that he loved me and respected that, but he never went this far to please Jack. He never offered him a car and really never held a fatherly conversation with him.

Elijah is twice the man Jack is, and even my dad seems to notice.

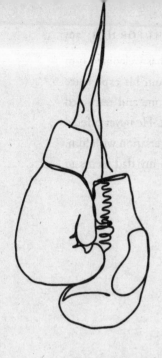

CHAPTER
EIGHTEEN

After a night of endless dreams about Max, wondering what his last moments could have been like, I make my way downstairs. I greet my mom in the kitchen. When she hears me come into the kitchen, she moves her attention from her phone to me, and I see the guilt still hidden in her eyes. I sit down next to her at the table.

"Good morning," she says, hesitance in her voice.

I want to be mad at her and my dad. They kept Max's entire life from me. A part of me will always be upset with them for that, but losing Max brought my family undeniably closer in times of need. As angry as I could be, I know I can choose to forgive and move on.

"Mom, you don't have to be so guilty. What you and dad did was wrong, but I don't want the burden of that to weigh on you two anymore."

She is clearly shocked by my straightforwardness, and soon that shock melts into tears of relief and gratitude.

"I don't know how I raised you to be the strong young woman you are today."

I hug her from my chair.

"I love you, Mom."

"I love you, too, sweetheart."

A knock at the door pulls us from our hug, and I glance down the hall at the front door with a smile.

"Elijah is a good guy, Scarlet. I'm glad you found him," my mom says.

"Me too."

I walk to the front door, a new feeling lighting my body. After learning all of these discoveries about Max, one would think I'd have the weight of the world on my shoulders. But, if anything, I think it's made me feel lighter. Free. I know more about my brother, and I feel closer to him because of it.

I swing the door open to reveal Elijah standing tall on the other side, his new Corvette sitting comfortably in the driveway behind him. He's wearing loose jeans and that same size-too-small jean jacket, but it doesn't matter because he's still more than attractive and I wonder yet again how no girls at school notice.

I squint at his jacket, one of the only two he has, and then a lightbulb goes off; my dad has an old leather jacket he never wears that may possibly fit Elijah. Their body types are stark opposites today, but my dad was a little buffer around the shoulders back in his glory days.

"Wait right there!" I say quickly, before sprinting up the steps and into their room. I swipe through his and Mom's closet and find the jacket sitting at the back, untouched for the last at least ten years. I grab it and rush back downstairs to Elijah.

"It's a leather jacket," he deadpans.

"For you."

"For me?"

"That jean jacket is a little too small," I say gently, and he glances at it with a frown.

"That obvious?"

"It looks more my size than yours."

For a second I worry that he took this in the wrong way, as charity of some sort. But I only gave the jacket to him to be nice and because I know he could use it. Slowly, though, he smiles and holds it out in front of him as he inspects it.

"Isn't it a little cliché for me to be wearing a leather jacket?"

I laugh. "Only if we were in some teen angst book."

He shrugs off his jean jacket and pulls on the leather one. "Thank you, Scarlet."

Okay, *damn.*

Anything looks good on Elijah, as I've learned, but there is something about a buff guy in a leather jacket that makes me, and most likely any other girl, weak at the knees. He looks undeniably *sexy.* I've always noticed his exceptionally good looks, but something about that leather jacket accentuates them all. Cliché, right?

He looks down at himself and then lifts his dark-green eyes to meet mine. "How do I look?"

"Good," I stammer.

Smooth. Elijah notices my stutter but he doesn't comment on it.

"Ready?"

"Let's go."

We drive to school and I can sense the pride radiating off of Elijah because of this new car—I'm sure it's nicer than anything he's ever had. I tilt my head to the side and watch him as he now drives with a set of old sunglasses on; he suddenly looks like something straight out of a '60s movie. Vintage sunglasses, a leather jacket, loose jeans, and the perfect '60s Corvette. All he's missing are the Converse.

I honestly think it'd be impossible for anyone *not* to think he was the most handsome guy alive right now.

We pull into the school's parking lot and circle around to find a place to park, though I notice plenty of spots closer to school that Elijah avoids. As we drive, I feel every single pair of eyes land on us and this new car, and the whispers start circulating as to who the new guy is. It's amazing the difference a new car and a leather jacket make.

We park and every student watches Elijah as he opens the convertible's door and fixes the leather jacket, casually taking off his aviators and placing them back inside the car. Everyone goes silent when they realize it's Elijah Black who's caught their attention, but he barely notices. Figures other people would only notice him in an expensive car and leather jacket.

My smile disappears as I look behind him to Jack's truck at the other end of the parking lot. He has one of my old friends pinned against his truck with a devious smirk and his hands on her waist, and my heart breaks a little when I see him lean in and start to make out with her. Elijah notices my mood drop and frowns, somehow instantly knowing what I saw.

"I was hoping you wouldn't notice them. I tried to park as far away as possible."

"It's that obvious that I saw them?"

He walks around the car and closer to me. "Heartbreak has a distinct look."

"I'm not heartbroken. I ended things, remember?"

"That doesn't mean it doesn't hurt."

"I can't argue that fact."

Was our relationship really so unimportant to Jack that he gets with another girl only a couple of days later? Elijah tenses slightly as he watches me, and then looks back over at Jack.

"Wait here."

He walks across the parking lot toward Jack and I wonder what the hell he's doing. Then I notice the clenched fists by his sides, so I quickly run after him. I gently place my hands on his arms to get his attention, and he stops walking and turns to me with confusion flickering across his face.

"It's okay, Elijah."

"He's hurting you for no reason."

"I'm not his to hurt anymore. And if I'm strong enough to be standing tall after what I learned about Max, I'm strong enough to move past that breakup."

"You know, when you're not rambling, you're pretty mature. And, for the record, he didn't deserve you."

Somehow, I barely notice the hundreds of eyes stuck on us as we head into school. However, I can't avoid hearing the rumors already circulating. They range from wondering how Elijah got so hot (again, I literally gave him a leather jacket and he was driving a nice car) to if this is some sort of version of *Geek Charming*: Freak Charming.

Rude, but even I can admit it's clever.

The one that catches my attention the most, though, is when

people start to suggest that I cheated on Jack with Elijah. And as I listen to where they all heard it from, my blood boils. Jack himself.

So, after Elijah and I go to our classes, I walk out of mine in search of Jack, who I know always skips his first class and wanders the hall. I walk up and down a multitude of stairs, since we have three stories to this building. I search the cafeteria and say a quick hello to the lunch ladies preparing today's meals, and finally I spot him coming out of the locker room just seconds before the bell rings. I storm up to him and I sense his surprise when he sees me suddenly in front of him, and a flash of hope crosses his face as if this is me asking for him back.

"Hey, Scarlet—"

I cut him off by grabbing his shirt and dragging him into a nearby closet as the hallway starts to fill with students; I'm tired of the entire school knowing every detail about my relationship, so this conversation will be a private one.

"Why didn't we ever do this in here when we were dating?" he smirks, reaching out to grab my waist.

Oh my God.

"You don't seriously think I want to have sex with you right now, do you?!" I exclaim, shoving him away from me and into a wall full of brooms, which fall on top of him.

"Okay, what the *hell*!" he yells, moving them off of him in one swift motion.

"You've been telling people I cheated on you with Elijah. And you *know* that isn't true."

"Do I? You spent more time with that freak than you did with me toward the end of our relationship."

"You were always busy!"

"Because *you* were always busy!"

"Stop! I am not having this argument with you again. But you need to stop spreading these rumors. You know I never cheated on you."

He glares at me and I heave a heavy sigh, taking a step closer to him as I calm down.

"Jack, please. Don't make this any worse than it already is. I'm sorry things between us ended the way they did, but can't the worst of this be over already?"

If he's guilty at all for spreading rumors about me and making the breakup so dramatic, he doesn't show it. He does the exact opposite actually. He scoffs and shoves past me to open the door to the closet, and as we both fall out into the crowded hallway everyone stops and stares at the two of us with wide eyes. So much for avoiding attention.

Jack notices all the eyes and smirks at me. "Jesus, Scarlet, I know you miss me but quit begging that I take you back! We're over, okay?"

My jaw drops. He. Did. Not. Farther down the packed hallway I catch sight of Elijah staring at Jack through guarded eyes, but his jaw is clenched tightly and his body is stiff. I keep my head held high and decide that he isn't about to win. So I come up with something snarky to say in response.

"*I* miss *you?* Says the one with a tent in his pants."

His face pales and his smirk instantly drops as he looks down at himself, and then the entire hallway starts to laugh. I just wink and then walk down the hall, adrenaline coursing through my veins as the entire hallway cheers me on. Even Bryce can't stop himself from laughing.

Elijah is waiting for me, clearly impressed, and we walk off together.

"I hate him," I mutter once we're far enough away from everyone else.

"I can't say I particularly like him either."

"I kind of figured that. I don't know when he turned into such an asshole."

"I don't think he suddenly turned into one, I just don't think you ever noticed."

"You're probably right." Suddenly, the grim thought of Elijah's need for money to pay off his brother's debt worms its way into my head, and I flinch. "So, Saturday is the last day, isn't it?"

Saturday is supposed to be the deadline for the debt money. Of course, Elijah had already paid the original amount, but with Alejandro constantly raising the price, he has had to keep fighting. Saturday, though, he has to have whatever amount they need. After Saturday, Alejandro shouldn't be able to increase the debt amount any more. After Saturday, Elijah should be able to stop having to fight for the money.

Most of Elijah's features harden as he nods.

"Do you have enough?"

"No. I'm taking a fight on Wednesday to get the rest."

"That can't be a safe or legal fight."

He doesn't reply.

"Who is it against?"

"Don't worry about it, Scarlet."

"Can I come?"

"Not this time."

Well, that's not reassuring.

I know that a thousand dollar fight isn't going to end well. Even if he was to win, I'm beyond worried he would have some

life-threatening injuries. One thousand dollars must mean that
the challenger would pull a knife or something crazy; how else
would the fight be worth that much? And if Elijah was to lose,
he would be both very injured and out a lot of money.

There's no way I'm letting him fight, and I know just what
to do.

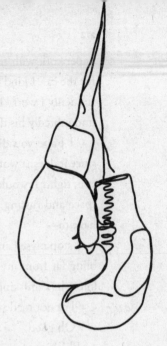

CHAPTER
NINETEEN

Later that night, I meet Elijah at the garage even though we've both decided his truck will never run again. He pulls up in his Corvette with the leather jacket still on and the top down, the wind blowing through his hair even as he parks.

"Hey." I smile, almost unable to hide the excitement coursing through me.

"What's got you so excited? It can't just be me."

Well, part of it definitely is just seeing him.

But the other part is the excitement of knowing he won't have to risk his safety ever again after this. He won't be at the risk of meeting the same fate as Max.

"You know how we decided your truck would never run again?" I ask.

Elijah looks at me suspiciously and nods.

"Well, since you have that new Corvette and did all that

paperwork with my dad to hand us over the truck in exchange for the car, I kind of got rid of your truck," I deadpan, and then suddenly I worry he may be mad that I sold something that was undoubtedly his despite the paperwork saying otherwise.

"I hope you didn't want to keep it! I figured you wouldn't since it doesn't work anymore and who wants a truck that doesn't run, right? It wouldn't be good for anything other than taking up space and rusting away, and then if it did that then you would have to—"

I stop myself and shut my eyes when I finally realize I'm rambling far from my point. I don't even have to look at Elijah to know he's smirking at me.

"I'm not mad you sold the truck."

"Oh good."

Elijah continues to watch me as if expecting something and I blink in confusion.

"So . . . why?"

Oh right. The point of this story.

"My point is that I sold your truck and it had a lot of really nice parts, and I was able to get nearly a thousand for it. I knew that wasn't enough, considering you said you needed the complete one thousand, so I went into my savings and took out the remaining amount, and well . . ." I say, picking up an envelope from on the table and handing it to him. "Here."

His eyes widen to the size of the moon as I place it in his hands. "Scarlet, there's no way I can accept this. You've already done enough for me; your dad gave me that Corvette, you gave me the leather jacket . . . I can't take this."

"I'm not taking it back."

"Scarlet, take—"

"What are the chances of you winning your fight tomorrow night?"

"I won't take this money."

"Answer the question."

He stares at me for a few seconds. "Let's just say for the bettors there's higher odds and a higher payout if they bet on me."

Meaning he's not expected to win.

I step closer to him and close his hands over the envelope. "You're not risking getting severely hurt when I have the money right here. You're taking this, and I won't take no for an answer."

Elijah stays quiet for a few moments and then responds softly.

"I know I said Jack didn't deserve you, Scarlet. But it isn't just him. No guy deserves a girl like you."

～

Elijah promises to come see me after he gives Alejandro the money tonight, and I can't deny how nervous I am. Things could go wrong. Alejandro could potentially say Elijah needs another thousand by midnight, the gang could take the money and hurt Elijah anyway, or he could be walking into some weird trap where he gets jumped and taken hostage by the gang and left for dead.

My knee keeps bouncing up and down from my seat on the couch, and my lip is numb from how much I've been gnawing on it. *Why isn't he here yet? It shouldn't have taken this long to give the money to Alejandro. So why—*

My thoughts are cut off when I see Elijah pulling into the driveway. Relief floods my body and I let my tense muscles relax and let out a breath I didn't know I had been holding. He's at least okay, not taken hostage.

I run to the door to let him in, ready to let out a flurry of questions as to what happened. However, when I open the door, I hesitate. His face is a bruised mess, bringing my fears of him getting jumped to life. His right eye is purple and blue, and his nose has dried blood caked around it. What I notice the most, however, is his expression. I can't read him at all. There's a stone-cold look in his eyes, and he's refusing to let me see past it.

My heart drops to the pit of my stomach.

"Elijah . . . what happened?" I ask, my legs shaking to match my voice.

Elijah shifts his eyes to mine, not saying anything. There's no mistaking the determination hidden beneath his stare, more defined now than ever before, which leaves me questioning even further what happened with Alejandro. He was only supposed to give Alejandro the money and finally pay off the remainder of the debt.

"Elijah, talk to me. What happened with Alejandro?"

With my hand on his arm and my worried gaze refusing to leave his, I can see his struggle to keep his expression stoic. He's having an internal battle, and I just want to know what about.

"Did they make you fight? I thought he would take the money . . . why would they make you fight even more?"

His jaw clenches painfully and his arm tenses even more underneath my hand, but for a small second I see past his walls. The raw emotions in his eyes would be hard to miss—the worry and guilt and fear, but I have no clue what it's all for.

"Elijah, talk to me," I plead, lifting my other hand to rest gently on his cheek. "Please."

He melts into my touch, closing his eyes for a brief moment as he takes in a breath. He opens his eyes and lets his emotions stay for me to see, lifting his scarred hand to cover my own as he responds. But his response suddenly makes me feel hopeless.

"I have to keep fighting."

"What?"

He steps away from me. "I just . . . I have to keep fighting."

"*Why?*"

But he doesn't provide me with an answer. Instead, he makes his way back down the front porch steps, pausing at the bottom and turning back to me as a chilling gust of wind blows around us.

"I can't answer your questions yet, Scarlet. I'm sorry."

And just like that, he walks away.

~

I haven't spoken to Elijah at all today about any of it. I can't imagine he was so worked up simply because Alejandro didn't follow their deal—there had to have been something else. He had an expression on his face I still can't quite decipher. There's more going on, but it seems as though Elijah doesn't want me knowing.

I'm jostled from my thoughts when I hear a student down the pristine hallway of Royal Eastwood take in a sharp breath of shock. I shake my head slightly to completely clear my mind and get accustomed to my surroundings, and I center my focus on the shocked student. I see her, along with all the others in the hallway, staring straight ahead with ghastly expressions on their faces. My expression soon matches.

Elijah is walking down the opposing end of the hall with a new set of grotesque stitches running down the bridge of his nose, curving under his black eye and extending at least two inches in length. My heart drops—he just got the last set of stitches on his forehead out a few nights ago.

It takes Elijah a moment or two to notice that all eyes are on him. This is the first time other students at Royal Eastwood have actually seen his stitches. Normally, he hides them beneath his black hoodie, but today he has on the leather jacket, which basically puts the stitches on full display. He stops walking. No one says anything, and then his focus lands on me. I see the small amount of panic hidden on his face; he's not used to anyone noticing his injuries.

He's not used to anyone noticing him at all. Unless it's Jack and his constant belittling. Instantly my feet carry me toward him to save him from the blatant stares that no one would feel comfortable under. Suddenly, the warning bell blares into the silent hallway, and the students around us begin to rush off in their own directions to get to class. Elijah and I stay still, ignoring some people making sure they walk past him in order to get a better look at the stitches. Once the hallway clears out, I walk the final few steps to him and silently lift my hand to rest on his cheek. I gently brush the pad of my thumb just under the stitches, and his eyes flutter shut.

"What happened?" I ask quietly.

"After I stopped at your place last night, I had to go back and take on a fight."

My stomach drops with my heart and I let my hand fall. As far as I know, I've been to every single one of his fights since I first found out he even fought. It was like an unspoken agreement that I would always be there for him.

"Why didn't you tell me?"

"I didn't need you to worry."

"How did it happen?"

Elijah turns his head to the side and walks to the balcony that overlooks another hallway, leaning forward on his forearms.

"I had to take on an illegal fight after I talked to Alejandro; part of the upped ante. I was prepared for knives, not to get double teamed," he admits, slightly clenching his jaw, and he drops his head. "They needed to send me a message."

"A message about what? You've kept your part of this debt deal, you've fought more than they originally asked to get back the money. Why can't they just let you be? What else do they want from you?" I ask, my voice rising toward the end because I don't understand why this is happening to him.

"Something I have to give them."

"Which is . . . ?"

He smashes his lips together in thought, glancing down as he forms what to say.

"You can't come to my fights anymore."

I recoil a bit. "What?"

"I mean you can't come to any more fights, Scarlet."

"Why?"

He finally looks at me and I meet his troubled expression with confusion.

"It isn't safe for you."

"For me specifically?"

He hesitates in his answer, and my thoughts go to Max. He was murdered by the gang, and now suddenly after Alejandro cryptically questioned why I'm still coming *and* forced Elijah to keep fighting, it's not safe for me.

"Does this have to do with what Alejandro talked to you

about last night? You're trusting anything that comes out of his mouth?"

"He knows more than you think, Scarlet. This has become more than just Oliver's debt."

"Between this conversation and how affected you were last night, I'm starting to feel like something big is being kept from me. Again. And if it's about Max, don't I have the right to know?"

Elijah doesn't answer me, just continues to stare straight ahead. I may not be able to see his eyes, but I can tell how tightly his jaw is clenched, how stiff his posture is. So, I can tell how much this is bothering him, and I just want to be let in so I can try to help.

"Whatever it is, why can't I be there for you?"

"You *can* be there for me by not coming."

"I know you're keeping something from me, and you can't keep me away. I can be there to help or *something* even though you're keeping me in the dark about what's going on. I mean, of course I can't fight or anything like that, but never underestimate the power of words! Words are what get the bad guy out of the life or death situation in movies nine out of ten times. They just talk and talk and buy themselves time and—"

"Scarlet," Elijah says, only this time he doesn't sound so playful as usual. "You need to listen to me."

"How am I supposed to listen when you're only giving me half the story?"

"Just stop arguing with me, okay?" he finally snaps. "You can't come to any more fights, period. From now on I go on my own, I fight on my own, I do it all on my own. Okay?"

I'm shocked into silence by the harshness of his response. He looks at me for a few seconds longer, and then he shakes his head and walks away.

After Elijah walked off yesterday, I couldn't get my mind off of what he was saying. Clearly, there's something Alejandro told him the other night that he's keeping from me. I think there's more to Alejandro's piece in this story than I originally thought. If Elijah was this upset over just having to fight more to pay back his dues, I don't understand why he suddenly took away my ability to attend the fights with him. The only clue is the fact Alejandro was surprised Elijah continued to let me come to the ring. I try and figure out why Alejandro could want to keep me away so badly.

My mind circles around Elijah cryptically telling me this has become more than Oliver's debt. But the problem is, I have absolutely no clue as to how or why. My gut says it in some way has to do with Max. My mind goes to the stitches extending across Elijah's face yesterday. He is clearly an amazing fighter, and the fact he had such serious injuries scares me. The fights must be getting more challenging; they must be worth more money. Or maybe they aren't worth money at all. Maybe this really *has* gone deeper than Oliver's debt.

But *how*?

What am I missing?

I grit my teeth. How could Elijah leave me out to dry when he needs me the most? I know he's at a fight tonight. I asked him to come over and he never answered. Knowing him, he wouldn't want to upset me with a lie, and he wouldn't want to tell me the truth about being at a fight.

I abruptly stand up from the couch and walk determinedly to the front door, grabbing my jacket and my mom's keys on the way.

I'm going to that fight. That may be the only way for me to get answers.

However, because of my abrupt movement, my parents shift their attention to me. My dad pauses the TV and sits up, eyeing the jacket I'm putting on with more force than necessary.

"Where are you headed?"

"The ring."

"No. Had we known before that the gang was still there, we never would have let you go in the first place. We thought they cleared out after the police started their investigation, not to mention Elijah reassured me they were mostly gone."

"Elijah is fighting tonight and I'm worried about him, Dad. He's been taking on harder and more illegal fights, he needs me there."

"Did he say you could come? Normally he picks you up," my mom says skeptically.

I frown and kick at the floor. "He doesn't want me coming."

"Why?"

"Too dangerous or something, I don't know," I rush out, trying to play it off as a nonissue.

"If even Elijah doesn't think you should be going, then I'm sure as hell not letting you out of this house tonight," Dad says.

"Dad! I think there's more to Max's story that we don't know."

"Scarlet, I can promise you we have told you everything about Max. We kept it from you for as long as we could."

"Well, maybe this is something even you guys don't know."

"You aren't going."

"Elijah can't be there alone."

"Kevin is there, right?"

"Well, yeah."

"Good, then you're not going."

I storm up to my room in a fit of angered stomping. My dad doesn't understand. Elijah is hiding something from me, something my gut is telling me may be imperative to completing the puzzle of Max's life. I have to find out what that is. I pace my room as worried thoughts rush through my head. Then my eyes land on my balcony.

Five minutes later, I'm leaning off of the balcony, trying my hardest not to look down so that I don't faint. I carefully climb down, all the while chanting to myself about how dumb I am and how demeaning the headlines would be if I fell.

JULIET FALLS TO HER DEATH WITH NO ROMEO IN SIGHT

After a heart-stopping climb down, I hit the ground without a single injury. I smile to myself as I dust off my shirt and pants. I just did that. Then I rush to the fight in my mom's car since my dad never took the keys from me, and since they're watching TV, they somehow don't hear it start up. When I arrive, I see both Elijah's and Kevin's cars, proving my theory of them being at a fight.

I ignore the painful sting in my heart that Elijah really did want to leave me out of this, and I run inside. My blood runs cold when I see Elijah in the ring. Blood is running from the opened stitches on his face. His hands are completely and utterly torn and ripped, and every punch he throws just spews blood on any member of the crowd standing too close.

His opponent is barely hurt; brass knuckles giving him an unfair advantage. He lunges for Elijah again, landing a crunching uppercut that pushes Elijah back against the ropes and instantly to the ground. The opposing fighter smirks down at him and spits blood onto Elijah's broken form, rearing his foot back and slamming it forward into his ribs. I jump when Elijah grunts in pain, and watch as he curls into a ball on the floor, barking relentless coughs. I've never seen him so beaten down. The fighter laughs and goes to kick him again, but I snap out of my state of frozen panic. I rush to the ring, heart pounding painfully from seeing the pain Elijah is in.

"Elijah!" I yell hysterically, efficiently stopping his opponent from sending another kick at his no doubt already broken ribs.

When he sees me, his eyes widen in shock and then fear. "Scarlet?"

Then he shifts his worried gaze to the other side of the ring, and before I can say anything or follow his eyes, I feel a grimy, calloused hand grab my face from behind. It covers my mouth, the salty sweat hitting my lips and making me grimace in disgust. Then the other hand grabs my arms and pins them behind my back before I'm dragged backward into the oblivious crowd while Elijah frantically yells my name.

Despite me being dragged through the crowd in such a violent manner, not a single person says anything. Most of them are still focused on the fight, and my best guess is that those who do notice are part of the gang and clearly don't want to help me. I can still hear Elijah calling my name, but he's too far away to be of any help. So if no one is able to help me, I'll have to help myself. I continue to kick and struggle, making it as difficult as possible for this man to drag me away. His hand gets tighter around my mouth and some of the sweat seeps past my lips. I clench my eyes tight and try my hardest to avoid getting the grimy taste on my tongue.

Oh my God, that didn't work and I tasted it. Oh my gosh, it's so disgusting.

Wait. Mouth . . . hand, teeth.

I snap my eyes open and do the only normal thing to do in a situation like this. I open my mouth the best I can, avoiding the vile taste of my assailant's muddied and clammy hands, and then chomp down on his fatty skin. He rears his hand back in shock with a deep yelp, and lets me go with the other. All I focus on is the fact I'm free from his grip. Without looking back, I dart in the direction of the ring, praying that Elijah is still there.

Suddenly, I run smack into someone, and I look up to see Elijah, whose eyes are lit with frantic worry as blood pools around his open stitches, caking the grooves in his skin.

He reaches out and grabs my arms. "Are you okay?"

I swallow and nod quickly, and he scans me over to make sure nothing happened.

"Why are you here? You shouldn't be here!"

"I—"

"You need to get the hell out of here. Now!" he says before I can even speak a single syllable.

"Look, I didn't plan on getting *snatched by someone*!"

"This is exactly what I was worried about! I told you to stay away from here for a reason, Scarlet!"

Before I can say anything back, Elijah pushes me behind him and next thing I know his fist flies across someone's face and a sickening crack follows.

"You stay the hell away from her," Elijah growls.

I peek around him to see a man with a bloody bite mark on his hand falling to the ground, clenching his face with his mangled hand. The rest of the crowd cheers Elijah on, unaware of what's actually happening. He whirls back around to me and places his hand on my shoulder, continuously looking around the crowd as though searching for someone.

"We need to go."

I don't offer any rebuttal and he gently, but frantically, pulls me out of the building and to his car. I get in, forgetting about my mom's car, and he rushes us to my house. Once we reach my house, he shuts off his lights and parks at the entrance of the driveway so we can't be seen from the house, and then we get out of the Corvette.

"Wait!" I call quietly as he goes to the front door. "They don't know I left. We can't go through the front door."

"How did you get out then?"

I sheepishly look up at my balcony and he follows my eyes.

"You jumped from the third floor?"

"Half jumped, half descended."

Five minutes later, somehow, we've climbed back up my balcony and are in my room. I don't know how Elijah did it with such serious injuries; I could barely do it without anything impairing me. Maybe it's the adrenaline. After we reach the top and enter through the balcony doors, he starts pacing my room. He runs his hands up and down his sweaty, dirt- and blood-stained face and I can tell his jaw is in pain by how tightly he's clenching it. He's not happy.

I go into my bathroom to grab supplies to fix the cuts on his face. Without words, I walk over to him and begin to clean his wounds, but I can feel anger radiating off of him. The silence between us is not comfortable; it's electric with emotion. He sits down on my bed, his disheveled look contrasting with my pristine sheets, and tensely allows me to tend to him. When I finish,

I awkwardly step back, eyeing the carpeted floor instead of him. I can't take the silence anymore.

"I'm sorry."

"I told you not to come."

"I couldn't just let you be alone."

"How many times do I have to say it isn't safe in order for you to finally understand?" he yells, his pent-up anger exploding out of him.

The stuffed animals on my bed would have cowered underneath the covers to escape his outraged tone if this were *Toy Story*. I'm thankful that we're on the third floor and protected by the surround-sound system my parents are using while watching TV downstairs. Hopefully they can't hear us.

"You can't just keep me away, Elijah. And it's a good thing I was there! You were about to get seriously hurt! What if something even worse had happened to you?"

"What if something happened to *me*? I fight every week, Scarlet! Nothing is going to happen to me whether you're there or not!"

"You can't say that. Anything could happen to you."

"The same goes for you!"

"For God's sake, look what happened to my brother! I wasn't there for him, Elijah, but I can be there for you."

He falters slightly, but that doesn't make him stop.

"Don't you get it, Scarlet?"

I narrow my eyes in question.

"The gang wants you!"

"*Really?* I had no idea after being basically kidnapped!"

"I told you to stay home. Had you listened then this wouldn't have happened!"

"You should know by now I'm not the best listener!"

"That doesn't make this any better. You put yourself at risk and I almost couldn't help you."

"Well, if you had just told me what's going on, maybe I wouldn't have been as curious and wouldn't have felt the need to go searching for answers."

He throws his hands into the air. "I didn't tell you anything because I didn't want to worry you!"

"Yes, because telling me you want me to have nothing to do with you is so much better."

The mood in my room changes. It suddenly feels smaller, our voices filling the space to an almost deafening level.

"Scarlet, I told you that because I knew if I could keep you away from the fights, then I could—"

"Continue to keep secrets from me? Keep me in the dark? Maybe not have a distraction anymore?"

"*Seriously?*"

"What?"

"Then I could keep you *safe*!" he yells, his voice cracking. "I don't know what I would have done if something had happened to you tonight."

Oh.

I falter in my argument. I see the raw emotion in his eyes but that doesn't change the fact I need answers.

"Safe from *what*? What did Alejandro tell you that has kept you there?"

He doesn't say anything.

"Elijah," I say firmly, my voice made strong by anger and frustration. "I know you and Kevin are keeping something from me. I have been kept in the dark about Max and the ring for too long, and I'm finally getting answers. And just when I thought I knew it all, *this* happens. I thought you were the one who was helping me decode Max's life, and now all you're doing is keeping more from me!"

"Scarlet—"

"No! I'm *so* tired of not knowing! I'm tired of his life being some mystery to me! All I know is that you're still fighting for some unknown reason! It's not for your brother's debt. You're getting hurt, and it *hurts me* to see you this way and not even know why! Did you ever think that maybe *I* want to keep *you* safe? That I *care about you*?"

He stares back at me through shocked eyes, no words coming to him. The room feels still as his entire demeanor changes, and I continue.

"I gave you the money because I wanted to help you stop fighting! Because I hate seeing you in pain! And now you refuse to even tell me why! If you don't tell me, I'm going to continue to believe you're fighting for no reason and—"

Elijah cuts me off by taking a few confident strides toward me and slamming his lips onto mine.

He places his hands on the wall next to my head so that I'm trapped, his lips begging to be kissed back. My shock instantly diminishes and my thoughts focus on his lips on mine. So I tangle my hands into his hair and move my lips against his. His body presses into mine. It's not a soft and loving kiss, but that's not Elijah. It's hard, rough, and filled with pent-up emotions. Frustration, anger, worry, and an indescribable amount of passion. He tastes faintly of blood, and for some reason that makes me crave his kiss even more.

But he pulls back. Both of us are breathing heavily, and he

rests his forehead against mine. He shuts his eyes tight as he catches his breath.

"I'm not fighting for no reason, Scarlet. Trust me."

Despite the shock of everything that just happened, my curiosity stirs. This kiss only leaves me wanting more answers.

"Then tell me what you're fighting for."

He takes a few steps back. "Scarlet, I can't—"

"You can't keep me in the dark after what happened tonight, Elijah. I have the right to know, especially if this involves me. Why are they after me?"

He keeps his eyes locked on mine, studying me to see if I'll back down. When he quickly realizes I won't, he sighs.

"Because of Max."

Though what Elijah says stuns me, my curiosity keeps me asking questions and not stopping there.

"What do you mean?"

He clearly does not want to have to say anything on this subject. But he knows I'm not going to stop until I get all of the answers I want.

"Do you remember the day you met Alejandro?" Elijah asks.

A shudder racks my body as I imagine his cold eyes. "He was surprised I was there and then later dropped the bomb about how Max actually died."

"I was confused as to why he seemed surprised to see you, but he answered that question the day I went to turn in the last of Oliver's debt. He warned me how dangerous it was to bring you to the fights—how dangerous it would be if people recognized you as Max's little sister."

"What did he tell you? Did he tell you why Max was killed?"

"He didn't tell me much. All he told me was that Max was

killed because of some sort of information he had on the gang. Information he shouldn't have been able to obtain. Information worth killing over."

"I assume Alejandro didn't say what that information was?"

"I don't know what specifically. But it's something that could expose the gang, according to him. Once Max was out of the picture, they agreed to forget about the whole ordeal. The cops stopped snooping around, and that information was gone with Max, as far as they knew. No one from your family came forward with it, and they deemed it no longer a threat after a few months had passed. But then . . ."

I take in a sharp breath as I realize where he's going with this.

"But then I showed up, and we told Alejandro exactly who I am."

Elijah shuts his eyes for a moment, as though wishing more than anything to take that moment back.

"Exactly. According to Alejandro, if they find out who you are, they're going to come after you. Because, to them, there's no other reason for you to be at the ring than to finish whatever Max started and do something with that information."

"So, according to Alejandro, if word gets out that Max's sister is attending the fights, the gang is going to come after me because they assume that I'm finishing what Max started?" I end in complete confusion.

I don't know what Max had to do with any of this aside from fighting at the ring.

"What did Max *do*?" I ask, trying to find clarity in this situation.

"I'm sorry, Scarlet, but I really don't know. Alejandro wouldn't tell me. All he would tell me is you have some sort of information that they need and were willing to kill Max for. He seems to think they won't hesitate to do the same thing to you."

Chills run up and down my spine as the severity of this situation sinks in. I feel like the walls are closing in all around me. My life is in danger because of some sort of information I didn't even know existed until now. The more Elijah tries to clarify for me, the more confusing it all becomes. I thought I had finally figured out everything about Max's life. Turns out there is still so much more.

"What does this have to do with *you* fighting? Can't we just stay away from the ring and let them forget I was ever there?"

Elijah chuckles humorlessly and looks away from me, clenching and unclenching his jaw before responding.

"Alejandro will do anything to make a quick buck. He doesn't have a fighting bone in his body, so he makes his money off of others. A true con man. He's making me fight and get him money in exchange for him keeping his mouth shut. If I was to stop fighting and he tells anyone . . ."

"Then they come after me."

Elijah doesn't respond but I can see from the fear in his eyes that I'm exactly right. I can practically hear my heartbeat in my ears. This is surreal.

Elijah is fighting for my life.

He takes a few steps closer to me, eyes flickering to my lips for a moment or two. When his gaze meets mine, I nearly let out a small gasp at how tender it is. He reaches out his hand to gently cup my face, thumb brushing my skin and setting my body ablaze as he responds.

"And I can't let that happen."

We both decide it's too late to make Elijah go home. Especially with his injuries, I can't sneak him out, and I don't want my parents to kill me for going against their orders and sneaking out to go to the ring. I was able to avoid getting caught taking my mom's car, and I devised a plan to tell her I had to take it into the shop early tomorrow morning since she won't see it when she goes outside.

I also don't think I can be alone with the crazy thoughts rushing through my head. But after Elijah gets set up in the guest room, I finally allow myself to sort through all of the danger I'm in. Both Elijah and I know that I'm wanted by the gang for some sort of information, but neither of us knows what that information is.

Who did Max rub the wrong way for them to want me so badly? And what information did Max gather that is so important to them?

I brush some hair out of my face as I collapse onto my pillow in a huff. Except for one time in elementary school, I've never had to play detective in my own life. My third-grade teacher, Mrs. Butts, had us all play detective to find out who put a roach in the sugar bowl she kept for her coffee. She deserved the constant pranks for going into an elementary school with a name like Mrs. Butts. All I know is that no one in the class was a good enough detective to rat me out.

I told Max about it after school, and since he was just as much of a troublemaker as me when he was in elementary school, he took me out for ice cream to celebrate a hilarious prank and a clean getaway. I wonder now how many hilarious pranks he played and how many clean getaways he had in his mystery of a life.

The chilling thought passes through me that maybe Max was a part of the gang. And maybe that's why they want me so badly. I have something they need, something that maybe Max took from them, yet I have no way of knowing what it is. And I have no one to answer my questions.

Except maybe Kevin. He was friends with Max in the thick of it all. He knows better than anyone what happened to my brother; more than he's letting on, I'm sure. If I want questions answered, I need to call him. Just about giving myself massive whiplash, I grab my phone from my nightstand and dial his number.

"Little Tucker?" He answers, his words jumbled and barely intelligible from the grogginess of his speech. Oops, I woke him up. "Are you okay?"

"You're not telling me something about Max and I need to know the full story. Elijah told me why he's fighting—if you know something about Max and that information, I need you to tell me."

He's silent on the other line, the only sound between us the slight static on the call. My palms turn sweaty in anticipation. This is it. I may finally find out what information is so desired from me.

"Scarlet, I've told you everything I know. Max kept secrets from me too. But I know who you can find out from. Alejandro."

"You've *got* to be kidding me," I mutter to myself. "He's the only one?"

"He knew Max and he's a part of the gang. He knows a lot more than he lets on. I'll send his number, go ahead and call him."

I hear him move the phone and then I hear light tapping sounds across the screen, and soon my phone lights up with a text from Kevin revealing Alejandro's number.

"He knew Max personally; he can answer all of your questions, Scarlet. Be careful, okay?"

I trust Kevin. He wouldn't tell me to go to Alejandro unless he was certain he could tell me everything I've been waiting to know.

"I will be."

Against my better judgment, I call Alejandro. Turns out I have a knack for doing things that probably don't ensure my safety.

"Hello?"

"What do you know about my brother?"

He doesn't say anything else, but I wait. I stay deadly silent, trying to calm my racing heart and ignore the red flags going up all around what I'm doing, and he finally replies.

"Meet me at the ring in an hour. I'll tell you everything."

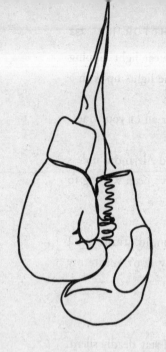

CHAPTER
TWENTY

I tiptoe into Elijah's room before I leave to make sure he's asleep and won't see me sneaking out. As I quietly open the door, I see him passed out, a beautiful, snoring mess. Seeing him sleeping peacefully, as though we weren't in the middle of a life or death crisis, almost convinces me not to leave and instead curl up next to him and fall into an equally peaceful sleep.

But then I remember why I'm meeting Alejandro in the first place. I need to get answers about Max. Hopefully, what he says will help me find the information the gang is looking for and save Elijah from having to fight ever again. So, instead of snuggling up with Elijah like my heart is screaming at me to do, I grab his keys and sneak out. I take his car in order to make others believe it's him driving. People associate this beauty with Elijah. When they see it, they think of him, and when people here think of Elijah, most of them get scared.

I slowly roll into the parking lot, my hands shaking on the steering wheel. I'm used to the lot being packed with cars belonging to people from different social statuses, but at this hour, nearly two in the morning, it's almost completely vacant. As I park, I shift my gaze to an alleyway between two buildings, one of which houses the ring. I see Alejandro emerge from the shadows of said alley. Great. I'm already creeped out and this man just literally *came out of the shadows*. Way to make a girl feel safe, dude. I step out of the Corvette and Alejandro scans the car with his snakelike brown eyes.

"I was thinking you'd bring Eli."

I stand tall, refusing to let my fear shine through any of my actions. "We agreed it would just be me."

"I'm surprised you listened."

I keep a safe distance from him and get right down to the point.

"What do you know about Max? Was he involved in all of this?"

He smirks and walks over to me and leans against the Corvette. I try to spot any dangerous items he may have on him. Instead, I just see his ripped jeans and tucked-in T-shirt, which is tight enough to show his muscles underneath.

"Beautiful, your brother is the reason for all of this."

I gnash my teeth together, rage filling my chest.

"How was he killed?"

"He went into a fight and never came out. They made it so that he never even stood a chance."

My body stiffens as he explains, and I take silent note of his constant referrals to the gang as "they."

"How? Even the illegal fights have their limits. The only thing that makes them exciting is the fact they use illegal weapons, but even those fights are ended before a person can die."

I see sympathy cross his gaze. "They did stop the fight before Max died. But they forced Will to clear everyone out, convincing everyone it was the last fight of the night, and then forced Will out. Once there were no witnesses . . ."

A shiver shoots up my spine, causing my body to feel numb.

"They beat him down to his last breath. Only one officer came when 911 was called, and when he saw Max, he couldn't do much. He called it in, said it was a fight gone wrong, and, well, that was the end of that. No questions were raised about the gang, and Will was barely questioned since he wasn't there to witness it. It was played off as two guys who broke into the ring to fight, and one met a fatal end."

My breath shortens as I hear how Max met his end. I was partly hoping for Alejandro to tell me the death never occurred, that Max was being held hostage by them and had been for the past three years, and that all I had to do was hand over the information to release him. High hopes just to get completely crushed by more of the truth.

"Why? Why kill Max, what did he do?"

"He crossed them. He found out what the gang stood for, found out about the drugs and the deaths. We all thought he just found an interest in the business and that's why he joined them. He worked his way up that ladder like no one else before."

I start shaking. My legs can't seem to stop, and I know my eyes have widened.

Max joined the gang.

"Turns out he had a secret agenda—he recorded everything

that happened in the gang. Took pictures, recorded conversations, took notes on every member. He was careful doing it too."

"What was he doing all of that for?"

"He really didn't tell anyone, did he? Max was working as an informant with the narcotics division of the Houston Police. Some cop sought him out, asked him to work for them and gain intel on the gang. The cop apparently had a tip from his son about the drugs. He worked closely with Max, told him everything to do."

I press my teeth together and swallow down the tears that want so badly to appear.

"So Max was trying to stop them? He was working with the police?" I ask, practically pleading with Alejandro to be telling me the truth. That Max was the kindhearted older brother I remember, not a gang member.

"He was—he didn't join the gang because he agreed with what they were doing. But they didn't know that; only he and that cop knew."

"Why . . . why didn't they come after my family?"

"They didn't think you knew. They thought they destroyed all of the information when they killed Max, figured he died with it only in his memory. They didn't know he had a flash drive that held those secrets. Didn't know that he didn't have that flash drive with him when he died. Only I knew."

"How did they find out then?"

He looks away, and suddenly his voice takes on a softer tone.

"Well, you started showing up and told me who you were. I never told them about you, but I didn't think any Tuckers would ever come even remotely near the ring. I figured you knew what had happened to Max, and I thought that chapter was over with. Once I found out who you were, I was worried the secret I kept about Max's flash drive would come back and bite me in the ass, so I had to tell them it existed."

My heart stops.

"*You* told them about it?"

Suddenly I notice the dark circles under his eyes. The permanent regret hidden behind his tough facade.

"I outed your brother, Scarlet. I told them he was only with the gang to gather information and give it to the cops."

I came here only to get answers. I didn't come to hurt anyone, because what good could a teenage girl with no fight training do? But at this moment, all I want to do is hurt Alejandro.

He's the reason Max is dead. He's the reason my family was put through hell after losing someone so close to us. He's the reason I no longer have a big brother.

"*You asshole!*"

Before I can run toward him, trying to inflict some sort of damage like how he's done to me, but Alejandro speaks up.

"I didn't want to, Scarlet!" he says, sudden, raw emotion in his voice. "I liked your brother. He trusted me. I trusted him. That's why he told me all about his plan—how that cop asked him to be an informant—and I vowed to keep it a secret. I was the only one he ever told; not even Kevin knew. But the gang threatened my little sister. They knew something was up. It was him or my family, and I'd never let anything happen to my Isabella, just like Max would have never let anything happen to you.

"That's why I had to tell them about the flash drive when I learned that you're Max's little sister. I had to assume you were here to leak that information. I couldn't risk them finding out that I kept that from them when that information is now in jeopardy. I knew if they found out I lied they'd go after Isabella.

I couldn't let that happen. I'm not going to tell them who you are, but if you keep coming, they will find out on their own and assume you have that information. Of course, I know now that you don't, but they won't just take your word for it."

I just want Max back. I want to be with him on the way to get ice cream after another successful prank in Mrs. Butts's class, where he laughs and ruffles my hair as he lets me get whatever I want. I want to pretend like none of this ever happened. I want to believe everything my parents once told me. I want to forget everything I've found out about Max.

Some secrets are better left unsaid.

"If this is some sort of way to make an excuse for what you've done . . ." I say, my voice so strained from anger I can barely make out my own words.

"Words won't condone what I did to your brother. But you have to understand that I'm trying to make things right this time while still protecting my own ass. I haven't told anyone about you, have I?"

"You're forcing Elijah to fight to keep me a secret just to make some money!"

I have never felt so much hate inside of me. He practically kills my brother and then forces the guy I've come to care about to fight nearly every night?

"You've got that all wrong."

I can feel my body physically shaking from both fear and anger. "*All wrong?* Elijah is only fighting to keep your mouth shut about who I am. He told me himself."

"Yes, he's still fighting for money. But it's not because I want some extra cash in my pocket, Scarlet. Don't you think it'd be a little suspicious if I told the gang about the flash drive and then one of the ring's top fighters suddenly stops fighting there? They're not dumb, they'd figure out it was someone close to Eli, which indicates either you or Kevin. I need him to stay fighting so that they don't come questioning me about why the ring's star fighter suddenly stopped showing up. So that they don't make that connection."

"Why not just tell Elijah that, then? Why lie?"

"They already know something is up. Why else would Elijah be fighting such harsh opponents? They know you're around; they just don't know exactly who you are. Which is why you weren't supposed to come back to the ring."

He pauses and sighs, running his hands over his face.

"After you barged into the ring today, they may already have figured you out. Considering someone grabbed you—"

"What now, then?" I ask carefully.

"I can hold them off a while longer, but it won't be easy. You need to find the flash drive and give it to them. That's the only way to truly end this."

"There's no other way? I have no idea where to even find this flash drive. I don't know where I'd look. I'm only just learning about Max's secret life—he kept all of that stuff completely hidden from me."

"The cop," Alejandro says suddenly. "Max said he worked day and night to try and get justice against the gang. He would never tell me the guy's name, didn't want anything bad to happen to him if the gang somehow found out, but if you find him, you may find a way to that information."

"Well, how am I supposed to find him? Do you have any contact information?"

"I don't. When he came the night of Max's last fight, no one suspected he had been working with Max. And after that, he just disappeared. Stopped trying to infiltrate the gang with any other fighter. I guess he realized the danger he was in when his intel went bad."

Internal alarms blare through my ears. "Why should I trust the cop who covered up my brother's death? Why would he have even covered up Max's death in the first place?"

"I wish I could tell you, Scarlet, but I don't know. I only know what I've told you, and he seems like the easiest way to get that information. It's up to you to find out how to contact him; if he was the one who worked with Max, I'm sure you've crossed paths with him before."

Just as I open my mouth to argue more, someone else calls out.

"*Alejandro! You out here?*"

I hear the voice somewhere in the distance, and I snap my eyes back to Alejandro, who lets out a rather loud, whispered string of curse words under his breath.

"You set me up!" I hiss.

However, when I meet his eyes he seems just as panicked as I am. Confused worry crosses his expression, and it heightens all of mine.

"Someone must have seen me come out here," he says, his eyes darting around. Then they land back on me as the voice calls out again.

"Scarlet, you have to trust me."

"Trust *you*? I bet that's what you said to my brother, isn't it?"

"I'm trying to right my wrongs. Just trust me."

His friend appears from the shadows. "Alejandro, what are you doing? There's a meeting going on inside and—Is this the one we've been looking for?"

In that exact moment, Alejandro pulls out a gun. And turns it on me.

Alejandro keeps the gun steadily on me but shifts his focus to the man. My entire body goes into shock, I couldn't move even if I wanted to. Every hair on the back of my neck is standing straight up as I stare down the silver barrel of the gun, but I force myself to rip my gaze away long enough to look at Alejandro's friend.

He's tall. Gelled blond hair, dark clothes, raggedy facial hair, and a tattoo crawling up his neck. When I meet his eyes, I stop breathing from fear. There's nothing friendly about this guy; even his eyes have his thirst for blood written all over them.

"This is her," Alejandro confirms.

"Does she have the information on her?"

"No. But I have this under control, Raymond. Go back inside before you complicate things," Alejandro says, his previous tone replaced with one of sinister violence that makes my blood run cold.

"You should know the boss doesn't like you doing things this big on your own. You go inside, Alejandro. Nice job finding her, we've all been looking. You've done your part, so let me handle her."

My panicked eyes shift to Alejandro but he doesn't let any worried emotions show, which causes me to fear all the more. Maybe I should have run away the second I heard another voice. I shouldn't be trusting Alejandro; he has a *gun* pointed to my head for God's sake.

"If he doesn't trust me to do these things, then this is my chance to prove it to him, yeah? Go back inside."

Is he . . . is he protecting me somehow?

Raymond narrows his eyes. "Don't test me, give me the gun."

I see panic flash across Alejandro's eyes for a split second as he realizes this Raymond guy isn't just going to leave.

"Raymond, I've got this—"

Then, out of nowhere, sirens fill our ears. I don't see police lights anywhere, but the sirens signaling my safety blare out all around us. Alejandro snaps his eyes to mine, and much to my surprise his expression mirrors mine: relief.

"How the fuck did she call the cops?!" Raymond screeches. "Let's get out of here!"

Alejandro sends me one last look before running off after his friend, quickly placing the gun back into his waistband as he turns away. But, for a fleeting moment, he turns to me and opens his mouth to say something.

"*Police!*" We hear from somewhere down the alleyway along with an engine roaring toward us. It cuts Alejandro off and shows him that he has almost no time to run away if he doesn't leave right now.

I stand there, stunned into silence and stillness as Alejandro sprints away. I hear footsteps rushing toward me, the sound of heavy boots on their way to save me. I don't know how the hell the cops knew where to find me—maybe Kevin sent them after me—but I am relieved they are here. They just saved my life, because even if Alejandro told me to trust him not to pull that trigger, I'm not so sure his friend would have been as generous.

Maybe this is the cop Alejandro spoke about. Maybe he came back, had a gut feeling Max's undercover life was being spoken back into existence and knew he needed to show up here just one last time. Maybe he has the information on him, and I can end all of this tonight.

"Are you okay?" The cop rushes out as he reaches me.

I lift my eyes to thank him, but my words catch in my throat and I momentarily forget everything that just happened.

"*Jack?*"

A flashback from a few months ago, when I was still dating Jack, hits me. He came to see me while I was working at the auto shop, with lunch prepared for the both of us. He made a makeshift picnic in the vacant section of the garage even though Archie advised us not to, and as we ate, he asked if I could install police sirens in his truck in order to play a joke on all of his friends at parties. I did it, only this time they weren't used for a silly prank, but to save my life.

"Scar! Oh my God, come here. He just fucking held a gun to you," Jack says in disbelief. "Who *was* that guy?"

I blink at him, worried that my fear has caused me to start hallucinating.

"What are you doing here?" I ask instead of answering his question, still in a daze from the fact that *Jack* is the one who just saved my life.

"Apparently I'm saving your life."

"How the *hell* did you even know I was here?"

"I saw the car and noticed you inside instead of Eli."

"So, you just happened to be in the worst section of downtown Houston and just happened to see the Corvette and decided to go check out if I was in the car or Elijah? Let me tell you why that's bullsh—"

"Okay! I saw you at a stoplight closer to home as I was leaving a party and I was wondering, first of all, why you were out so late in Eli's car without him, and second, why you were going straight when I know you would have to turn right to go home.

I was curious as to where you were going, so I followed you. No big deal."

I blink at him.

"Why did you feel the need to follow me?"

"I don't know, Scar!"

Either he's gone insane, or I am a lot more affected by having a gun pointed at me than I thought and am talking to myself right now and Jack's not actually in front of me. Either way, I'm out of here. I turn away to go back home to Elijah and try to piece together how to solve this. To try and figure out where to find this flash drive Alejandro told me about. But I suddenly remember the fact that there is a huge gang of psychos after me that are apparently having a meeting inside the very building whose parking lot I am standing in. I can't stay here. My life is in danger, and so is Jack's if he doesn't get out of here right now.

Alejandro must have convinced Raymond to run far away upon hearing the sirens. If they were still nearby, Raymond would have seen that Jack was a phony and come back for me. That being said, there's no way I'm sticking around to find out if I'm right or not.

I start on my way to the Corvette, walking past Jack to get there. "Well, thanks for the whole saving-my-life thing, but we should really go."

"I can't stop thinking about you!" he blurts out.

I stop and slowly turn around to face him.

"I—I just can't. I can't stop thinking about what happened between us, Scar."

There have just been so many confessions tonight.

"I see you with *him* and I get so angry."

"I've noticed."

"I'm sorry. I've never felt this way before and I'm struggling with how to deal with it."

"You've never felt anger before?"

"Heartbreak."

I'm silent.

"Look, Scarlet, I still love you."

Add that to the already huge list of confessions from random guys in my life today.

All of the sudden he steps forward and tries to kiss me.

Oh my gosh, he's actually trying to kiss me.

My brain finally connects with the rest of my body, and instead of my lips, he's met with my hand as I smack him. My eyes widen and I quickly cover my mouth in surprise.

He opens his eyes and glares at me, lifting his hand to his reddening cheek. "What the *fuck* was that for?!"

"Just because you saved my life doesn't mean you can kiss me!" I exclaim. "You've made my life a living hell at school with all of your rumors!"

He runs his fingers through his hair out of frustration. "I know! And I'm sorry, Scar. I just didn't know how to handle seeing you walk around with such a frea—I didn't know how to handle seeing you walk around with Eli."

"Anything would have been better than what you're doing."

"I'm so sorry, Scar. He took a lot from me, and it hurts a hell of a lot to see that he took you too."

I can tell he's being genuine, but this apology is too little too late.

"Jack, he didn't take me. You lost me."

"I know," he says, and then glances back at me through pained eyes. "Blaming Eli just makes losing the best thing that ever happened to me a little bit easier."

∼

After Jack's unwanted confession, we booked it out of there with the threat of Alejandro, Raymond, and the gun still looming over both of our heads. All Raymond had to do was come back to check the scene and see that instead of the police there was just two unarmed teenagers arguing over a lost love.

Because my mom's car was still parked here in the lot from when I'd left it earlier, I had two cars to choose from: my mom's and Elijah's. In order to keep this little adventure hidden from Elijah, I chose to drive his Corvette back home. My mom will buy my excuse that I woke up early and took her car to the shop, right?

I shut off the Corvette's headlights and pull almost silently into the driveway, inching up the pavement and trying to get it back in the exact same spot as before I left. Elijah is observant. He'll notice if the tire is an extra inch from the lone rock in the driveway than it had been before I left.

I carefully make my way inside, closing the front door behind me as quietly as physically possible, and then tiptoe up the steps. I avoid every creak I've come to know by living here my whole life, and I suddenly wonder if Max had to do this exact same thing when coming home from fights. As I pad down the hallway that holds my parents' room, I hold my breath and tread lightly. Then I reach the final staircase that leads to my room, and I notice that the light is on. I definitely turned that off before I left.

Elijah noticed I was gone.

I flinch at the idea of him finding out I went on my own and debate running into Max's room and hiding beneath his covers. But I have to face my problems. I can't wish them away anymore; they've become too real. So I go up the final few stairs into my room and sheepishly walk inside. Elijah is sitting there with his shoulders sagging. He looks disheveled with his hair a small mess but his eyes are alert and worried. As soon as I step through the door, he abruptly stands up and strides confidently toward me.

I open my mouth to defend my actions, ready for him to yell at me for putting myself in harm's way again, but I swallow every word as he reaches out and pulls me into his arms. He wraps them around my body, nuzzling his face next to mine, and I rest mine in the crook of his shoulder, allowing his warmth to blanket me. The hug both comforts me and makes me feel guilty, guiltier than I felt after putting that roach into Mrs. Butts's sugar bowl. I shouldn't have gone without telling him.

"I'm sorry," I murmur, hugging him a little tighter. "I should have told you."

"I woke up and came in here to talk to you, just to see that you weren't here."

"I went to see Alejandro," I say as we pull apart.

"I know. I called Kevin because I knew you'd done something stupid. And I was right."

"I'm sorry."

"What happened?"

"I wanted answers. He gave them to me—told me everything about my brother—but then another member of the gang showed up and Alejandro pulled a gun on me," I explain, swallowing down the fear that is washing over me again. "He didn't shoot. I think he only pulled it to get the other guy to leave. He was somehow trying to keep me safe."

"*Alejandro?* Keeping you safe?"

"I know, I know. It sounds crazy. But he tried to explain all of this to me, explained why he is doing what he's doing. He refused to leave me alone with Raymond, the other guy."

Elijah looks away from me, consumed by his thoughts. But I reach my hand up to his face to pull his focus back to me.

"I'm okay, Elijah. I got out safely and got the information I wanted. I know how to end this now."

"Why didn't you tell me? I could have helped you."

"I was just trying to find out more information so that I could keep you from fighting. I hate seeing you hurt like this."

"Did you get the answers you wanted?"

"He told me everything, Elijah."

I can see the strain standing up is putting on his injured body, and I'm sure the lack of sleep isn't helping, so I walk us to my bed and sit down as I dive into everything I learned. He listens patiently and silently as I give a play by play of what Alejandro told me.

"How did you get away?"

I internally groan. I'm not looking forward to this explanation. Moving my gaze down to my comforter, I purse my lips and mutter my answer.

"Jack."

"What?"

"He followed me there for some reason."

"Your ex-boyfriend mysteriously followed you to the ring in the middle of the night?" Elijah echoes.

"That sounds even more strange every time I hear it. . . . Yeah, he followed me out of town because he was wondering why I was in your car without you at two in the morning."

"How did a punk like Jack scare a guy with a gun?"

I would have snorted if the situation wasn't so serious.

"He pretended to be the police using a siren I installed in his truck months ago. Pretty sure what he did was illegal, you know, impersonating a cop and all that, but it saved me."

"What was Jack's reaction?" Elijah asks stiffly.

I awkwardly scratch my head and fumble for something to say. "Um . . . he—well, he said some things . . ."

"That he still loves you."

"Yeah. How'd you know that?"

"No guy is going to follow his ex-girlfriend in the middle of the night all the way to *that* end of Houston without having some sort of feelings, and I'm sure he was feeling pretty confident after saving your life when clearly it should have been me there. What else did he say?"

"That he hasn't stopped thinking about me. It was stupid, and really caught me off guard. I mean, of course it caught me off guard. I heard sirens and thought I was saved, just to get attacked with confessions I did *not* seek out. I'm still partly convinced that I was hallucinating and . . ."

I trail out of my ramble when I feel Elijah's calculating gaze stuck on me.

"He kissed you. Didn't he?"

My jaw drops. "How? *How* did you know that? Oh my God, do I still have Jack slobber on me? No, that wouldn't make sense, I smacked him before he ever got the chance to kiss me."

Elijah smiles at me. "You smacked him?"

"I did. How'd you know he tried to kiss me?"

"Because when we look into those beautiful blue eyes of yours, it's damn near impossible not to."

I don't know how he's not angry at me. I don't know how he doesn't want to yell at me for putting myself in such a dangerous situation. Or how he isn't mad that Jack was the one to save me.

All I know is that I've never felt more gratitude toward anyone.

My lips match his soft smile. "Is that why you kissed me earlier?"

And, wouldn't you believe it, Elijah actually blushes.

"That and the fact I'm kind of crazy about you."

I know my cheeks mirror his from the warmth that spreads up my neck, and for once I don't know what to say.

"Scarlet?" Elijah says quietly, eyes flickering down to my lips. "It's getting damn near impossible again."

I don't hesitate. I close the distance between us and kiss him, gently but hungrily pressing my lips to his. He rests his hand on the corner of my jaw, his palm brushing my neck and fingers slipping under my hair as he tenderly kisses me back.

"You scared me, Scarlet," he admits as we pull apart. "I wanted to come after you and make sure you were okay, and I went outside just to see that *someone* took my car."

I sheepishly bite my lip and he watches as I roll it between my teeth, forcing his eyes back to mine.

"I don't have my own. Oh, and we still have to go get my mom's Escalade."

He rubs his thumb along my cheek. "Only you."

"Would leave her mom's car at the site where she almost got murdered? Yeah, sounds about right. She doesn't know, so I can tell her it's in the shop for now."

He laughs and moves in to kiss me again. And again. And again. And again, until a few innocent pecks turn into a passionate locking of lips. His hand moves from resting on my jaw to resting on the bed as we slowly lie back. He moves between my legs, his body hovering so closely to mine that I can feel the heat radiating off of him.

"We should get some sleep," he says. "It's past three."

I regretfully nod. I'd much rather prefer to make out with Elijah, because *goddamn* he's a good kisser. I don't know if Jack was just bad or what, but Elijah's kiss sets a fire in my heart that turns my whole body into a hot mess.

He shifts and lies down next to me, flinching from the still terrible bruise on his torso. I frown and eye the wound, taking a second or two to admire his beautifully sculpted stomach in the process. Instead of saying anything else, I pull the covers over us and lay my head on his chest. We lie there for a while, more than enough time to fall asleep, but so much has happened to me in the past twenty-four hours that my mind refuses to rest.

"You know," I say quietly through a yawn, not even sure if he's awake to hear this, "Max really would have liked you. He was a teddy bear, aside from the whole underground fighting/gang stuff, of course." Another yawn. "But, still a teddy bear. He hated it when . . ."

My words trail off into soft snores as sleep takes over.

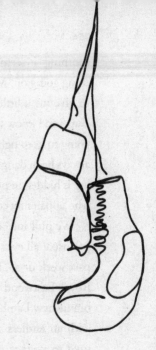

CHAPTER
TWENTY ONE

The next morning, Elijah and I wake up for school and try to keep his staying over a secret from my parents. I don't know how they didn't hear any of our conversation last night, me sneaking out, or me sneaking back inside. Elijah apparently keeps clothes in his car at all times, so he went to get his things and change, sneaking past my parents, who were downstairs and awake. He tried to play it off by acting as though he had just arrived, coming to the door to "pick me up."

When I come downstairs, I see him wearing the leather jacket and old, ratty jeans, aviators in their natural place on his worn shirt. He looks rugged, and the scars on his face add to it.

"Ready?"

"To attempt to live a normal high school life despite being sought after by a gang?" I ask. "Yeah, let's go!"

Elijah frowns deeply as we get in his car; when we woke up this morning, it seemed that he didn't want to have to discuss every-thing going on. Maybe he wants a normal day, or maybe he wants to give me a little bit of time to decipher it all in my own head. But even I know this is a situation we can't just ignore. He is always going to keep fighting until this whole thing ends, and my life will always be in danger until I find the mysterious flash drive I'm pray-ing is hidden in plain sight, and if not, then I have to contact a cop who apparently convinced my brother to put his life on the line.

We pull into the school parking lot a few minutes later, and per usual all eyes turn to Elijah's car. He's been driving it for the past week or so, but it still seems to amaze the students here at Royal Eastwood. Which is odd, considering one girl drives a brand-new Lamborghini to school every day and the lot is filled with an endless supply of new BMWs. I guess they just aren't used to vintage cars like this one. I turn my head to him and eye the fading bruises, my mind going to the worst one on his stomach.

"How are you feeling?" I ask gently.

"I'm okay."

"I'll find that flash drive, Elijah. I'll stop all this."

We both get out of the car and he leans his arms on the top, staring at me from across it.

"I promise," I add.

"And I'll keep you safe until then."

Without saying anything else, Elijah disappears in the back-seat to grab our backpacks as I lean against the cherry-red paint.

"It's nice to be back at school." I hum as he walks around the car to my side. "It makes me feel normal. Like my life isn't being twisted upside down because of a crazed gang that's after a flash drive I didn't even know existed until last night."

Elijah lets out a sigh and drapes my backpack over his open shoulder. I cross my arms as I look across the parking lot at the other students living normal lives.

"All we have to worry about here is the petty drama," I say, my eyes falling on Jack at his truck with his football buddies. Flash back to when the breakup was the worst of my problems.

Elijah silently follows my eyes to Jack and then looks back at me, playful interest sparking across his eyes.

"Can I be a jerk for a second?"

"How so?"

"Is he looking?"

I move my gaze to Jack for a second, noticing his eyes trained tightly on the two of us, and then I look back at Elijah with a nod.

"Good."

He steps closer to me, rests his hand on my cheek, and kisses me.

I grin against his lips, having to stop smiling in order to keep the kiss going, and I slide my fingers into the hair on the back of his neck. His hands drop down to my waist, leaning into me as I use the car for support. People around us catcall and cheer us on, as though they've never seen anyone make out in the parking lot before. It causes me to laugh against his lips, so we have to pull apart, but he doesn't bother to hide his grin.

"For the record, that's the first and last time I'll ever kiss you for a reason other than to show you how much you mean to me. *But* that felt good."

From the corner of my eye, I notice Jack stomping away and I smirk at Elijah.

"Is that how you repay him for saving my life?" I tease.

"I'll thank him for that another day, that was payback for years of insults."

I laugh and pull him back for another kiss, and the people in the parking lot go nuts again. I'm pretty sure everyone thought we were dating before this because of the amount of time we spent together, but this is the first we've been to school as a couple, and apparently, we've become the talk of the school before first period has even started. Rumors regarding Elijah have shifted from him being the freak of the school to the hunk of the school. I just don't understand how others didn't notice sooner.

~

By the end of the day, the rumors about me and Elijah haven't died down like I expected them to. There are also a few circulating around Jack's story of how he got the pretty handprint on his cheek. His story has to do with a fight with some majorly buff guy, and not his ex-girlfriend smacking him after he let his hormones take over his brain cells. Normally, I would hate having rumors circulate about me. However, these are able to momentarily take my mind off of the overriding doom of being taken by the gang.

As I walk down the hall, my eyes land on a body walking around the corner. Per usual, my heart rate increases tenfold when Elijah comes into view, a reaction I can't control. When he walks up to me, I notice the tense vein in his temple that only comes out when his jaw has been clenched for quite some time.

"You look tense, is everything okay?"

He shakes his head but doesn't say anything. I frown at him, trying to read through his tough facade. As I study him, I notice the clenching of his fist and the stiffening of his posture, and I purse my lips.

"When is your next fight?"

He shifts his eyes to mine, and I realize I asked the golden question.

"Tonight."

Hopelessness settles in in an instant.

"Alejandro called earlier. I know I have to stall until you find that flash drive. It'll be okay."

His reassurance doesn't change my worried expression and he steps closer. "I should be okay tonight."

"I feel like I need to help in some way."

"Unless you get into the ring with me, I don't think you can help, Scarlet. And clearly that's not going to happen."

I know there's no use in arguing with him. There isn't much he can do; he won't change his mind. So instead, I decide to lighten the intensifying mood.

"I don't know, I pack a pretty mean punch."

His whole demeanor softens once he realizes the tough conversation is over and he snorts. "Hit me then."

I freeze. "What?"

"Hit me."

"Hit *you*?"

"Yes."

"*Hit* you?"

He crosses his arms over his broad chest. "If you can smack Jack hard enough to leave a mark, I want to see how hard you can punch."

I blink at him. "So, you want me to . . . *punch* you?"

"That's what I said."

"Punch you?"

"Scarlet."

"Make a fist and then propel it forward with a fast momentum toward you?"

"Would you please shut up and punch me?"

I finally stop asking questions and form my hand into a fist, hesitating for another second before punching his chest as hard as I can.

Okay, *ouch*.

He doesn't even flinch, but I'm pretty sure he broke my damn hand. I open my mouth in pain and cradle my hand against my body.

"I think it's broken," I whine loudly.

Elijah takes my hand into his hand to examine it. "I think you'll live."

I pull it back to my chest, frowning at it. "Tell that to the blood cells you just destroyed with your freaking chest of steel."

"This is why you should stay home; you can't even punch right."

"I guess you're right."

He gently takes my wounded hand in his and tenderly kisses my knuckles, and a blush takes over my face from such a simple action.

"I have to do this, Scarlet. I can't let anything happen to you."

I don't know how much more grateful I can be for someone, but there has to be a way because Elijah Black keeps making me unbelievably grateful every day. I can feel my affection for him rumbling in my chest and stomach. Seeing him is something I look forward to every morning when I wake up, and he's my last thought when I go to bed. But he rips out a little piece of my heart every time he leaves to go to a fight with no guarantee of coming back, and the thought of losing him sends a cold shiver down my spine that doesn't go away until I see his confident face again, sending me a smile of reassurance that he's okay. It's impossible for any words to do justice to the way my heart speeds up the second he steps into a room or explain how I feel when we touch. It's impossible to put a word to the way I feel about Elijah Black.

Then my thoughts freeze.

There *is* one word.

Love. I love Elijah Black. And I *have* to find that flash drive.

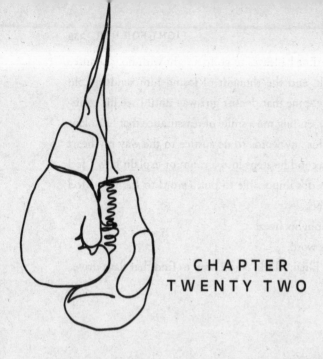

CHAPTER
TWENTY TWO

Elijah promised to come over after his fight. I didn't ask to go with him because after looking down the barrel of a gun I don't really want to take my chances going to the ring. Plus, he'd never let me go. He's made that clear enough times for me to finally listen. After my revelation of being in love with Elijah, I came home to search frantically for that flash drive.

I didn't tell him that I love him yet. I don't know how or when to tell him. I mean, how do you tell someone you love them? Especially when you've only just kissed for the first time the day before? I could come right out and say it; it has the same amount of meaning no matter how you reveal it, but that doesn't make it any less nerve-racking. Anything I do will be better than Jack's confession the other night, but that's not a very high standard. Even when he and I admitted we loved each other for the first time, it wasn't this hard.

Despite tearing my brother's room apart for the past two hours, I can't find the flash drive. I come to my room to try and brainstorm, thinking of places Max may have hidden such important information. The issue with that, however, is the fact that I never knew this part of his life existed.

My mind may not want to sleep, but my body is exhausted. I've been tossing and turning, trying to rest my eyes until Elijah gets here, but sleep seems to be off the table. There's too much on my mind. Being in love, being sought after by murderers, Elijah fighting for his life as well as mine, and what to wear tomorrow to school. It's a lot.

I sit up in bed when I hear feet on the stairs leading to my room, and seconds later Elijah opens the door, trying to be as quiet as possible. I left a key under the mat outside so he could get in, since I knew he wouldn't be here until late; and I was right. It's twelve. And I didn't want him to have to climb up the balcony; that was *not* a good experience.

I scan his face for new injuries, and the first thing I spot is his freshly blackened eye. It had just begun healing from the other night. My heart sinks. I want to ask him what happened but he doesn't look like he wants to talk about it. So instead, I mask my concern with a smile and move over in the bed, and he seems grateful that I choose not to question him. Lying down on his uninjured side next to me, he rests his head on his respective pillow and reaches for me to come closer.

"Any luck?" he asks, referring to the flash drive.

"Not yet."

He nods, expertly hiding any reaction from me.

"I'll find it. I will."

He knows there's no guarantee, but he should believe me

when I say I'll find it. Because I won't stop looking until he no longer has to risk his life fighting to keep me safe.

"Alejandro suggested I reach out and find who that cop was. That's my next plan of action, and then I'll have the flash drive," I reason.

I reach out and lightly trace my finger around Elijah's black eye. He barely hides a flinch and I quickly stop. I move to an old scar under his cheekbone, letting my thumb gently stroke it. The only noise between us is the sound of our breaths and the occasional car driving by outside, and we stay like this for a long time. I let my eyes dance across every scar on his face, picking out many faint ones I never even knew were there.

Elijah suddenly leans forward and kisses me sweetly, resting his head back on the pillow as he pulls back. I shift my hand to another faded scar on his forehead.

"Where did you get this one?" I ask.

"First fight—he got the first shot in, and his ring caught my skin." Then he smirks. "It was his only shot of the fight."

"I want to hear the story behind every scar."

"There are a lot."

"I want to hear every one."

He smiles tenderly. "Okay."

He explains every scar I trace on his face. Some of the stories are difficult for him to tell, and some get gruesome, but the hardest is from a scar on his shoulder.

It's from when he was a little kid, when he was still best friends with Jack, still had two loving parents, and lived in a house larger than mine. He and his older brother, Oliver, were wrestling, and Oliver took things a little too far and they went tumbling into the living room where his mom's favorite coffee table was, which just so happened to be made of glass.

His brother flipped him onto it, trying to mirror a move by his favorite wrestler at the time. But Elijah was bigger than Oliver expected the table to hold, because he went crashing through it and it shattered around him. The first person to hear the crash was his dad. He came rushing into the room, frantic, and saw Elijah sitting among broken glass and his brother with a pale face from what he just did. He quickly picked Elijah up and took him to the hospital to get his shoulder—where the largest piece of glass cut him—stitched up, and they treated the other small scratches along his body.

I know the story wasn't hard to tell because of the fact he got hurt, but because he had to bring up a life that he'll never get back. His brother is gone, and his dad left. He goes quiet after the story.

"Are you okay?" I ask.

His tough facade cracks a bit. "It's just hard to talk about him."

"Oliver or your dad?"

"Both."

"I'm sorry."

He offers a sad smile. "I don't know how you talk about Max so much. It hurts to even think about Oliver."

"Different people have different ways of coping."

"You didn't even have to ramble for that one."

"What about your dad?" I ask, instantly regretting it from the way his eyes darken.

"What about him?"

"What was he like?"

Elijah rolls onto his back, shifting so that he has one arm behind his head, and stares at the ceiling.

"Cold. Often distant. Jerk to my mother, jerk to my brother, jerk to me."

I sit up and prop my head on my arm, studying his face.

"Before that."

He stares at me, trying to decide whether or not to say there was nothing before, or to tell me the truth.

"Before, when I was very little, he was a good man. Was very affectionate toward my mom, loved to wrestle with me and Oliver and spoil us to no end, and was the dad all the neighborhood kids secretly wished was their own. He treated them all like he was."

"What happened?"

He purses his lips and his gaze hardens at the ceiling. "The business he had with Mr. Dallas failed. He moved to the police force, since he had experience under his belt from before he went down the business track. Then Oliver took up drugs, and it caused a lot of arguments between my dad and my mom. They got bad. He got incredibly busy at work, and then suddenly he wasn't. I don't know why. Then once Oliver overdosed—well, that was his breaking point. He left soon after without a word. We didn't hear from him for months, and then we got a letter telling us all about his new life."

I furrow my brow and wait for him to expand.

"He was having an affair before he left. Then he left my mom—" He pauses and adds, "left me—to go live with the new woman and her two kids. A drug-free son, and a little baby girl that was apparently his. I guess he was tired of our family."

He stops there, and tears well up in his eyes, causing my heart to crack. He has literally been through hell and he's barely even eighteen.

"Elijah . . ."

"I'm okay, Scarlet," he says, and just as quickly as the tears welled up, they go away.

I stare at him to make sure no more tears come, and then I lean down and gently kiss him. I lightly kiss his lips, then I move and kiss every scar on his face, the scar on his shoulder, and then back to his lips. He smiles softly at me and brushes some hair from where it fell in front of my eyes. His eyes slowly rake over my face, lingering on random spots, and I feel myself blush.

"What? Is there something on my face? Oh my gosh, do I have a booger?"

He shifts his eyes back to mine and chuckles, quickly shaking his head. "No, I just wanted to admire."

"Admire . . . ?"

"You."

He rests his hand on my cheek and rubs his thumb along my skin. "You're beautiful, Scarlet. I don't think I've ever told you that, but I think you're absolutely beautiful."

Before I can answer, though he rendered me speechless, he rests his hand on the back of my head to pull my lips to his, this kiss deeper but just as tender as the others. I place my hand on his chest to support myself, and he lifts his head, so I slowly retreat back to my pillow with his lips still on mine. He hovers over me, resting his hands on each side of my face as we kiss. He slips his tongue past my lips, and I trail my hands up and down the muscles on his back, smirking at the goose bumps that rise on his skin.

Thank God I decided not to wear my retainer tonight.

But then he pulls back, and I notice the guilty look on his face.

"I talked to Alejandro tonight."

"And you decided to tell me that now?" I deadpan, glancing at our position. "In the middle of making out?"

He shifts so that he's sitting up next to me and runs his hands over his face.

"I'm sorry, I just—I wanted to tell you. We set up a fight, Scarlet."

"What do you mean?"

"To end all of this. I was able to get Alejandro to convince them to leave you alone if I win. You haven't done anything with the information thus far, so I think they believe that you won't do anything if I win the fight."

My blood runs cold.

"Elijah—what happens if you lose?"

He doesn't answer me.

"I'm sorry, Scarlet. But I'm doing whatever I can to keep you safe."

"I want *you* to be safe!"

"I stop fighting and then they kill you to get rid of that information."

"You lose this fight and they kill *you*!"

"I won't lose."

I feel that same pit of hopelessness settle into my stomach. "I can't lose you."

"I would never leave you." He doesn't miss a beat.

The black eye he endured tonight doesn't dare interfere with his handsome features, and despite what we're going through, the brightness in his eyes hasn't dimmed. Despite what he's had to go through his whole life, he's still such an amazing man. I love him. And I want to tell him, but all that comes out is, "I care about you a lot."

"You mean everything to me, Scarlet."

I stay quiet, trying to figure out how to tell him that I love him. How to tell him the exact way he makes me feel, because just saying those three words wouldn't be enough to describe my affection for him. But he must take my silence as annoyance.

"I'm sorry for all of this, Scarlet. I dragged you into this. You deserve someone better than me."

"No, I don't. I don't want anyone better. Mainly because no one better exists, because you're literally the most amazing guy I've met. You're selfless, you're so kind, and you're hot as hell. Which is a great plus, because, like, I'd feel this way about you even without the abs, but they definitely help. I mean, what girl doesn't like a guy with abs, you know? A sculpted body is always a bonus to a relationship, because it's a great turn-on and—" I realize I'm going completely off topic and shake my head. "What I'm trying to say here is that—"

"I love you."

"Yes, exactly!" I exclaim, relieved I was finally able to get it out. "That's all I'm trying to say."

Then I pause.

"Wait. Were you filling in my blank or were you saying—"

"That I love you? Both, I hope."

I attack him with kisses. I kiss his forehead, his cheeks, his nose, his eyes (careful of the black eye), and his lips over and over again. He laughs and captures my lips so that I can't pull away, but neither of us can stay in the kiss for long because of our smiles.

Then the thought of the flash drive hits me again.

"Don't go to that fight. I'll find the flash drive before so that you don't have to fight anymore. Just . . . don't go."

He replies by kissing me again, but I can't pretend I don't see the look in his eye that clearly states he is going to the fight no matter what.

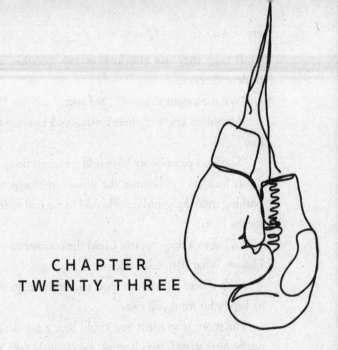

CHAPTER
TWENTY THREE

The fight is tonight. I have been searching for the flash drive all day, but to no avail. I only have one option left: I have to try and find the cop who Max worked with. I've held off for this long because doing that means involving my parents, and as far as I know they don't know about Max working as an informant. But now that Elijah has set up this fight, I can't be afraid of anything anymore. I have to do all I can to keep him safe, just like he's trying to do for me.

With heavy feet and sweaty palms, I travel downstairs and into the living room where my parents are lounging clueless as to what is at stake for us.

"Mom? Dad?"

"What's up, sweetheart?"

"Why did you never try to look further into Max's death?"

To say they are shocked at my question would be an understatement.

"What brought this on?" Dad asks.

"I need to know if there's more you two are keeping from me."

"Scarlet, I promise we have told you everything we know. We didn't look into it because the officer in charge said there was nothing more he could do. He told us we had to let it go, it was for the best."

Taking in a deep breath, I find the courage to tell them what I know. What Alejandro told me.

"The officer didn't want you asking more questions because he kept a lot from you two."

The room is so silent you could hear a pin drop. I can practically hear their hearts beating ridiculously fast, almost as fast as mine.

"Max was working as an informant. He was a part of the gang, working with that officer to get information on the gang so that the cops could bust them. The gang found out and they killed him before he got the chance to turn that information over."

The whites of their eyes have never been so defined.

"How—"

"Did I find out? The guy at the ring who told me Max was murdered—Alejandro—I contacted him. He's in the gang, and he knew Max. He told me everything. I know it was dangerous, and I know sometimes there are things in life maybe we aren't meant to find out, but now Elijah's life is on the line and I'll do anything I can to make sure he's safe. As well as this family."

I go on to explain to them the danger we are in, the flash drive Max supposedly had, that Elijah's life is also hanging in the balance, and the urgency to find this flash drive before his fight tonight.

"And you didn't think to tell us this earlier?" my dad says, overwhelmed by everything I just dumped on him.

"Look, I know I should have involved you two in this since it's all of our lives at stake here, but I at least included you now, right? So, can you help me find that cop Max worked with? Because at this point, I think he's our last hope. Elijah is going to fight tonight no matter what, and the gang will continue to come after us until we get that information, despite what Elijah says the rules of the fight are."

"The officer left his card with us," Mom says frantically. "Remember? He said if we heard anything else to call him."

"Okay, this is good. Where did you put that card?"

The lines on their foreheads are clearly defined as they concentrate on a memory they probably tried their hardest to forget. I sit there and try to rack my brain, too, recalling the day we found out Max was gone from our lives.

Suddenly, Dad pulls out his wallet, quickly opening the worn leather and searching through his cards until he finds the golden ticket. "I always kept it on me in case we did hear something."

This is it.

With shaky hands, I lift the card to my line of sight and scan it. And what I see makes my body go still. I can't look away.

CHARLES BLACK
DRUG ENFORCEMENT TASK FORCE

"Scarlet? What is it?"

Elijah said his dad was a cop for the Houston PD. Alejandro

said the cop found out about the drugs being sold at the ring through his son. Oliver bought from the dealers at the ring. Charles Black. Elijah Black.

"Scarlet?"

"He's Elijah's dad."

"*What?*"

"The officer . . . the one who worked with Max. Charles Black, it's Elijah's dad. He walked out on Elijah and his mom a couple of years back, Elijah hasn't talked to him since. Elijah must not have known—he said that his dad was becoming distant before he left and didn't talk much with the family. He must have never told them what he was doing at work."

"So, you're telling me the cop who convinced Max to be an informant and convinced us to stop asking questions is Elijah's father?" Dad asks incredulously.

"Apparently that's exactly what I'm telling you."

"And Elijah has no idea?"

My body is shaking from adrenaline and shock, my hands frozen to the touch from clenching the business card so tightly.

"There's no way, he would have told me if he did. I—I have to go call his dad, he needs to stop this before Elijah's fight tonight," I rush out, running upstairs for my phone.

My hands shake as I start to type in the number on the card. What do I say? What do I do?

Hello, this is Scarlet Tucker, Max's little sister. You know, the guy you worked with who died doing what you asked him to do and then you never told his family what truly happened and covered up his murder, oh, and I'm the girl your son is in love with! You know, the son you left when he needed you most! Great to meet you.

Yeah, that sounds perfect.

"Hello?"

My mouth goes dry and my breath gets caught in my throat, shutting out my sarcastic thoughts.

"Uh, hello. Is this Officer Black?"

"This is him, who is this? If you have a police issue you should have dialed 911."

With a deep breath to calm myself, I close my eyes and speak clearly into the phone.

"I'm Scarlet. Max Tucker's little sister."

I don't hear anything but the static between our phones for a few moments, and I worry he hung up on me. But, finally, he responds.

"I'm sorry, Scarlet, but if you're asking for more details on the accident, I just don't—"

"I know Max was murdered, Officer Black. I know the gang did it, and I know he was an informant for you."

Again, silence. A cigarette cough.

"Can I meet you in person to discuss this?"

My pounding heart resonates through my ears, drowning out my own response.

"Yes."

We decide to meet at Harold's Coffee Shop here in Conroe, overlooking the lake and very much a public place so that nothing bad can go down. Dashing downstairs, I throw on my coat and shoes to go out and meet Officer Black and find the key to unlocking our safety.

"Scarlet, what—"

"Can't talk. Coffee shop, Elijah's dad, secrets!" I rush out, nearly falling to the floor as I pull on my right boot.

"Slow down. What happened?" Mom asks.

"I told him that I knew the secrets he kept from us, and he asked me to meet him at Harold's Coffee Shop over on Lake Conroe."

"Hold on, you aren't going there alone. Not with everything going on right now and your safety at risk," Dad says, taking broad steps toward me.

"Mom, Dad . . . I *need* to do this. Elijah is going to a fight tonight to attempt to save my life, but even if he wins, the gang won't stop until they find that flash drive. I can't let Elijah fight tonight; I can't let him suffer the same fate as Max. Elijah's dad may be the only one who can give us the answers we need—he may finally give us clarity. Don't you want that?"

They don't answer me right away, but from the softening of their expressions, I know I got through to them. This is about more than just me and my safety.

"We shouldn't let you go at all," Mom says. "And we definitely won't let you go alone."

"You can talk with him on your own, but you're crazy if you think we are going to let you just go without us," Dad adds.

"Let's go."

I look out at the lake, watching the leaves from the trees float down and land on the water, disrupting its peace. When we arrived at the coffee shop, I sat down at a table overlooking the lake, and my parents sat in the back, out of view from me but where they could clearly see my table. I can't stop my leg from bouncing up and down, giving away my nerves. The caffeine from my coffee probably isn't helping.

I don't particularly like this man. He got my brother to be an informant, a job that ultimately took his life, and then left Elijah and his mother. I have no idea how this is going to play out. I don't know if I'll be able to control my emotions.

"Scarlet?"

As I turn my head, I swear I'm met with a carbon copy of Elijah. If I wasn't sure this was his dad before, now I have no doubt. Their posture, their height, but mainly their eyes.

"Officer Black?" I ask; he's not wearing a police uniform. He's in black dress pants and a light-blue button-down, and that's when my eyes land on the badge attached to his belt.

"Please, call me Charles." He gestures to the seat across from me as a silent question to sit. I nod and he quickly sits down, hesitance evident on his features.

"So . . . you know. How?"

I drop my eyes to the coffee in my hands. He doesn't know about Elijah. He has no idea his son is fighting at the one place he probably wanted him to stay far away from, and now I have to be the one to tell him what he's missed in the time since he left his family.

"Elijah."

His face glazes over with shock.

"You know my son?"

"I'm in love with your son," I clarify.

The creases in his forehead are prominent as he raises his brows.

"How does he fit into this? I kept this from him."

"He is a fighter at the ring. The top fighter, much like Max. I know a lot more than you probably think I do, Officer—I mean, Charles. But I still have my questions."

"It's better that you don't know."

"No, it's not better that I don't know. I haven't known for the last few years, and I'm finally learning the truth about my brother. It's not up to you anymore what my family gets to know and what we don't."

He sits silently, jaw clenching and unclenching. "I know you probably think I'm a bad person."

Understatement of the century.

"I know I had a part in Max's death, and I know I kept details from you and your family, but I have my reasons."

Anger boils inside of me. "There is *no* reason not to tell a family how their son and brother died. And to even *cover it up*? There is no justification for that."

He presses his lips together, again looking everywhere but me. The crimson-colored table, the lake outside, the hardwood floors.

"Your brother asked me not to tell your family, Scarlet. When he agreed to be an informant, he begged me never to tell anyone what he was doing no matter what happened. I was trying to uphold that wish."

"Why didn't you keep investigating? Everything he died for, it was all in vain because of you."

"When he died all of the information he gathered died with him. I was there the night he died, I searched him for that flash drive but I never found it. I hadn't a clue where it could be, and I spent a while searching, but eventually the case was dropped by my superiors and went cold. I didn't have a choice—without any evidence to arrest the gang members, I had to move on."

I clench my coffee, trying to keep my emotions at bay the best I can.

"Why not try to get information on your own?"

"The gang discovered Max was working for the police. They're smart. Once they learned we were trying to bust them, they scattered. I couldn't do anything without that flash drive."

I digest all of the information he's just fed me, thankful for the caffeine boost to help it flow together.

"Look, Scarlet, that case was the hardest thing I've had to deal with my entire career. I liked Max, a lot. He was a great kid and reminded me of my own kids, Elijah in particular. I took the case to save my other son—he became addicted to the drugs that damn gang fed him, and Max was more than willing to help me. When he died I had a very hard time dealing with knowing an innocent kid died because of my own personal ambition. I started slipping away from my family, Oliver got deeper into the drugs, and I worked day and night to try and find another way to bust the gang despite the case being dropped. Then Oliver overdosed, and I had to finally give up. I failed. I couldn't handle being home anymore; everything was a reminder of what I had lost."

As much anger and resentment I harbor toward this man, I can't help but sympathize with his situation. I've been so caught up in trying to detangle Max's story that I didn't stop to wonder who else was affected. I didn't stop to wonder why I was lied to, why things were kept from our family. Charles lost a son, too, and if Elijah fights tonight, he could lose another.

"You have the chance to right some of your wrongs. If I can get that flash drive, can you help put an end to this once and for all?"

He looks at me, intensity falling off of him in waves, but even I can see his fear.

"Getting that information will put you and your family at great risk. I promised Max to keep you out of this, I can't let you—"

"This isn't just about me and my family anymore. Elijah has gotten tangled up in this mess. The gang thinks I have that flash drive and they've begun threatening to come after me. Elijah . . . he won't let them. He's been fighting gruesome matches to try and keep them away from me, and tonight he took a fight to supposedly end this for good. But after learning how Max died, I know this gang doesn't have an ounce of integrity. Whatever deal they struck with Elijah, they won't uphold it. And I won't let him go to a fight where the outcome has already been decided."

Charles is silent. I don't know if he's unsure of what to say or is so overcome by emotion that he can't speak.

"You may not have been able to save Oliver, and I am truly sorry for that, but you have the chance to save Elijah. Help me find that flash drive and we can stop Elijah from having to fight. We can save him."

Charles finally looks at me, determination written all over his face.

"It's time to finally finish what I started."

Relief washes over me. We actually might win this battle.

"But in order to find that flash drive, I need more heads. I could never find it on my own because I didn't know Max's personal life. Get your parents here and any of Max's friends," Charles says.

"Yeah, about that first one . . . look behind me to the back of the restaurant on the right."

He has to angle his body oddly in order to see the table my parents are located at. "Ah, not so easy on the trust, are you?"

"Can you blame me? I have a gang after me."

I twist my body to catch my parents' eyes and wave them over, and they shoot out of their booth.

"Mr. and Mrs. Tucker, it's good to see you two again. I'm sorry it's under these circumstances."

"Why didn't you tell us?"

As Charles talks with my parents, I step outside and call Kevin. I explain to him everything I've discovered, not really even giving him time to be shocked that the officer is Elijah's dad. We don't have the time for surprised reactions. He rushes to meet us at the coffee shop since time is ticking away. Elijah's fight is in a mere four hours, so every second counts. As soon as Kevin arrives, he hands over his phone to Charles, who is going through all of our pictures, searching for some sort of clue.

"This is what I didn't have when I was investigating. Without much insight into Max's personal life, I couldn't figure out where the flash drive was. And since the case was dropped, I wasn't allowed to get any warrants for these things."

"What are you looking for?" Kevin asks.

"Some sort of clue, anything. Maybe the flash drive itself, hidden in plain sight."

Kevin rolls his eyes, "You really think you'll actually find the flash drive in one of the pictures on my phone? I've looked through those pictures more times than I can count, there's no way—"

"Here," Charles suddenly states, turning the phone for all of our eyes to see.

He shows us a picture from Kevin's phone of him and Max by Max's motorcycle, his keys dangling off of a chain attached to his waistband. Charles zooms in on the key chain, glancing up to watch our reactions. I'm the first to see it.

"The key chain. He kept the flash drive on his key chain."

"Hidden in plain sight," Charles says.

Kevin takes his phone in awe, staring at the picture with his mouth agape. "How did I never see this? This picture was my wallpaper for months after his death."

"You didn't know what to look for. None of us did."

"This won't help us unless we are able to find that key chain," Charles chimes in. "Mr. and Mrs. Tucker, what did you do with Max's motorcycle when he passed away?"

"We kept it in a storage unit, to go along with the story of it being a motorcycle accident," Mom says.

"Are his keys with it?"

My parents look at one another, and slowly I see smiles fill their faces.

"Yes."

Charles's face floods with relief, and he turns his attention to me.

"Scarlet, meet me at my office as soon as you get it. I have to see what's on it in order to get approval from my new superior to infiltrate the ring before Elijah's fight. We can devise a plan once we get that information."

I don't wait any longer. My parents give me the address to the storage unit, Charles gives me the address to his office, and Kevin offers to come with me. We get into his Mustang and rush off to the storage unit.

～

Kevin speeds us to the storage unit just outside of our small town. Time is against us. Four hours have dwindled to three, and we still have to deliver this information to Charles.

"Can't you go faster?" I snap.

"I'm already pushing ninety!"

"Why not make it a hundred?"

"Do you want me to get pulled over?"

"I don't see any cops. Plus, we have one on our side, we'll be fine."

"Scarlet. We'll get there, okay? We're going to get the flash drive and save Elijah, don't worry."

"I'm worried."

He sends me a flat look.

"What if we don't get the flash drive? What if someone came and took it? What if the storage unit burnt down without anyone knowing and the motorcycle and flash drive exploded along with it?" I gasp. "What if the motorcycle and the flash drive are the *reason* it burnt down?! What if Max put a timer bomb on the flash drive so that no one could find it and we waited too long and the timer went off and it exploded, taking everything else in the storage unit along with it?"

Kevin glances at me, eyes wide from all of the rather ridiculous questions.

"How does Elijah usually react to these things?"

I blush and smile sheepishly at him. Kevin isn't used to my rambles. "Oops."

"Just . . . don't worry. The flash drive is fine."

We reach the storage unit and go to my parents' unit. We walk down a few hallways filled with garage doors, searching for #422.

I see #400 and break into a jog, scanning the numbers for the one we need. My eyes land on #421 and I rush to the one next to it, only to see that it says #423 and my heart drops.

"Kevin, there is no number 422. It's gone!"

"Scarlet—"

"The gang must have known and somehow gotten rid of it! They already have the flash drive, so why do they want me? They must have come here and threatened the workers to cover up unit 422 and—"

"Scarlet!"

He's standing in front of an open unit across from me.

"The numbers go in a zigzag fashion, Little Tucker. It's across from 421, not next to it."

Oh.

I smile sheepishly at him and scratch the back of my neck awkwardly, walking past him and into the unit. I see Max's motorcycle sitting there—it's the only thing in the unit. It looks the exact same as it did three years ago before I thought it was mangled by an eighteen-wheeler. And sitting on the seat are Max's keys.

Kevin and I share a look of relief and excitement, and we run forward to snatch the keys, as though at any moment someone else could take them from us. I grab them—they're freezing cold to the touch since they've been sitting here for however many years, and eye the jet-black flash drive sitting between the motorcycle key and house key.

We found it. We actually found it.

"Let's get this to Charles and figure out a plan for tonight."

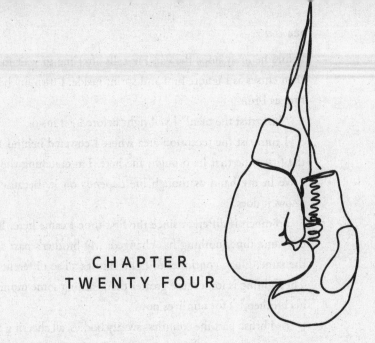

CHAPTER
TWENTY FOUR

Kevin and I make it to Charles's office and hand over the flash drive, which he then hands over to his superiors after looking it over, gaining access to his case once again. His excitement is hard to miss—the pure energy radiating off of him when he realizes all the work that he put in years ago isn't going to go to waste anymore.

After devising a plan, Kevin and I book it to the ring. The fight has already started. Our prep took longer than anticipated and I haven't been able to calm my racing heart ever since ten o'clock hit.

Elijah is already fighting for his life. I'm just praying that he's winning.

Kevin speeds past the endless cornfields in this end of Texas. They eventually turn into the outer sections of Houston, and next thing I know he's pulling into the parking lot. I jump out before he even stops the car. He calls after me to wait for him then curses as I ignore him and sprint inside. I turn my head to him as I run.

"Just trust the plan!" I yell right before I get inside.

I run past the reception area where I cowered behind Elijah the first time that he brought me here. I'm clutching the flash drive in my hand as though life depends on it. Because, you know, it does.

So much is different since the first time I came here. But at the same time, nothing has changed. My brother's past stayed the same, Elijah continues to fight, but it's all so different now. The fighting is for a cause greater than earning some money for his brother. It's for our lives now.

As I brush past the countless sweaty bodies, all cheering at the top of their lungs and pumping their fists in the air from adrenaline of the fight, I slip the flash drive into my pocket and shove my way through. It amazes me how these people can't feel the shift in the atmosphere. How they don't recognize the number of angered faces that don't belong to excited viewers.

They don't know what this fight really is.

The crowd is thick tonight, and I have to literally throw myself into the small gaps between the large bodies to move anywhere, and even then, I have a tough time running through the crowd. It's dark and stuffy in here, more so than usual, making the mood even darker. Suddenly, over the chants of the crowd, I hear the sickening blows in the ring. I hear the painful grunts, the impact of each hit, and it makes all of my hair stand on end. That's Elijah in there, and I don't know if he's the one throwing the punches or the one receiving them. I'm afraid to find out, because I think I know the answer.

The closer I get to the ring the louder the grunts get. My stomach churns as I recognize the painful groans as Elijah's. It wasn't often in past fights that he got hurt, but when he did, he had a distinct grunt of pain, and it's something I never want to hear again. As I hear Elijah cry out, I knock someone over to get closer to him, and now I can see what I didn't want to.

Elijah is lying on the floor of the bloodstained ring.

He's clutching his stomach and his face is pulled into an expression of complete agony as blood slowly trickles down his swollen lip. His left eye is swollen shut, the rest of his face a discolored mess, and his shirt is discarded somewhere in the ring, showing that his entire torso is a sea of blue and purple. There's one spot in particular that's almost black, and my stomach aches when I realize he must have a broken rib. His opponent has no mercy and slams his heel into Elijah's back, causing him to cry out again and arch it as he shouts in pain.

"*Elijah!*"

Someone screams his name, and my heart clenches at the fear laced into their voice.

When his eyes lazily move to mine, I realize I'm the one who yelled. I see surprise flash across his face, and he tries to stand up, shaking his bleeding head.

"*Scarlet! Get out of here!*"

Instead of listening to him, I run forward and try to climb into the ring to tend to him. There's no way he can get out of here without me. I have to trust the plan and do what I can to keep him safe until it's put in full force. But the minute my hands touch the ropes, Elijah's yanked up from the pool of blood and into a headlock, his neck seconds away from being snapped.

"Stop!" I scream.

The minute Elijah is lifted into the headlock the entire room goes silent. The oblivious crowd is *finally* realizing that this isn't just an ass kicking. This isn't a normal fight; it never was.

I lift my gaze to the man who's about to take Elijah's life and I meet his sickening blue eyes. One is clouded over, the other piercingly evil, and my blood runs cold all over again. But upon seeing me, he drops Elijah from the death grip. Elijah falls into a heap on the floor, clutching his neck while gasping for air.

His loud gasps fill the silent space and my heart drops out of my chest.

"It's about time you showed up, Tucker." The fighter smirks. Alejandro appears in the ring too.

The crowd suddenly parts, and from the shadows emerges a man dressed in a perfectly tailored suit. His black hair is slicked back, his high cheekbones are almost too perfectly sculpted, and his smile is too calm to be natural. His walk is laced with power, and it causes the hairs on the back of my neck to stand on end. He must be the boss.

"Alejandro, why don't you two make sure everyone leaves," he says.

His voice is just as calm as his walk. It holds an entitled tone, as though he comes from money and has learned he can get what he wants no matter the consequences. I rush to Elijah as the ring clears out, but the leader lifts his hand.

"Ah, ah, ah," he says, and suddenly I'm pulled into a tight grip by Alejandro.

I thought he told me to trust him.

"Don't touch her," Elijah growls.

I hear him struggle and see him trying to get to me, only to be held back. The leader calmly steps into the ring and stands next to Elijah, who's still struggling. But he's too weak to get free, and I see the defeat in his eyes.

"Scarlet, I assume?" the leader says with a sickly sweet smile at me. His words are too smooth and too persuasive to be authentic.

I know what he's capable of.

I grind my teeth, refusing to answer.

"My apologies, I should introduce myself first. I'm Deke, and I'm hoping you've come with what I want?"

From the corner of my eye I can see Elijah trying to catch my gaze, maybe to tell me not to comply, but I know what to do. We have a plan. Charles is a cop; we have the police force on our side. I'm ignoring the pit of doubt in my stomach and promising myself that it's going to work. I reach into my pocket and pull out the little black flash drive. Deke reaches forward to grab it, but I grip it tightly in my palm.

"Let him go," I demand.

Deke smiles and calmly places his hands back by his sides. "You're in no place to be making demands, Scarlet. You think I'm just going to take your word for this? Give me the flash drive, let me look it over, and he can go."

There's no threat behind his words, and that alone is the biggest threat he could give.

I hold his gaze, trying to think of an alternative, and I realize there isn't one. So, I unsquare my shoulders and toss the flash drive to him. One of his men instantly comes with a laptop, and he snaps to the fighter to let Elijah go. Elijah falls to the floor and I rush to him, noticing for a fleeting second how Alejandro just let me go with no struggle. I grab the lone rag in the corner of the ring and instantly tend to the countless scrapes on Elijah's face to try and stop some of the bleeding.

"Scarlet," he coughs, and I wipe the blood that seeped out of his mouth. "Why did you give it to him? That was everything your brother worked for."

"Don't worry, Elijah. I know what I'm doing."

He scans my face, trying to read what plan I have hidden up my sleeve. "I didn't want you to come. This is life or death, Scarlet. You shouldn't have come."

"I wasn't about to let you tackle this one on your own."

"They aren't just going to let us walk out of here. They tricked us. This is exactly what they wanted, for you to show up."

"I know that."

"I really hope you know what you're doing." He sighs, instantly erupting in a coughing fit that has him clutching his ribs in pain, crying out.

My heart breaks at his agony and I rub his back to give him some sort of relief, but it's pointless. He's hurt very badly, and he needs to see a doctor right away. I don't know how he hasn't passed out.

"Just trust me," I whisper as his breathing calms after the coughing fit.

He reaches out to take my hand and weakly squeezes it. "Always."

Then he's ripped away from me again. This time by Alejandro. Elijah is yanked by his arm into the air and held in a tight grip that refuses to allow him any movement. He clenches his eyes shut from the sudden movement, and I can see how hard it is for him not to cry out in pain again.

"Stop! You're hurting him!" I scream.

Alejandro glares at me, something hidden in his eyes that is impossible for me to detect.

"Be quiet, Scarlet. He's going to get what he has coming to him, and so will you," he adds loudly, so the gang crowding around us to hear.

Suddenly, Elijah slips free and lands a weak, but still effective, punch on Alejandro's jaw. It doesn't get him far, and seconds later Alejandro reacts and restrains him again. But not before sending a blow to Elijah's already broken ribs. He instantly falls to the floor and curls up to try and protect himself, clenching his entire body in agony. I watch in horror as he coughs up blood, laying his head on the mat as he groans loudly. Fear creeps up my spine all over again. Elijah may have been right. There really is no way for us to get out of here. Even with the plan, I fear Elijah and I may have no hope.

"It's all here, sweetheart, I'll give you that," Deke says. "But that doesn't change the fact we still need you gone. How do I know you didn't make copies?"

"I didn't."

"Tuckers are known to be liars," he says, and for the first time I see anger slip across his gaze.

"He was doing the right thing by trying to expose you."

"That, sweetheart, is exactly why you giving us the flash drive isn't enough to get you out of this situation. Did you really think that even if your little boyfriend here won that we would just forget about you? No, we knew making him fight would bring you in, trying to play the little hero."

He suddenly pulls a gun from the back of his suit pants, and my entire body goes numb.

Kevin, Charles, now would be a really good time to get the ball rolling on our plan . . .

Deke slowly wipes off the top of it, as if getting rid of dust, and lifts it toward me. From the corner of my eye, I notice Elijah on full alert, as though he hadn't been coughing up blood seconds ago. Deke smiles that same sickening grin, and instead of aiming for me he tosses the gun to Alejandro.

"I'll let you finish what you started five years ago, Alejandro. You've earned it," Deke says, unplugging the flash drive from the laptop. "As for this . . ." he says as he throws it on the ground and steps on it with a sickening crack that echoes throughout the now empty room, "well, at least this copy is now gone."

Alejandro walks toward me silently and with no emotion on his face.

"Alejandro, you get the hell away from her," Elijah spits, finding the energy to stand up and stumble toward us, but someone from the gang instantly restrains him. "You're not one of them, man."

I suddenly feel the terrifying coolness of metal on my temple, applying light pressure, and my heart stops beating. I stop breathing. My entire body freezes.

There is a gun being held to my head right now.

Kevin, where the hell are you?

Alejandro presses the gun against my temple and I feel my body start to shake. Elijah is still struggling against the guy restraining him, but I keep my eyes shut tight and try to picture myself anywhere but here.

"The guilt of betraying Max never leaves me, Scarlet," Alejandro says, his voice shaking. It soon reaches his hand, and the barrel starts to shake against my temple.

"I'm the reason he got murdered. But it wasn't because I wanted him to be killed, Scarlet. You have to believe that! I never wanted anything bad to happen to him! I saw him as a role model, as a brotherly figure—he took everyone under his wing and made us feel safe in this hellhole."

I swallow back another wave of fear, and slowly he starts relieving the pressure of the gun against my temple as his rant continues.

"I did it because my sister was threatened. Because she was put in danger. Because of *you*." He spits, and suddenly I'm let go and the gun is no longer pointed at me.

It's pointed at Deke.

"You're the reason so many people have been killed!" Alejandro shouts, holding the gun with two shaking arms. "I promised I'd put an end to this. An end to you."

His finger reaches for the trigger, sweat dripping down his face as he makes a decision that he can never go back on. But he doesn't shoot, because someone else shoots him. He drops the gun and clutches his gun-shot hand to his chest, falling to his knees.

Suddenly, the room is swarmed by armed men dressed in black bulletproof vests spelling out our saving grace: Houston PD.

The plan will work.

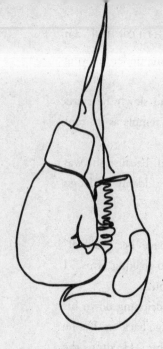

CHAPTER
TWENTY FIVE

With horror-filled eyes, I watch as Alejandro clutches his bleeding hand. Whoever shot him has impeccable aim; they shot his hand so that he would drop the gun. Charles was right, this is about to end once and for all.

Suddenly I hear Elijah shout my name.

"Scarlet! Get down!" he yells into the chaos.

I snap my eyes to him, and in the process, I see Deke grab the discarded gun and lift it toward me. I hit the floor at the same time the gunshot rings out.

I wait for it to hit me.

When I don't feel my body break into agonizing pain, I slowly lift my head and see Elijah tackling Deke. The gun flies across the floor of the ring, and suddenly Deke is swarmed by the police. Elijah rushes to me and drops to his knees as he reaches me, worry evident in his frantic eyes.

"Are you okay?" he says, scanning my body to see if any part of me is injured.

The fact that he's not unconscious amazes me. Adrenaline is a serious force to reckon with.

"He missed me," I breathe out shakily.

Relief floods both of our bodies and we cling to one another. Elijah wraps me in his arms, his heart pounding too hard and too fast to be safe. But I know mine is doing the same.

"Thank God you're okay. You were never supposed to come here, Scarlet."

"I wasn't going to let you do this on your own. You should have known that."

Suddenly, we hear a loud groan behind us. It makes all of my hair stand on end; I thought Elijah's grunts of pain were the worst noise I've ever heard, but this agonizing groan may top it. We pull apart to find the source of the noise and our eyes land on a sight I wish a thousand times over that I could unsee.

The bullet didn't hit me.

It hit Alejandro.

His bleeding hand is clutching his bleeding stomach as he lies in a pool of his own thick and sticky blood. Alejandro may have done a lot of things wrong. He may have outed my brother and he may have held a gun to me on numerous occasions, but despite all of that I can't find it in me to hate him. Despite the things he's done wrong, there's no denying the fact he was trying to help me and Elijah. He was trying to keep us safe, as well as his family.

I can't hate him. He was taken advantage of and had to make difficult decisions in his life. He had to choose the lesser of two evils, and either option was going to hurt someone. I can't hate him for choosing me to get hurt over his sister.

"Alejandro . . ." I breathe, rushing to where he lies on the ground. Elijah follows behind me, still on alert.

Tears are running down Alejandro's pale cheeks and I can already see the life slipping from his dark-brown eyes. Then they focus on me, and I see how broken he is. How broken he has always been.

"Scarlet, I'm so sorry. For everything. I tried to make it right."

"You're not a bad guy, Alejandro."

His chin quivers as more tears blind him. "I truly hope one day you can forgive me for what I've done. I never meant to ruin your family, and if I could go back and change all of this I would. I was never going to shoot you tonight or the other night, Scarlet. My plan was always to get you and Elijah out of here. This whole time I was just trying to find a way to help you. I know that's what Max would have done for Isabella."

I feel tears slipping down my cheeks. "Thank you."

Suddenly he reaches out with whatever strength he has left and clutches my hand in his bloodstained one. Thankfully, he reached for me with the one that didn't get shot. Because of his sudden movement, Elijah tries to rip him away from me, worried he's going to harm me, but I stop Elijah. Alejandro's not a threat.

"Please . . . please tell my sister how much I love her. Tell her how sorry I am. How much I'm going to miss her."

"I will. I'll find her and tell her."

"I'm sorry, Scarlet," he whispers, choking on his own words.

"It's okay," I cry. "It's okay."

Then I watch as the life slips from his eyes. His grip on my hand loosens and his hand falls to his side. A sob escapes me and my body shakes as more sobs take me over. I lift my hand to cover my mouth, hoping that will in some way stop my cries.

"Scarlet," Elijah says softly, his deep voice calming me.

He gently pulls me away from Alejandro and into his arms, and I sob into his chest. He combs my hair to try and calm me down.

"It's okay, Scarlet. We're okay."

"He didn't deserve this."

"I know, Scarlet. I know."

"His sister doesn't deserve this."

"She's going to be okay."

I continue to cling to Elijah. My rock. Who somehow, despite taking a massive beating tonight, is still able to stand tall for my sake. Who somehow, despite getting bullied every day by a guy I used to love, found it in his heart to love me.

I pull back just enough to look at him and my heart sinks as I once again take in the havoc that they did to him. His entire face is one swollen mess with bruise after bruise dotting his skin. Anyone else should be on the floor right now. But Elijah never stops fighting. And that's what I love about him.

"I can tell you're rambling in that head of yours—"

I cut him off by throwing my hands (gently) on his face and kissing him. He's shocked for a second from the sudden outburst of affection, especially considering the fact there are arrests going on all around us, but places his hands on my cheeks to kiss me back. I laugh and rest my forehead on his, breathing in a huge breath of utter relief as we break the kiss.

How did we just escape a near-death situation like this?

"I love you."

"I love you too." He smiles.

"Elijah!"

We pull apart at the sound of his name being called frantically, and Elijah glances around confusedly. However, as I watch his eyes dance around, I notice that the confusion isn't being caused only by his name being called. His eyes are starting to get glossy and I watch as he has to set a hand firmly on the ground to support himself, his mouth hanging open and eyes blinking rapidly.

"Elijah, are you okay?" The words rush out.

He tries to set his focus on me, which takes a few seconds longer than it should, and nods. "Yeah, I'm okay. Who—"

"Elijah!"

His name is yelled again and he snaps his head back around to try and see who is calling him, nearly falling because of how dizzy he's becoming. But then he must realize where he recognizes the voice from because he turns back to me.

"You called him?"

His dad.

"He was the cop who worked with Max."

"My dad?" he asks, his voice beginning to slur. "And Max?"

"Yes, Elijah. I was just as shocked as you," I say, my voice becoming frantic as his blinking begins to slow way down.

Elijah drops his hand into mine, so I give it a squeeze and he attempts to squeeze back but his adrenaline rush is over, and he has no strength to do so. And then suddenly Charles is here, kneeling over the both of us.

"Elijah," he breathes out in relief. "Son."

"So, you've decided to start calling me that again?" Elijah asks, but his words come out slurred and panic washes over me.

Charles furrows his brow, not about Elijah's words but about the quality of his speech. Elijah attempts to stand up, but just collapses back onto the ground and groans in agony as it jars his broken ribs. Then we watch in horror as Elijah spits up blood and goes into a coughing fit. He coughs up blood while groaning and clutching his ribs.

"Someone get me an ambulance!" Charles shouts, his voice booming with authority. Elijah lets out a small scream of pain and takes my hand, squeezing with a new strength that comes from his pain, and his dad clenches his jaw.

"Now, goddammit!"

He holds Elijah up so he's not lying on his injured side, trying everything in his power to relieve some of his pain. "I am *not* losing anyone else to this place," he says, mostly to himself. "I'm here. You'll be okay, son."

The ambulances get there within minutes. The first one takes Alejandro and the crew from the second one rushes to Elijah. I watch as Elijah is lifted onto a gurney and rushed into the ambulance while Charles hops in with no hesitation. At the last second my feet connect with my brain and I rush after them, jumping in just before they close the door, ignoring their questions as to who I am.

When we get to the hospital, Kevin having followed in his Mustang, the paramedics waste absolutely no time and rush Elijah into surgery. They're all spitting out what could be wrong with him and I try my hardest to cling to what they're saying. My heart sinks as I focus on the many options, including his broken ribs damaging major blood vessels or even his lungs.

None of the options sounds ideal.

Charles, Kevin, and I follow them until the door labeled HOSPITAL STAFF ONLY slams shut on us.

"What do we do?" I ask into the sudden silence that falls upon us.

Kevin reaches out and once again puts his arm around my

shoulders as a form of comfort, and I gladly accept it, curling into the man who has become like a second brother to me.

Charles runs his hands over his face and then sets them on his hips, staring past the doors in disbelief that this all just occurred. I'm sure this is a lot for anyone to comprehend. The little sister of the boy he asked to be an informant calls him up randomly one day, calls him out on all of his lies, and then tells him the son he abandoned might get killed unless he helps find some flash drive.

That's a lot to deal with.

Charles turns to look at me after a few minutes and his eyes drop to my bloodstained clothes and bruised wrists.

"You should go get all of that checked out. I'll call your parents and get them down here, explain what went on. But you need to make sure you're okay physically."

Kevin glances down at me and instantly agrees.

"It's not my blood," I say in an emotionless tone.

"And I suppose those aren't your wrists, then?" Charles asks, gesturing to the purple bruises.

"I need to stay here and wait for them to tell us what happened to Elijah."

"Little Tucker, you should get yourself checked out," Kevin advises.

Though all I want to do is wait for Elijah, Kevin insists I go get checked out. The bruises on my wrists are only getting worse with each passing second, so I oblige, and he walks with me to find a doctor.

I had a gun held to my head—for the second time in my life—and somehow, I came out with nothing but a sprained wrist. The doctors give me a nifty wrist brace to show off, but of course they can't do anything for the bruising other than hand me a bag of ice. Kevin gives me his sweatshirt so that I can change out of my bloodstained clothes, though my jeans are still spattered. After changing and getting my wrist brace, Kevin and I are quick to go back to the waiting room, where we walk in on Elijah's mom staring in shock at Charles.

This is awkward.

Kevin and I glance at one another, and we agree silently to back out of the room to let the two of them have this moment without any spectators. We stand in the hallway, both of us leaning against the stark white walls, taking in the scent of antiseptic.

"Kevin?"

He rolls his head to the side. "What's up, Little Tucker?"

"How serious are broken ribs?"

I know nothing about the seriousness of Elijah's injuries. All I know is that he was clearly in unbearable pain, then adrenaline snapped him out of it, and after the adrenaline was gone, he collapsed and coughed up blood. I don't need to be a doctor to know there is something seriously wrong with him.

"It depends on what his ribs punctured, if anything at all," he says carefully.

I fiddle with my hands nervously, trying to keep my thoughts in my head. But that's never worked for me.

"He was fine, beaten and bruised but still standing and defending both himself and me. He wasn't coughing up blood or keeling over in pain until his dad came over, and it seemed to come out of nowhere, Kevin. He was fine. He was talking to me, joking with me, one moment and then the next . . ."

"His adrenaline finally wore off once he realized the both of you were safe."

"He fell on his ribs, Kevin. He was starting to pass out before that, but he didn't start coughing up blood or sweating profusely until he fell on his ribs."

Kevin furrows his brow and takes in a deep, slow breath, but he lets his worry shine through. "That fall could have moved the ribs to puncture something, then."

A chill passes down my spine. "What could it have punctured?"

"We shouldn't play the guessing game anymore."

I stare at him and then my eyes shift to the clock taunting me on the wall.

"He's been back there for two hours."

Instead of answering me, Kevin reaches out and takes my hand in his, his silent way of telling me it's all going to be okay. With a heavy sigh, I rest my head on his shoulder and try to keep myself calm. And that's when my parents come running down the hall toward the waiting room.

"Scarlet, honey, oh thank God," Mom says upon seeing me, making me her new destination, my dad following. "Officer Black told us everything, thank God you're all right."

I hug them both close to me, allowing myself to feel a little of the relief I deserve. Though Elijah is in surgery right now, potentially fighting for his life, I at least know that I finished what Max started. He didn't die in vain.

"How is Elijah?"

"He's been in surgery for a while now. We are waiting to hear the news."

"Where's Officer Black?"

Kevin takes this one. "Ms. Black just got here . . . we're letting them hash it out on their own."

Suddenly, a surgeon passes us on her way into the waiting

room. We realize she could be the surgeon reporting about Elijah's surgery, so we quickly follow her. Our suspicions are confirmed when we see her talking to Elijah's parents.

"—and he broke three of his ribs, one of which punctured his lung and another that punctured some major blood vessels. Thankfully, the third didn't do much damage aside from provide him a lot of pain, but the other two were serious injuries. He—"

I break down.

She may have never said he wasn't going to be okay, but because I'm tired and worried and frantic, that's what I convince myself of.

"Oh my God, he's not okay. We were too late. I thought he was going to be okay, Kevin, you said he would be okay. But he punctured his *lung*. We need those to breathe," I sob, not realizing how hysterical I sound. "No wonder he was gasping for breath, and the coughing up blood . . . I *knew* that wasn't good! He's not okay and it's all because we didn't get there in time!"

Suddenly, I feel a hand on my shoulder that shuts me up and Kevin furrows his brow at me. "Little Tucker, she already said Elijah was fine. He just needs rest."

"Scarlet, honey, he's all right," my mom adds.

I nearly collapse onto the floor in tears of utter relief, but somehow, I hold myself together. He's okay.

The surgeon continues, "He's asleep for now, but family members are allowed in. Mr. and Ms. Black? You two can follow me."

"You go ahead, Janet. I . . . he'll want to see you first," Charles says.

She doesn't argue with him, and I really can't blame her. Just because he did his job as a dad and job as an officer doesn't mean he's suddenly forgiven for walking out on his family. Ms. Black just turns away and follows the surgeon to go see Elijah, and I long to be the one going with her.

"As a matter of fact," Charles starts, grabbing his coat with an awkward cough. "I should probably get going."

"Wait, what?"

"Scarlet, I appreciate you coming to me and allowing me to finish this, but I can't face Elijah. I'm sorry."

I thought this was over, but it's not. Our lives may be safe now, and Max's life may no longer be a mystery, but there's still one loose end that needs tied.

"So you're just going to leave him again when he needs you?"

Charles stops in his tracks, his tense back facing me.

"I said you had the chance to right your wrongs earlier today. I didn't just mean saving Elijah. You have the chance to have a relationship with your *son* again. Saving him was only half of this battle, Charles."

He turns around, and for the first time I see tears in his eyes.

"He won't forgive me, Scarlet."

"How do you know if you don't try?"

He glances around, at my parents and at Kevin, who back me fully, and then slowly nods.

"Okay. I'll go see him."

I spend the night at the hospital, in the waiting room, with Kevin and my parents. I refuse to leave before seeing Elijah, and they refuse to leave without me. This morning, the nurses inform me I'm finally able to go see him.

I follow the nurse down the stark white hallways that reek of bleach, trying to focus on her rather than the abundance of nurses and doctors all around us. Just a few short seconds later she stops at a room and opens the door for me to go in. I was preparing myself during this short walk to see someone who didn't even resemble Elijah. I had built up this image of what he was going to look like after surgery—a cut-up mess of a man.

But then my eyes land on him.

Elijah is sound asleep. Instead of his normal fighting attire, he has on a hospital gown void of blood. I let my eyes gaze on his beaten face and my heart sinks at just how bruised it is. His eyes are swollen, his nose realigned but now off center from being broken yet again, and his cheeks are purple with bruising, but he's still Elijah. He has been through a lot; I don't want to wake him.

"I'll leave you two. If you need anything, just call for a nurse," she says before stepping out of the room.

I take the chair next to his bed, which is somehow more uncomfortable than the waiting room seats, and quietly sit down. Though the chair couldn't have been worse to fall asleep in, considering I barely got any sleep last night, I doze off into a restless sleep almost the second my butt hits the springy cushion. I wake up a little while later when I sense Elijah stirring in his sleep. He whips his head to the side, agony etched on his features, and I instantly sit up. He mumbles incoherent things as he tosses and turns, and I try to figure out what he's saying in such distress, and the second I make out my name I take his bandaged hand in mine and try to soothe him awake.

"Elijah, it's okay!"

He doesn't come out of his slumber, so I keep trying, and

eventually he wakes up and when his frantic eyes land on me he relaxes. I reach out and comb some hair off of his forehead as he continues to regulate his breathing. He shuts his eyes after a few silent moments and keeps them shut for a while. I assume he's faded back to sleep, but I continue to comb my fingers through his hair.

"What time is it?" he asks into the silence as his eyes open, startling me.

I jump slightly and I see the twitch up of his lips from my reaction, and then I clear my throat.

"I'm not sure, sometime in the early morning. Maybe eight? It's been a long night."

"Did that all really happen?"

"Which part?"

"It all seems a little crazy, huh?"

Crazy is not a strong enough word to define what happened.

"But we did it," I say.

He squeezes my hand and offers a small smile, but his expression soon turns troubled as he studies my face.

"What's wrong?" I ask softly.

"I told you not to come."

"Had I not then they would have killed you."

His eyes trail from my face to my wrist. "You got hurt trying to play the hero."

"You're really saying *I'm* hurt with this little brace while you just had surgery for three hours?" I snort, lifting my pathetic injury in comparison to what he sustained. "Elijah, you scared me to death. One minute you were fine and the next you were collapsing, coughing up blood . . . I didn't know what was going on."

"I'm okay, though."

"I didn't know if you were going to be."

"Scarlet, I knew what I was getting into when I went."

"So did I."

"Then why did you go?"

I scan his face and then blink a few times. "Elijah, you're usually pretty perceptive."

"I'm aware—what if I just want to hear you say it?"

"Here I was thinking you were tired of my rambling."

His eyes soften a considerable amount. "I will never get tired of any part of you."

My heart melts. "I went because I love you too much to let anything happen to you."

"Funny, I went for the same reason." He trails his hand up my arm, tugging slightly so that I'll come closer. "Come here."

Of course, I have no hesitation, and he moves his hand to rest on the back of my neck as he kisses me sweetly. One kiss after the other, we both allow ourselves to realize that it's almost all over. We got through the lies and secrets and we can finally relax.

"How much pain are you in?"

"I'm so hopped up on pain medication that I can't feel a thing," he says. "Lie down with me?"

He doesn't have to ask me twice.

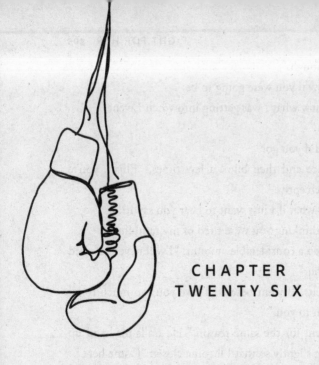

CHAPTER
TWENTY SIX

After having to stay at the hospital for a couple of days to monitor his injuries, Elijah is finally able to come home. With the injuries he sustained, he needs constant care, and his mom is unable to provide that since she needs to work. Unfortunately, she was only able to get a few days off, and spent every one with Elijah in the hospital.

She would keep him at the hospital to get that care he needs, but their insurance won't cover any more nights there. My dad was quick to offer to pay for him staying longer, but my mom stepped in and suggested that Elijah stay with us instead, since she doesn't work and could take care of him. This way both parties save some money and he can be taken care of.

Charles offered to take Elijah in, but Elijah made a rather easy decision to turn down his offer. I asked him about the talk with his dad, curious as to why Charles wasn't there the morning I went to see Elijah.

Elijah is a very stoic and strong man. He doesn't give anything away to anyone he doesn't want to, and he calculates every move before he does it. Aside from me and Kevin, he never lets his guard down.

He doesn't let things affect him, but his father leaving him and his mother was too big to ignore. So he pushed it to the back of his mind for so long, and it stayed there while everything else happening around him became his priority. But seeing his dad again forced the situation to the forefront, and though Elijah is the strongest man I know, even he has his moments of weakness.

He told me that they talked. They yelled. Charles cried. Elijah said the things he has wanted to since it happened. Charles gave up defending his actions. And, in the end, they hugged. They held each other tight (but carefully, considering Elijah's broken ribs) and hugged one another for long enough to make up for the lost time. Elijah didn't forgive him for leaving their family, but he was open to giving him a second chance at being in Elijah's life. The way he explained it to me was that it's better to have a father again than to go on hating someone he should love.

Kevin and I offer to drive Elijah to my house since Elijah's parents were forced to leave the hospital for work and my dad left for New York to settle a deal with some company for a new line of oil products for our shops. We pull up to my house and drive slowly down my extensive driveway.

Kevin throws the car in park. "Home sweet home. Come on, Eli, let's get you inside."

Kevin and I get out and walk to Elijah's side of the Mustang.

I step back as Kevin carefully helps Elijah stand up without putting too much strain on his ribs,. I can tell from the frustration on Elijah's face that he hates this. I know he does. I've learned he likes to play the hero, and in his eyes a hero doesn't need help from others.

His face is still bruised, but the bruises have turned yellow instead of purple and blue, which means he's healing. That's what his doctor had to keep repeating over and over to me every time I buzzed for a nurse to come check on him because his bruises were changing colors.

I didn't realize that was a good thing. But in my defense, WebMD told me his skin was going to fall off after I typed in the symptoms.

I do as much as I can to help get Elijah to the extra bedroom on the second floor. We get him settled on the bed, listening to him grumble things to himself about how much he hates being this needy, and Kevin goes back to the car to get Elijah's things.

"Hey, if you keep pouting, your face is going to stick that way," I say as I sit down next to him.

"I hope I'm not coming off as unappreciative."

"I lost count of the number of times you said thank you to my parents when they offered to let you stay here."

"Your family has done a lot for me, Scarlet. I don't think I can ever repay them."

"You don't have to. My parents care a lot about you, they do these things for you because they want to."

He sits up enough to reach my lips in a kiss. I place a hand on his sturdy jaw, and he rests one on my waist, and when we pull apart, I comb my fingers through the hair on the back of his neck and smile.

"So, we're roommates now. There's no escaping me," I say.

"Too late for me to back out now, huh?"

I scoff at his teasing and he chuckles and kisses me again before resting his forehead on mine. But then a knock at the door has us both turning our attention toward it, and my mom walks in with a plate of cookies. My mom is not a baker, so the cookies are interesting.

I'll bet a hundred dollars she bought those at the store and is pretending to have baked them.

"Are you settled in nicely, Elijah?" she asks.

I set a kiss on his cheek and go over to help her with the plate, taking it from her and setting it on his nightstand.

Yep, she definitely bought these.

He smiles gratefully at her. "Yes, ma'am, thank you again for—"

She stops him by putting a hand up. "If you thank me one more time, I might kick you out."

"Yes, ma'am."

"I know the decorations in this room may not be the prettiest," she says, scrunching up her nose at the sailboat figurines on the dresser and the paintings of boats along the walls, "but Scarlet's father decided this is what he wanted when we built the house."

"I like it."

"You don't have to lie, I already like you."

He smiles bashfully. "It could be better?"

I zone out of their conversation as Kevin walks back into the room with a duffel bag of Elijah's clothes, and I help unload it all into the drawers. I listen absentmindedly to what Elijah and my mom talk about.

"Mrs. Tucker, you and your husband have really given me everything."

"Oh, honey, it's no trouble letting you stay here."

"I don't just mean the car and a place to stay."

It takes a few seconds for his words to sink in, but the second they do, I turn my attention to Elijah. I catch him staring softly over at me with a look that has me feeling every nerve in my body and then melting into the floor.

"Everything," he repeats, but I know he's not talking to her at this point.

The tenderness of his stare almost makes me cry, and I barely notice my mom back out of the room. Kevin must not realize, though, because he stays right next to me, oblivious to what's going on around him.

"Where should I put his sweatpants? In the drawer with his boxers?"

When I don't respond, he glances between me and Elijah, who haven't once looked away from one another, and from the corner of my eye I see his expression turn to one of awkward realization that he should leave, and he backs out.

But before he can leave, someone else shows up in the doorway —someone who is confusing enough to break our stare.

"*Jack?*"

What the *hell* is he doing here?

My eyes wander from his face to the card he's awkwardly holding in his hands and then drift back to his uncomfortable expression.

Kevin clears his throat and places his hand on the back of my shoulder. "I think I should go now, call me if you two need anything okay?" he asks, nodding over to Elijah.

I nod absentmindedly, my eyes still stuck to Jack, and Kevin walks out of the room, but not before stopping in front of Jack. Jack tries to seem nonchalant about someone who kind of looks like a bodybuilder staring him down, but I can tell how nervous he is. Kevin gives him a once-over, snorts, and then brushes past him to leave.

"What are you doing here?" I ask, the surprise evident in my tone.

"Word of what happened got out and I just . . . I wanted to swing by and give y'all this," he says, holding up the card.

I furrow my brow and walk over to him, feeling Elijah's eyes boring into my back. I know he's tense and probably ready to pounce, so I take the card from Jack and walk over to Elijah to hand it to him.

"Go on, clearly he wants to talk," he says quietly.

"He just wanted to drop off the card."

"Considering he's staring holes into you right now, I think he wants to talk, Scarlet," Elijah says with a hint of humor behind his words, knowing how naive I want to be.

I thought my talks with Jack had finally ended. All they do is stress me out.

I sigh deeply and then bend down to give Elijah a kiss, and he sends me a reassuring smile.

"I'll be here."

I smile at him, but the second I turn to face Jack the smile twitches away and I walk into the hallway with him following. I lean my hip against the wall to try and find a comfortable position for an uncomfortable conversation.

"I—I was worried about you," he says into the ear-splitting silence that has fallen between us.

"Thank you."

Jack sighs. "He really loves you."

Though I didn't know what this talk would be about, this is the last thing I expected.

"I can tell. He looks at you the same way I do."

I don't say anything.

"The difference between us and you two, though, is that you look at him the same way. You never looked at me like that."

I frown at the crack in his voice. "Jack . . ."

"It's okay, Scar. I screwed up; he'll treat you better than I ever did."

I stare at him, wanting to say something but not quite knowing what.

"Jack, I did love you."

"I know you did, Scar," he says quietly. "But never as much as you love him."

We fall silent and he glances at me, eyeing the brace on my wrist.

"I just wanted to come see for myself that you were all right—the story exaggerated your wrist a hell of a lot. I didn't mean to make anyone uncomfortable."

"Thank you."

He smiles sadly at me, and I really examine him, and I finally see the toll our breakup took on him. I never noticed the dark bags under his eyes or the patches of stubble he missed shaving. Even his hair looks a little unruly.

I debate what to do but end up opening my arms slightly. Jack's eyes widen in surprise and he hesitantly walks over to hug me. He carefully wraps his arms around me in a small hug that's both full of familiarity and foreign to me at the same time. He feels skinnier than he used to, and though we broke up, my heart breaks a little from the effects this all has had on him.

We both know this is the last time we'll ever hold each other again.

I pull away and glance up at him, and the pain in his eyes is almost too much for me to handle. So I don't push him away when he leans down to place a final kiss on my cheek, being smart enough to avoid a kiss on the lips. He sends me one last sad smile, and then his eyes drift to the room Elijah's in.

"There's one more thing I have to do."

Before I respond, he walks into the room and over to Elijah, with me following. Elijah seems a little shocked that Jack came back into the room at all, but he easily hides it until Jack sticks his hand out. I try my hardest to read Elijah's thoughts, but he's masked everything so well that I get no reading. Then he reaches out and takes Jack's hand, and I see Jack's entire body relax. As they shake hands, Jack speaks up.

"We don't deserve her," he says.

"I know."

"You realized that long before I ever did. You deserve her more than anyone."

Elijah doesn't respond but gives another firm shake to Jack's hand before letting go, and Jack nods once, sensing his cue to head out. After Jack walks through the doorway, I shift my gaze to Elijah and let every emotion show.

"So that just happened—" I walk to him and sit down on the bed, reaching for the card that he already opened. "What's it say?"

"An apology for everything he ever did."

"Seriously?"

"Seriously. Now come here," he says, turning onto his side so that I can lie down next to him.

I lie down and reach out to rest my hand on the back of his neck, playing with his hair. "I don't know why, but for some reason it didn't feel like everything we've been through was over until just then."

He places a hand on my hip and pulls me slightly closer.

"It's over, Scarlet. We did it."

"We went through hell and back and somehow came out on cloud nine."

"You know, it's kind of ironic. My body is littered with little nicks and bruises, endless scars—scars aren't pretty. But then you, *Scar*let, came and gave them a whole new meaning. I know I've never called you Scar, but you make anything beautiful. And you're the one scar I never want to lose."

"Now *that* was spoken like a true poet," I tease lightly, and he chuckles, but all too soon my expression drops.

"What's wrong?"

"Are you going to fight once you're better?" I ask vulnerably. "Because I mean we just went through hell when you were fighting. I know you liked it at first because it was a way to release all the stress in your life, but then it *became* the stress in your life. Plus, the ring is probably going to be a crime scene for a long time, considering we witnessed someone die there. Oh my God, Alejandro . . . I still have to find his sister and tell her everything he said. What if I never find her? What if she goes through life thinking her brother didn't say good-bye? What if—"

Elijah stops my train of thought by moving his head forward to kiss me softly and reassuringly. "Scarlet, stop worrying. We'll get to that. Right now we can finally relax."

"What about your fighting?"

He chuckles softly and shakes his head, letting his nose brush against mine.

"That's the best part. No more fighting. I fought for you and I won."

EPILOGUE

The wind whips past me, tangling my hair and making it do all sorts of weird dances. Thankfully, the wind in this sense is providing relief from the high temperatures. Though this land is beautiful—rolling hills with perfectly cut stark, green grass—it is anything but pleasant. The welcome sign is an oxymoron. It welcomes you to a place of remorse and sadness, a place where you don't *want* to be welcomed.

Meadow View Cemetery.

My eyes follow the seemingly endless tombstones. They mostly look the same, though each carries such a different story. I slowly let my eyes drift back to the tombstone owned by the Blacks, and my heart drops even more.

I watch with sorrowful eyes as Elijah kneels in front of his brother's grave. He's silent. I can tell he has an enormous number of thoughts running through his mind, and though he never talks about Oliver, I know they are all memories of what life was like when he was alive. Then he stands and wipes off the grass that collected on his knees. The second he stands up, I walk to his side and he perks up at hearing my feet crunching on the grass. Once he looks at me, he wraps his arm around my waist and kisses my temple.

"I'm okay, stop looking so worried."

I let my body relax into his. "I know you are."

"I miss him."

"I know," I say softly.

"I'll never understand how he could have fallen so far into the drugs."

"I don't think anyone does, but that doesn't change the fact you and your family loved him or that he loved you."

Elijah rests his lips on my head and holds me a little tighter. "Thanks for coming here with me."

"Of course."

"Are you ready?"

"I think so."

With a deep breath, I find it in me to force my feet to walk through the cemetery to my own family's grave site. Elijah keeps my hand held tightly in his, providing the extra strength I need. Dandelion seeds tickle my ankles on the walk before being blown away in the wind.

Maxwell Kurt Tucker

Tears well in my eyes as I stare down at what now represents Max. He had his whole life left. Could have gone on to be a professional boxer, could have taken over the family business, or even created his own. Maybe he would have sold motorcycles for a living. But that's what's so sad about this, isn't it? The fact that I'll never know.

Elijah and I came here today to say good-bye to those we loved, knowing we avenged part of their deaths. I figured out everything we didn't know about Max, and we were able to finish what he started years ago.

"He'd be proud of me."

"He would be. He'd be proud to see what a strong woman you are."

I don't know if closure has ever been a true thing. I don't know if it's something everyone has the opportunity to reach, but in this moment I finally feel like I've achieved it.

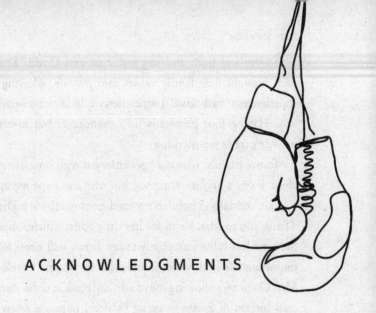

ACKNOWLEDGMENTS

First, I want to thank my mom, who took the momager role to the extremes when she discovered my books on Wattpad. She has always been there for me to talk her ear off, mainly about the petty boy drama that ultimately inspired all of my books. Without her (or the drama) none of this would have been put into motion.

To my dad, who has always encouraged me to go after what I want no matter how tough the road may be. He inspires me to diversify myself in as many ways as possible, pushing me to explore yearbook, writing, theater, and tennis. I am who I am today because of the values he taught me, and my dad jokes are nearing his in perfection.

To my brother, Taylor, for always putting me in my place and never sugarcoating anything. He is one of my biggest critics, and while that bothered me as a kid, today it's something I appreciate . . . to an extent.

319

To my stepmom and stepdad, Kris and David. They have each brought new family values into my life, allowing me to experience a traditional home lifestyle in a not-so-traditional way. Having four parents is unconventional, but something I wouldn't trade for anything.

To my friends, who may get annoyed with how often I brag about being a published author, but who also hype me up for it.

I am eternally grateful to my teachers throughout high school. Thank you to Mrs. Keith for her daily edits, which I dreaded at the time but value immensely today. I now will never forget an important life skill: when to use who vs. whom. Thank you to Mrs. Coiner for allowing me to edit my book at times during her class instead of always listening (which I hope she knew before reading this). And thank you to Mrs. Craft for allowing me to explore my creativity through ridiculous headlines for the school yearbook (TALLER BALLER will always be my favorite) and for being the first teacher to read my original book. Because of her, I started to feel tremendously confident in my creative writing and was inspired to write three more books. It means everything to me that they saw my potential and gave me the confidence to write my own stories.

To my editors, Kortney and Deanna, for pushing me way beyond what I thought were my limits and helping me discover the full potential of my writing. This experience has been nothing short of difficult, and they were there to help me every step of the way. Without them, this story never would have blossomed into what it is now.

To my lawyer, Kirk Schroder, for helping me secure this publishing deal. He took a chance with an eighteen-year-old amateur writer, and I am forever grateful that he did.

To Alysha D'Souza for getting me this opportunity as well as many others. And to I-Yana Tucker, for helping me through this process.

Last, but certainly not least, I want to thank the Wattpad community. Publishing one's work on a platform where anyone can comment whatever they'd like is intimidating, but the support from my fan base has been unbelievable. Thank you all for every comment, every vote, and every word of encouragement.

ABOUT
THE AUTHOR

Liz Plum is a young author from Hanover, Virginia, pursuing a bachelor's degree in marketing. Her stories on Wattpad have grossed over forty million reads and when she's not studying or watching romantic comedies for story inspiration, you can find Liz exploring every hiking spot within driving distance, bursting with Hokie pride at sporting events, or scribbling down ideas for her next novel. Connect with Liz on Instagram and on Wattpad at @Liz_Plum.

wattpad

Where stories live.

Discover millions of stories created by diverse writers from around the globe.

Download the app or visit www.wattpad.com today.

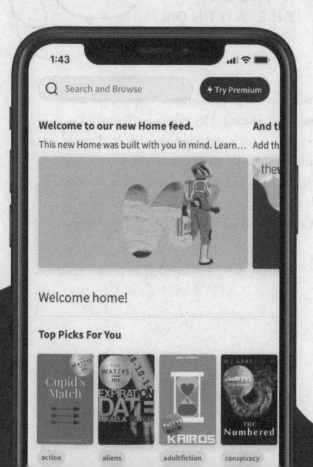

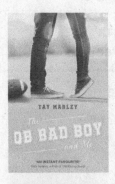

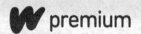

Want more? Why not try . . .

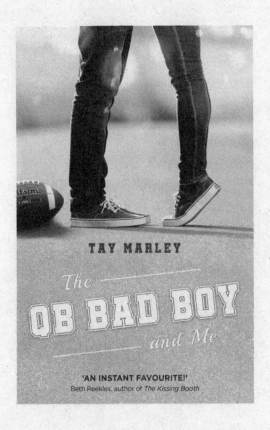

Sparks fly between star cheerleader Dallas
and bad boy Drayton. As opposites attract,
is their love destined for disaster?

Want more? Why not try . . .

Can Amelia hide her dark past from
bad boy Aiden?